High Hope Publishing
www.highhopepublishing.com

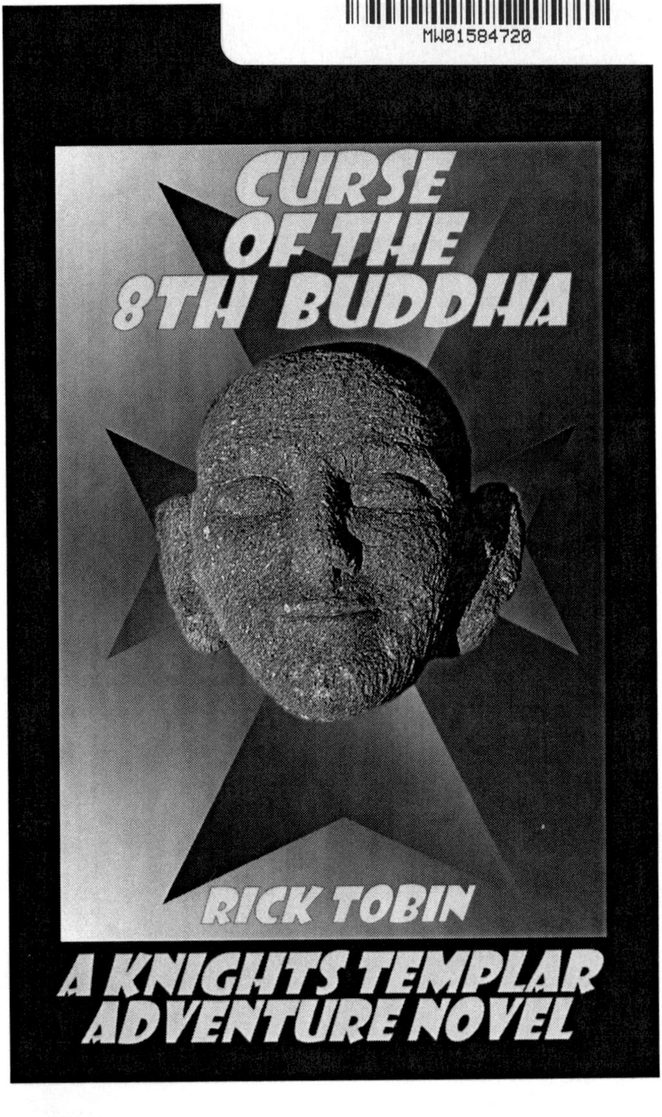

Curse of the 8th Buddha

Copyright © 2009 by Rick Tobin,
Published by High Hope Publishing,
318 Whitestone Drive, Spring Branch, Texas 78070
www.highhopepublishing.com

All cover art and internal design art copyright © 2009 by Rick Tobin.

High Hope and the portrayal of its logo are trademarks of High Hope Publishing.

All rights reserved. No part of this publication may be reproduced, stored in a retrieval system or transmitted in any form by any means, electronic, mechanical, photocopy, recording, or otherwise, without the prior permission of the publisher and author, except as provided by USA copyright law.

All of the characters and events in this book are fictitious, and any resemblance to actual persons, living or dead, is purely coincidental.

To

[Handwritten inscription: Roberta / for the ears to / Listen when / you didn't / need to / and your kind / and confident / Brad]

My wife Cinda and my son Ryan for continuing to believe in the dream and the dreamer.

Dorrie O'Brien for the dedication to the initial editing.

Paul Levine for insights and support.

Cathi Slaminski, Susan Santos, Josh Lichterman, and Jeff Narducci for their time and insights.

Ellie Crystal for her consistent vision and for letting me work with her on her book, *Sarah and Alexander*.

May you all walk in perfected light.

Curse of The 8th Buddha

A Novel

Rick Tobin

Chapter 1

"There's only one good thing about freezing in a San Francisco summer night," Richard Sinclair said, pulling on the ties of his black windbreaker so the hood snuggled tighter over the expanse of his broad forehead and thinning, salt-and-pepper hair. He peered up into the darkness above the steel stairway and over the head of his companion, Duncan Torres.

"What, it keeps the flies off you?" Torres muttered, pounding out each step under his squat, powerful frame, which he'd covered with a San Francisco '49er's football team warm-up jacket. "Maybe it'll keep you quiet in the control room for a change."

The golden script on the back of Sinclair's windbreaker read: STATE OF CALIFORNIA. It glinted sporadically in the faint glow from the construction lighting sixty feet below from where the two men climbed up the frigid steel stairway, suspended from the abdomen of the largest crane in San Francisco, near Chinatown.

"Nah, it keeps those damn black widows back in their corners. They're all over this damn scaffolding. Good thing they don't tell the tourists about this. I wonder what people would say if they knew about the bed bugs in our finest hotels."

"Yeah, well bugs are your problem, not mine. Hey, you need to keep up."

"I can't go any faster. My knees are killing me—torn meniscus."

"No shit, really? Well, Mr. State Emergency Manager, you better keep up or get left. I'm not here to take care of your ass while I freeze mine off up here. Never understood why they didn't put an elevator on this bitch." Torres grunted on each stair of the final flight.

"Don't worry; with that aftershave even a deaf man could track you in the dark. But you think this is cold?" Sinclair stopped a minute and caught his breath while hanging onto the frigid handrails. "I'll tell you what real cold is."

"Yeah, you keep talking, desk jockey," Torres reached for the door of the looming crane's control room. Light from a single fluorescent fixture pierced the wire-reinforced glass allowing Torres to find the scratched and weathered doorknob wrapped around an unforgiving lock.

Torres struggled to make his key work, jiggling and rattling it against the worn tumblers in the lock. His dark eyes and complexion fit his role as the pit bull of the site, always pushing his way around the other teamsters, even the union stewards.

"Hate this fuckin' piece of shit Japanese junk."

The open steel mesh floor beneath their boots held them over the reconstruction site of Embarcadero Center One. The grating gave no protection against the bitter winds shooting up their pants. Sinclair merely grimaced at these discomforts. They came with the assignment to oversee the retrofit improvements after the 7.5 earthquake of January 2012.

After Torres won the battle with the lock, the two men rushed inside to the space-heater warmth. Torres slammed the door behind him, kicking it hard enough to leave a new dent next to the pockmarks from previous outrages.

Sinclair got his bearings beneath the harsh fluorescent lighting of the exposed, dull-gray bowels of the crane's operation cabin. The space was tight for two men, with little room for movement.

"You just let me get my goddamn work done, Sinclair, and I promise not to have you buried in cement."

"Some work."

Sinclair hesitated as Torres fought a new foe. The key drawer for the crane control panel stuck half open and sideways on its runners. The crane operator slammed it open and shut until it rolled smoothly on its desk drawer guides. The keys were pulled out and shaken until the right one came free of its rings.

"All you have to do for an eight-hour shift is move one bunch of pylons from the side of the pit over to the other side. You move a few levers and presto, there it is: Another union job well done. What a sham."

"Hey, it's a living." Torres started charging the engines on the huge crane. "You have to pay your dues to get the sweet stuff."

Sinclair noticed a ring on Torres' right hand he had not seen before. It had a series of symbols inscribed on a blue field with a KC above it. "Nice ring. Knights of Columbus, huh?"

"Yeah, what's it to you? My great-grandfather was a Fourth Degree in the Knights back in the Great Quake in nineteen o'six. He saved a lot of people down on the piers. He was a great guy."

"Yeah, I really respect what the Knights of Columbus do with all their historical remembrance of Columbus finding America. I'm interested in that kind of thing, you know, like the Masons." Sinclair looked away, pretending not to watch for a response.

"The KCs are nothing like those faggot Masons running around hugging and kissing on each other. They're nothing but a clan of weirdoes."

"I don't think all the Masons are like that, but I can see how you feel that way, especially in this City. I'm a flaming heterosexual myself."

Torres turned around swiftly with a hard scowl for Sinclair, "You're a what?"

"Easy, Geronimo, that means I like women. Shit, you're touchy tonight."

"How come I don't see a wedding ring on your hand, buddy?"

"I had one. I won't again." Sinclair looked down and shoved his hands in his pockets.

"Oh, divorce, huh? Well, we don't do that if we believe in the Old Church. Must've been painful."

"Not a divorce." Sinclair could not look up as his eyes watered. "When the flu came through in twenty-eleven, I lost my wife and daughter. Strange, how I thought a new pandemic would take the very old, and instead it took mostly teens and women in their thirties. There I was, working in emergency management, unable to do a damned thing as my own family and two hundred thousand other people died in California. No wonder so many people have lost their faith in their religion, their government, and themselves. Ten percent of everyone in the U.S. died in six weeks. I think it'll take a helluva time to get over my pain, no matter what I do."

"Hey, you ain't alone, pal. That's one boat I share with you."

Torres stopped for a minute, turned around and sat hard on the padded steel chair next to the control panel as it blinked to life. "I lost a brother and a cousin that January. In fact, we were out at the graveyard memorial the day of the earthquake last year."

"A lot of us were. That probably helped cut the injuries. Most of the City was out at memorials; so many young lives gone from influenza. Then the quake hits right on the day of mourning. That was just about too much for me. I don't know how others handled it. Hell, the country's been damn near in a depression since the pandemic. Maybe the Daly City Shaker didn't cause catastrophic property losses, but the wound in morale, at least for me, just didn't heal. I don't know what to think about all this any more. What should I call it, fate?"

"I call it seriously fucked up. God's punishing us for something. Damned if I can figure out for what. I haven't been to communion since."

"Me, too. I thought about just letting go and checking out. Didn't seem to be a whole lot to stick around for—but some folks found me and saved me at the last minute. I've been on kind of a fast track recovery program with them since March. I owe them big time."

"We've been up here bitching at each other for almost two weeks now. How come you never mentioned any of this shit before, Sinclair? It isn't healthy to let all that sit in there and eat at you."

"Cause you're a crane engineer, not a shrink. You don't need to hear my problems, Torres. You have your problems just like everyone else. Besides, if I keep my mind on the work I get by . . . most days."

"Well, I've been around the deep darks myself. You need to just shoot the shit sometime. We'll talk during lunch. Glad somebody reached down and got you. Some don't make it back. I had a—what the hell's wrong now?" Torres turned and swore under his breath at some difficulty he was having with starting his crane, Betty.

"I can't believe you live up in this sky hog," Sinclair commented, trying to pull his emotions back inside. He had to keep his jacket on until the space heater reached the cold under his clothes. "It must have been hell in the aftershocks."

"Shake and bake inside my Betty Crocker," Torres joked. "Hey, those rumbles weren't as bad as having you snooping around here. Christ, it's like having a fresh grunt to break in. I have to watch your ass ever time you take a step out of my sight. Okay, c'mon, me hearties, let poppa move you into place."

Torres started working the controls at the same time he looked at a television next to a computer screen. There were lighted graphs and charts that moved as he adjusted a load of pylons six stories below. The floor and sides of the cabin were clear panels of glass giving him unrestricted views of the work below and the city lights. "So you don't call a nice July night in San Fran cold, huh? I'm wearing a '49er bench warmer. What's your wussie excuse for wearing that Eskimo Pie outfit?"

"Memories of the old 'Niners are probably the only warmth you'll ever get out of that old rag. I guess you've probably never been frostbitten."

"Can't say I have." Duncan turned away from Sinclair to his controls as he studied the hydraulic pressure gauges. His linebacker shape blocked Sinclair's view of his crane control manipulations.

CURSE OF THE 8ᵀᴴ BUDDHA

"Try the Dakotas at forty-five below zero with a forty mile-an-hour north wind," Sinclair suggested, as he took off his parka. "Your breath freezes in a long cloud in front of you. Your tires freeze square. You have to drive for miles before they round out. You touch a bare hand with sweat on it to anything metal and you're stuck, or your skin strips off. Now that, my friend, that's cold. These San Fran summer nights are just unpleasant."

"Yeah, well, I'll tell you sometime about being stationed in the fuckin' Antarctic for a year. Later. I got a problem here."

"Need any help?"

"Naw, just keep clear so I can move around here. I gotta figure out why I'm dropping power on the hoist."

Sinclair threw his jacket on top of the tiny table he'd been given to take notes on during this assignment. The warmth was finally reaching his chilled knees. He looked at the gray wall of dials to his left. The meters flashed red numbers as line voltage fluctuated on the cable motors. It was easier for him to focus on those. His fear of heights made the view below, through their glass cage, close to intolerable.

"Why the hell were you sent to be my goddamned shadow, anyway? I don't recall ordering an extra asshole." Torres's hands moved quickly over the console. Sweat beaded on his forehead in the warm control-room booth.

"If they find something of cultural significance under the ground while you guys are doing this retrofit, and you fuck it up, hey, you'll need an extra asshole, 'cause you won't have an ass left to sit on."

They both laughed. Sinclair shifted slowly to the side panel so he could see the gauge readouts a little more clearly and have less of the panorama in his view.

"Hey, did you forget? Don't fuckin' touch shit on the panel."

"I'm good. Just looking."

"What an ass-wipe generator." Torres pointed to the needle dipping on the generator's power gauge next to Sinclair's head. "It's supposed to be the backup if we lose the main bus. It's failing. In two or three more minutes I'm out of power and it's gonna get mighty dark up here. Did you sign on for that, college boy?"

"Maybe we ought to get out of here. And actually, I didn't sign on for this. This was my punishment for questioning the Governor's judgment—they don't like that too much in Sacramento when you work for the State. He heard that I talked to one of my media buddies about his personal use of earthquake insurance funds. That could have tossed him out for a recall. When he heard that the Tong had threatened to kill any white men digging into their old burial sites in San Fran, he probably figured this would be a nice clean way to get rid of my ass."

"Hmmm, you might be worth saving yet. Hate that prick. Never helped a union man in his life." Torres worked furiously on a set of controls for restarting the back-up power. Nothing. "I've never seen anything like it. I'll be go to hell, anyway. We're going to lose everything here. Those safety brakes on the cables better damned well work; I've got twenty tons of pylons hanging from the end. If they fall, it's gonna make one hell of a pile of splinters in that section we just cleared yesterday. I don't think your bone-chunking pet bitch is gonna care for that."

"Mary Beth is just doing her job. That's what archeologists do. She's actually on your side, if you'd give her half a chance."

"Half a chance? I'd drop these pylons on her scrawny ass if I thought it wouldn't miss. Ah, fuck, there goes the juice! Better grab the flashlights."

The men pulled two bright-yellow flashlights out of snap holders bolted to the control room walls. The fluorescent lights flickered and then fluttered dead. The exit sign was powered by its own batteries, making a spooky green glow over the door of the crane operator's cabin.

Sinclair wrapped himself back into the comfort of his lined windbreaker as they headed outside.

"Watch your step, Sinclair. Don't dent my Betty with that hard Irish head. Wow, look at that, half the City's out," Sinclair peered around, carefully, and confirmed the blackout, as his stomach came up to his throat with fresh vertigo. He made his way down the ladder to the side of the cabin and then onto winding stairs that had been specially constructed for the crane operation. He was glad for stairs instead of sixty feet of steel rungs to cling to all the way to the bottom.

"You have no idea what heights do to me. I was in one of those cars hanging from the Bay Bridge after the Loma Prieta quake. Karma, I guess, for being an emergency manager."

"You were in that little Pinto out on the Bay Bridge?"

"No, I was in the white van. I was driving over for a nursing home transfer for an ambulance company, trying to pay for my college classes. Guess it was better to be there and make it, than on the Nimitz Freeway collapse. Those poor bastards."

"Hell, yeah," Torres looked back as they worked their way down the iron stairs. Sinclair could not keep up with Torres. Torres slowed. "Oh Christ, there it goes. Feel that? Lost all of 'em."

They rested on a landing, catching their breaths in the cold, as the steel took its toll on both of them. They could feel the rolling thuds of the tons of pylons pounding into the excavation.

The men focused their lights on the unforgiving metal stairs as they descended the final forty feet to solid ground. Sinclair did a hop-step and bent down to kneel once he was off the reverberating platform. The dust from the collapse rose to meet them.

"Saying your prayers?" Torres looked down at Sinclair and shook his head.

"Never hurts, except on the knees."

"Well, let's go see the damage. Holy Christ almighty, if those pylons busted up when they hit—I can't understand why the auto brake on the cable pulley didn't stop this mess."

"So where are the pylons?" Sinclair asked, as Torres gave him a hand up.

"Looks like they went for a swim. Put your light over on this side—what the hell?"

They were looking at a series of craters where the pylons had struck the bottom of the pit and then disappeared somewhere underneath. The torn suspension cables drifted above like broken spider web threads, dangling aimlessly back and forth in the night breeze.

"Ever see anything like that?" Sinclair asked.

"Not really. This is just damn creepy. I better call the bone-snatcher. Looks like you might have found the rest of that Chink graveyard she was talking about. What's happening over there?" Torres swept his flashlight beam over a corner of the pit just at the end of the punctures from the pylons; a gaping hole was opening up around them like a hungry mouth. His flashlight started blinking off and on. He shook it. It went dead.

CURSE OF THE 8ᵀᴴ BUDDHA

"I'll have a look see," Sinclair said, pushing Torres behind him. "This is something I know about. I did a lot of caving when I traveled in the Southwest twenty years ago. We have to be damn careful here. That could be a cave-in or a wash-out from an underground drainage. We were getting pretty close to the water line from what the site engineer told me yesterday."

"Hey, better you than me. I don't like crawling in where I didn't come out of . . . kind of a birth trauma thing." Torres chuckled. "You go in there and you go alone, Bubba. I'll got get your other half. Maybe she'll fall in and I'll end the shift on a high note."

"She's over at the shack on the other side of the building. They've got an office in the back for her when she works graveyard shift."

"Speaking of graves, you smell that?"

"That's a new smell for me. I'm not sure I like that. Tell her to bring the site bag with the oxygen meter, the masks, some rope, heavy gloves, and the big flashlight. Oh, and tell her to bring me a flare gun. Don't call anyone else down here 'til we have a look."

"Hey, who's to call? Everyone else is off 'til next Monday. Remember, this is a holiday weekend: the fourth. Or did you just get dropped off on this planet?"

"Sure, whatever . . . just get her down here. Get Betty back running. I might need your help lowering me into that space. I know how to use hand signals. If you see the flare gun go off, pull me out, and I mean now." Sinclair was already on his belly, crawling back and forth like a desert sidewinder, as he pounded the end of the flashlight against the ground ahead of him.

Torres gazed in astonishment as Sinclair wriggled toward the pylon crash. "You gotta be shitin' me. I was just joking. You aren't really going down in that hole?"

Sinclair waved him off. "Just go get Mary Beth and hurry up. This sucker might close up before we find out what the hell we're dealing with and that could hold up this project for months,"

"Yeah, and maybe take that snooty bitch with it." Torres said, turning away.

"Torres. One more thing."

Torres turned back and looked up with rolled eyes, shaking his head. "Yeah, I know, don't piss off that whiny little poontang. I got it." He started to amble away, growling under his breath.

"No, once you get her down here, make sure you put a hook on the crane cable, on what's ever left of those lines. I don't want to go down there hanging on some loose cables with my skinny legs trying to hold me up. Remember, you see the flare you pull *my* bony ass out of that hole. Better hurry it up. I don't think this new space is going to hold up much longer."

Torres changed his steps to a lumbering trot through the darkness of the pit toward the State Archeological Society's personnel shack.

Fetid, black-and-gray speckled mud stuck to Richard like glue. It bonded with Sinclair's pants and coat, mixing with his sweat as he wriggled like a puddle-trapped earthworm. The soil's odors were soon overtaken by the curious, nose-bristling bitterness oozing its way out of the fresh pylon penetrations. Vapors crept along the ground to meet Sinclair, now covered in traces of clay and muck like a camouflaged jungle fighter.

On the far end of the construction site, Patrolman Henry Pfeister and Sergeant Arnie Johnson sat quietly in their black, polished squad car, slightly hidden behind some of the site's equipment storage buildings, near the edge of the construction pit.

Pfeister was finishing patrol reports when electricity failed, including the overhead light in the car's ceiling and the backup battery to his computer. "Jesus H. Christ, there goes another hour shot to hell."

Johnson tried to ignore the rookie's language. He had learned to build a thick shell over his religious sensitivities the last two months. It was a fine balancing act to ensure completion of his Deacon's training for his church. Pfeister was just a challenge the Lord had given to test his worth.

That concern passed quickly as Johnson watched a swath of San Francisco go black. Then they both heard the thud and crash from the falling pylons.

"Pfeister, get on the horn and find out what happened."

"Shit, Arnie, I just lost all my entries. Damn it! Hey, no radio. Is that possible? Listen. There's not even any static." He kept keying the hand piece and holding it toward Johnson's face.

"You may think I'm an old, deaf dog, but I'm not dead. Now get that damn thing— Just put the mike down. This doesn't make any sense. I'll check out the dig and see if someone got hurt and needs a hand."

"So, what am I supposed to do?"

"Play with your mike." Johnson paused. "Just keep trying to get dispatch." He said something under his breath, hoping Jesus couldn't hear it. "And hand me the shotgun."

Johnson used his flashlight to reconnoiter around the sharp edges of barrels, stacks of rebar, and rusting storage bins. His flashlight flickered and then failed as he approached the fence protecting the side of the hole. It took a minute or two for his aging eyes to adjust, but he could make out something moving below him in the excavation, close to the ground, near a new hole that hadn't been there earlier during a site surveillance patrol.

"Wow," he whispered.

A bluish-green glow started pulsing from the jagged edges of the puncture made by the pylons. That glow allowed Johnson a better perspective. There was a second form rushing across the site floor; it was smaller and wearing lighter clothing. He could hear a woman's voice cutting through the darkness, but it was too faint to pick out words.

Mary Beth Calvert stood over a prone, slithering Richard Sinclair. A green ruck sack hung over her shoulder. She crossed her arms in her blue pea coat as she bent down to get closer to his muddy face.

"Richard, what on earth do you think you're doing?"

Sinclair was just about to peer over the edge when that familiar, shrill, hawk-like voice caught him short. "For God's sake, Mary Beth, get the hell down. We don't know what's been exposed. Keep yourself close to the ground and spread your weight out." Richard fired the orders at her like a drill instructor.

She dropped like a bag of cats, squirming and mewing with discomfort and annoyance. "Hey, this is my site. You can't talk to *me* like that."

"Like what? Did you bring the meter and the flashlights?"

"You are insufferable. What a schmuck."

"I'll ask you one more time. Do you have them or not?"

His voice sent a chill down her spine. She felt her stomach muscles harden. "Yes," she said, lowly, "here's the bag with all the stuff and the air meter. But based on that smell, I think you'd better wear the filter mask, too. I brought it, just in case. It's good for a couple of the worst gases, but if there's no oxygen that's a moot point."

"Slide the stuff over here, and don't come any closer. Do you hear me?"

"Yes. Here's everything you asked for." Her voice was mechanical. "No wonder I couldn't stand to wake up with you. You're such an arrogant ass." She slid the equipment over to him hastily, causing the flashlight to roll and splatter mud on the lens.

Sinclair pulled the bag of tools, the flare gun, and the ropes to him, and then motioned her away like an idle tourist on the beach. He pulled the strap for the oxygen meter over his neck, donned the mask, and pulled the straps extra tight to get a strong seal. The flashlight refused to work even after a good shaking. He tried the crane flashlight. No good.

"Didn't you check the damn light before you brought it down?" She could hear his mumbling through his mask. Background construction sounds didn't block his masked voice because the hole was dead-still, except for aching groans of the crane generator as it failed to start.

"I'm sorry, Richard." She crawled away from her former lover and his madness. "It worked just before I left the shack. Screw you!"

He tossed the light back at her. A broken light was a nuisance, just like Mary Beth. The story of their affair was like the flashlight: worn, out of juice and annoying.

Sinclair finally worked his way to the edge of the growing maw. He peeked over the side while keeping an eye on the oxygen meter. He thought back on the men he'd pulled from confined spaces at industrial site accidents. He could still see their shocked faces after they fell dead from an invisible killer: no oxygen. He pursed his lips and looked deeper.

A bluish mist rose to the lip, like dry ice on a rock-and-roll concert stage. Along with it came an odor of ancient decay that the mask's organic gas filter wasn't trapping. It left an acrid taste in his mouth, but not enough to cause discomfort or pain. He made his final decision to proceed just as green phosphorescence began pulsing directly below and to the inside of the fissure. He remembered what happened in natural gas leaks, how methane sometimes rolled out in a mist. Richard started to put the flare gun back, hesitated, and then stuffed it deep under his belt.

"I wonder if Bisol would approve of his new Templar spy crawling into this mess. Well, I was sent to check this place for Drake's treasure, so I might as well do it as long as I have the chance. Something's down there. C'mon, suck it up Sinclair," he said to the yawning void, trying to build his courage. "Templars show no fear. Templars give no ground." He made the sign of the cross. "Do geese see God?" he whispered over and over again as he heard the crane's backup generator cough to life.

Arnie Johnson leaned over the dig's security fence and wondered if he could find a quick route to apprehend the trespassers. Nobody should be out there at night with the holiday coming. That new hole and the crash probably meant some kind of sabotage or even terrorism activity. There had been some threats from an off-the-wall environmental group that wanted San Francisco to go back to a natural forest after the quake. They didn't want any repair or reconstruction of any major buildings. This could be some of those wackos, or maybe even the Asian gangs that had pestered the reconstruction site last week claiming the State was threatening their birthright. To Johnson they were all nut jobs.

Before the officer could feel his way any farther around the fence, he heard the groan of the Cummins diesel generator spitting and growling from the top of the other side of the hole. A few lights came on here and there around the construction site, and in the crane cabin above, but the generator was struggling. Johnson could hear the whine of the engine as though the fuel was full of sand. He hoped a halogen construction light might come on and fill out the movement in the hole so he could see who to arrest.

As he got more accustomed to the dimmed security lights, he could make out a man and maybe a woman. She was crawling away, at least fifty feet from the man. Johnson was sure this was going to be a homicide until he saw the lone man reaching over the edge of the hole. Johnson could see the man's arm and face lined in a glimmering reflection coming from the gash in the ground. He examined the string of loose cables above the pit drift over to the work area on the side. These dropped completely away from the main boom. A sharp click followed as the operator used electromagnetic connectors to clamp a new end of cables to the hoist. The new line had a large hook suspended from the end, almost the size of the man lying in the construction mire. The crane operator skillfully brought the new line over so it rested within inches of the glowing arms of the intruder poised on the edge. Johnson kept testing the perimeter fence and finally spotted a stairway on his side of the hole.

"Pfeister, get your dumb ass down here." There was no response. Johnson's chest mike and radio were still out. His only option was to work his way down in the darkness by himself. He could barely see the outline of the man below him, grabbing onto the cable to pull up from the floor. The shadowy figure placed one foot in the belly of the giant, crooked bend while wrapping his other leg around the cable. One arm held tight on the steel lifeline while the other waved hand signals to the crane operator above. The last signal was a stiff arm flapping downward. The baited hook slipped into the strange alien glow, which, as far as Johnson was concerned, might be the entrance to Hell.

Chapter 2

Before Sinclair slipped his foot into the massive J-shaped hook, he tightened his facemask and filter. The mask canister looked like a sawed-off black tusk. He hoped the filter would protect him from any toxic trails drifting about. The mask cartridge cut most of the stench, but something in the vapors stung where it combined with his sweat. The corrosive irritation kept him aware of the risks, but at least he was sure now it wasn't natural gas. Methane didn't make acids like that. Maybe the flare wouldn't set off a methane blast.

He pulled the strap for the oxygen meter over his head so it hung freely in front of him. He checked the gauges. The air was good. At least it was safe on the lip of the new crevasse. Finally, he pulled on thick leather gloves and finished his preparations by shoving the flare gun tighter under his belt. He used the hook safety strap to secure his legs against the splintery steel cable. He clung to it tight as a tick. His right arm flailed downward as a signal for Torres to start lowering the line into the unknown waiting for his arrival.

It wasn't a smooth journey. The cable swung about in circles and in spurts. Sinclair's hands trembled. He didn't look down. The pain and cold in his hands ripped at his focus as he clung to the rusting, oily steel cable. The metal line reeked of construction mud and grime from years of heavy lifting and toil in filthy building sites. Vertigo writhed through him from his acrophobic frenzy.

His leather gloves didn't stop all the cable's steel slivers from reaching his palms. He grimaced as warm blood ran from his gloves down into his shirt sleeve. A few steel thorns stuck into his neck after a hard jolt. He breathed harder and faster after the visor fogged up with trapped moisture. The humidity and biting chill gave him an occasional shudder.

Billowing clouds continued to drift up and around him as the hook slipped silently below. The mask filters provided less protection than he had expected. He could feel a pinch in his lungs and a new, deeper burning in his throat and sinuses.

Sinclair was desperate to find some visual reference point. He still couldn't see specifics through the noxious, suspended dust-mist: a mix of sparkling particles drifting in layers after the pylons' impact into this void. It was impossible to pinpoint the exact source of the pulsing light through the multi-colored clouds. Sinclair explored with one leg, searching for a bottom to land on as the line descended ten, twenty, thirty and then forty feet. He came to rest with a hard thud that shook every disk in his back. His knees were burning knives that gave way as he slipped and fell onto solid ground.

He shook his head and stood back up. His hands ached from the metal splinter wounds, but that was overtaken by his curiosity about the lights. The oxygen meter still read fine for air, but the mask was little help against the smells and acrid vapors. Sinclair ripped the ineffective headpiece off and tossed it aside. A fresh onslaught of the caustic fumes made him turn quickly and vomit.

Even with the disorientation, and a new pounding in his head from the discomfort, he froze in place to concentrate on a hissing, high-pitched screeching. It was omnidirectional and bounced off the walls as it spun around him. Then the cave was silent. He knelt quickly, trying to survey the ground under the murky upper layers of suspended impact dust. There was a brief break in the dense cover, but only about ten inches above the soil, which was dry and caked to the point of being brittle and cracked. He had to depend on blind groping to find his way, just like in the caves that had almost devoured him in the Sangre de Cristo Mountains in New Mexico. He was grateful that he wasn't knee deep in bat guano filled with a sea of living, hungry, disease-infested insects.

He righted himself, again, after sensing something moving behind him in the shifting green-and-blue mists, but there was nothing to identify in the cloak of pulsing colors that coalesced into a dull, glowing center just ahead of his position. He was fairly confident the light was bioluminescence; there was simply no other explanation. He had seen similar effects in caves in the Caribbean from glow worms suspended from the ceiling, but nothing like this in North America. This was a find in itself.

He pulled a roll of nylon rope out of the bag and wrapped it around the cable. This would be his lifeline as he made short, steady scouting ventures in an ever-increasing circle. He needed a certainty of escape from whatever was scooting about.

Sinclair kicked up the cracked clay with his steel-toed boots as he carefully inched forward. He bumped blindly face first into a stray pylon. The shock tipped his balance and he landed hard on the floor. He noticed again the increased visibility across the void when he was under the overhanging fog. The main source of light was much closer than it seemed in the mists. His knees let him know they were fed up with his falls. They demanded a short rest.

There was a swift movement just in front of him, breaking the light along the bottom of the space. He caught a glimpse of multiple shadows, but not enough to form a distinct picture. It was a rapid, quiet silhouette.

He thought about his distance from the cable. Maybe escape was in order. Curiosity ate at him and tore away all his training for undefined situations in underground explorations. He had to know what was creating the glow. What was this space hiding? Then, just as he turned to rise, something gripped his shoulder. He spun wildly, striking out in the mist. His fist struck home and he heard something hit the floor near his feet.

"Richard! You bastard. What the bloody hell did you do that for? Ohhhh . . ." Mary Beth's muffled voice trailed off as she recovered from the blow to the side of her mask. He'd only grazed her but it was enough to knock her off balance.

"You're the one who snuck up on me. How'd you get down here? Don't you ever listen to directions?" He pulled her up to her feet and stood close so he could hear her. Mary Beth popped a yellow glow stick, blinding Sinclair. Its brilliance created a thicker blanket around them as it reflected back and forth in a flurry of dust.

"Toss that in the corner. It won't help us in this. Besides, it's interfering with the light ahead."

"Listen, Richard, you *putz*, the last time I remember, I was in charge of this site, not you. Where do you get off telling me what I can do at my dig?"

"Christ, Mary Beth, not now. I don't know why Torres let you down here, but we've got company, and I don't think it's friendly. This isn't a burial mound. I think we ought to get out of here."

"I'll leave when I'm damn well good and ready. Just move along the wall a little and explore toward that light. Why don't you just let a pro do this? You're still such a little boy, you *schlemiel*." She threw the glow stick aside. Richard kept the initiative and pushed her behind him as they and moved forward into the green radiance.

The pulses of light got brighter and more frequent. There were no signposts to give a sense of up, down, or sideways. Only their feet on the cave clay assured them they weren't floating in a cloud. As they got closer to the source, sweat poured out of his eyelids and nose, burning like liquid fire. He wiped it away, stopping mid-swipe as something swept past him, ghostlike in the mist.

"You ought to put this on," Mary Beth directed, handing Sinclair another mask. "I switched canisters. The others weren't working. It might protect those sensitive *goy* lungs."

"No, I need to keep clear so I can react. I know I heard something moving around here. I don't want any distraction. I don't think what's in here cares if you're Jewish, so you better watch your pretty little ass."

"Yeah, acid in your eyes, that wouldn't distract anyone, now would it? And keep your eyes off my ass."

"Hey, you dumped me. I got no interest now or ever. Just keep moving."

He poked ahead with his feet, just like exploring the underground limestone beds near the San Carlos Indian Reservation in New Mexico. A secondary crevasse could lay waiting, hundreds of feet deep, under a mere shell of a crust deposited slowly over the eons. He had sworn off caving after watching two of his friends fall to their deaths at the Reservation. Since then he avoided anything requiring a trek underground, but as a Templar he was sworn to overcome every fear by charging at the fear.

He took a deep breath and pushed forward with Mary Beth at his side until his feet were blocked by something between Sinclair and the brilliant glow ahead of his path. His boots crunched the restriction. It was something fragile as eggshells. He'd felt the same kinds of shards in a sacrificial cave in Arizona filled with human skulls. He hoped the ones below him now were from a sheep or pig, but he had no stomach to reach down and check. He'd let the wicked witch check it out. If they were human remains, that might distract Mary Beth long enough to let him do the reconnaissance he was charged to perform.

"Hey, check this out," he said, pulling her head downward while he tapped on top of the skulls with his boot. "It might be a real find, especially if it's early Maidu Culture."

"Nice, Richard. Probably just smashed it to smithereens. You go ahead, but quit crushing my work. I'll just take a few samples until we can get this fog out of here and light the place up properly."

Sinclair pulled his guide rope tight and stretched his gloved hand toward the throbbing light just ahead of him. It was there and real. It was solid. It was warm to the touch and he could lift it. He pulled it toward his face as his hands and arms began to shake violently. He could just make it out now—an odd figurine made of silver-green metal; the light beams emanated from its core. He'd never seen or felt anything like it. It was a Buddha-like statuette made of a lightweight alloy. It pulsed with a throbbing hum. It projected a wave of force that resonated within Richard's chest.

Sinclair saw the jewels in the eye sockets and realized that this was not a Buddha of love and forgiveness. This Buddha had the visage of a hungry, angry, demonic soul. The emerald eyes glowed independently of the metal's light. He could see facial features twist and grimace as if the object was alive. As he pulled it toward him a shot of excruciating pain tore through his hand. He screamed as the miniature mouth tore a piece of flesh from his wrist. He threw the statue hard against the ground, but in doing so lost his grip on his guide rope. Something slithered past him again, pulling his safety tether away.

"Richard, are you all right?"

He couldn't see her but he knew the general direction of Mary Beth's position. Moving without the rope was disorienting, but he took the risk and shuffled toward her.

A deep, melancholic moaning filled the void, vibrating back and forth. If he hadn't been terrified and deeply wounded, Richard would have laughed at what seemed a silly imitation of graveyard ghosts in a B movie; but, this was no movie. Something spun around him unimpeded by the walls and debris. It was invisible in the mist and coming closer as he retreated. He prayed his sense of direction would not fail him as he moved a little faster than he could clearly navigate. He brushed his face against one of the pylons. The cresol oil in the splinters burned his cheek—a minor irritation compared to the grinding, tearing spasms in his bleeding wrist and his burning lungs. The slow shuffle back was also tearing at his re-damaged knees. The fall from the cable was taking its toll.

He rushed pell-mell and blindly back to Mary Beth, his lifeline. His feet kept slipping on something. Now he realized that his ankles were covered in frigid water. The hole could be caving in and filling the void with seepage from the Bay.

He finally reached Mary Beth and held onto her.

She screamed in his face. "We've got to get out of here! Crap, you're hurt. It looks pretty damn serious. C'mon, let's go, I got my samples."

Her lead rope was still intact. She used the umbilical to lead them back to the drop line. The cable hook loomed directly in front of them. Sinclair wasted no time in pulling the flare gun out and firing it straight overhead. The response was immediate. The cable and hook began to pull up. He pushed against Mary Beth's back, forcing her forward to step into the hook. *At least she'll be safe*, he thought, as he put what pressure he could against the blood still spurting from his wrist.

He knew he was losing too much blood as he grew faint, waiting for the line to return. The hook finally descended for him. He fired off a second round from the flare gun. He used the last of his strength to grasp the cable with his good hand and his legs. The line rose slowly. *Just twenty more feet*, he prayed, *and there will be help*. Just as his body crested over the lip, a force from the mist below grabbed him violently. The cable stopped in midair as he felt the crush of a python-like grip on his left boot. Help was nearby, but too far away to assist the Templar in his life-and-death struggle.

By the time Johnson got to a flank position to the pit he could see the cable was deep into the hole, but the light from inside was brighter now, and moving around like a whirlpool. "It is hell," he muttered.

A flare shot out and lit up the excavation floor. The crane roared to life and lifted the cable up. There was a woman hanging tenuously from the end, flailing her free arm around wildly. There was a quick movement of the line. Johnson could see her as she flipped from her support about six feet to the ground near the glowing cave-in entrance. She didn't move.

The crane operator wasted no time dropping the cable back down into the cavity. A second flare flew up from below. The line pulled back up slowly and then stalled just as another figure peeked over the rim. Johnson could hear the back-up generator straining to support the demands of the crane. The flare faded but left just enough illumination so Johnson could see the cable come to a complete halt. He could hear the crane motors grind in agony to a new strain on the line. Then he saw the shadow of a man riding on the cable hook, but there was something else attached and squirming on the man's leg. It was something beyond belief.

Johnson rushed forward to attack. He needed to get closer for his shotgun to have any effect on the beast clinging to its victim, and still not kill its prey. He battled to maintain his own training. He denied that in front of him was a gigantic, twisting centipede trying to tear the squirming survivor off his perilous hold.

Sinclair was beginning to pass out from loss of blood, pain, and the venom from something that could not exist. The bulbous, gleaming face of the huge centipede passed him as it swung over his chest, trying to pull the line back into its lair. Richard knew he would fall as soon as the shaking became more violent. The source of the den's odor was evidently from this *thing*. Its scuttling, dagger-sharp legs cut into Sinclair's clothes and into his thighs and chest. Each pierce left a searing burn from a caustic chemical.

The thing was winning the struggle when Richard heard a shotgun go off nearby, followed by pistol fire. A spine-tingling, non-human screech penetrated the space around him. He was suffocating from new smells of decay and death as the monster bug disappeared in thin air. Sinclair immediately felt a new presence in his chest cavity, tearing and rushing within him. This venomous attacker was making the Templar's insides its new home.

The sides of the abyss crumbled and collapsed into the entrance below Sinclair, as he was still dangling and losing his hold. He could see Mary Beth lying flat with her mask torn away. Dust and thick, rolling, black clouds rushed up around Sinclair. Torres struggled to swing the hook and cable carefully to the closest wall of the pit, near Mary Beth and Johnson. Sinclair collapsed the last few feet before the hook reached the excavation floor. The other side of the site roared as the ground folded over the buried pylons. A fountain of dark water surged up from the rupture.

Johnson dragged Mary Beth next to Sinclair's limp body. Richard's mind was already drifting in a painless coma.

Chapter 3

A haze of fog rolled through Richard's brain as the pains of the attack drifted in and out through rippling layers of darkness. Silence reigned over him, interrupted occasionally by whispers or echoes. His hands thrashed wildly in the middle of hallucinations of shadowy beasts. He would rest only when there was no denizen to strike. He cursed at the terror in the silence. He was alone, trapped, the only one listening in this eternal fog; unfettered by nothing but the cool drape of moisture. Sinclair was a lost soul in the land of coma—the almost death.

Smoking castle battlements rose over him. He felt the cold, rough-edged stone on his burning hands as he tried to rise. The screams of the dying were at every side: the last moans of the butchered and the unmerciful growling of swordsman slicing life from the wounded. He was trapped in a battle of carnage.

"Gaspard, Gaspard! What of him?" Richard's cries echoed in a narrow street, his nostrils near suffocation with the smell of fresh human blood and offal.

Sinclair felt the warmth of his own blood drifting down his face and hands as he swung his sword wildly against his foes. His twelve-pound blade shattered armor and sinew before him. Cries rolled from his path hewn from men's flesh.

Then there was darkness and terror as the night cries faded away. Bodies were piled on him, wriggling in their last futile moments; but, he was not dead beneath their weight and rigor mortis. Every movement in the pile of corpses awakened him to his comrades' grim endings and possibly his own.

Sinclair sprang upright in the hospital bed, trying to scream through his dry, wizened vocal cords. He felt the agony on his wrist wound and knees as the leather restraints pulled him back. Unfamiliar noises of monitoring equipment and hospital hallways rolled around him, but he was alone. There were no buttons to push and no strings to pull for aid. Sinclair felt abandoned as he struggled in vain. The wrinkled, drab-green drapes encased the bed. They only let through a few peeks of the room as they fell around the handrails with their occasional gruesome stain. Behind him rose a wall of cracked and chipped paint that separated him and whatever remained of the world.

He lapsed back into darkness. The mist burned off into another world of unconsciousness.

"How's the head?" A cool, deep voice cascaded over Richard, who fluttered his eyes open. He wanted to say something, anything, but could not.

"You've been through hell and back, buddy. Hell and more. When you get back to yourself a bit we'll have a good debrief. You just get better."

Sinclair could feel a strong hand on his shoulder. It could only be Alex Bisol, his recently assigned mentor and guide through a new life as an initiate Templar. Bisol was charged to look over Richard's progress after Sinclair's return back to California. It was a relief after his whirlwind, three-month, global training tour. Sinclair took a deep breath, sighed, and fell back to sleep. He imagined in his stupor that this was all a fantasy and he had successfully committed suicide on his little sloop off Catalina Island. He prayed for release and peace, and to meet his wife and daughter on the other side.

Sinclair could feel himself stretch, stretch, and stretch again, almost touching his mother's fingertips. How he longed to see her. She was just as he remembered her in his childhood; pleasant, calm, deep-chocolate eyes embedded in pale, clear skin, and framed by flowing, black wavy hair. Her full, rich mouth didn't move, but Richard could hear her voice calling him lightly, "Richard, welcome home."

He heard the words again, but then realized it was another woman calling him.

A throbbing headache pummeled him as he tried to sit up straight. Spittle ran down the side of his cheek. Sinclair felt the cool sponge drift over his mouth and forehead. The nurse leaned over him, supporting the back of his head. She replaced the pillow soaked in Richard's sweat.

"Can you hear me, Richard?"

He could barely make out her white uniform as a film was still heavy on his eyes. He blinked again and again to clear them. A soft tissue dusted against his check and dabbed at the corners of his eyes. Her name tag read MARIE HALLERAN.

"Here, let me clear some of that sleep for you."

He could see her young, vivacious figure. Her blond hair was in pillows and puffs, barely restrained behind her headpiece. She was a pale blond angel leaning over him with warmth and caring. He could feel her heat. Her breath was sweet and her light scent reminded him of his mother's perfume, Evening in Paris.

"Can he hear me now?" A voice rose from behind her.

"I think so."

"Good, you can go now. We need to speak alone for a while." Alexander Bisol moved forward, touching the nurse lightly on the shoulders to show his confidence and support for her attention. She shrugged off his hands with a look of disgust and stepped away from Bisol.

"All right, Alex, but only for a few minutes. He's still very weak and you know we still haven't managed to find a way to control the—"

"That will be enough for now."

As she walked away, taking the plastic pan with gauze, medications, and used needles, she looked back once more and smiled pleasantly at the patient, tilting her head a bit so he could see her interest. She frowned at Alex Bisol.

After the door of the private hospital room closed, Bisol moved closer to Sinclair. His right hand sought out Richard's, as he pushed his thumb into the hollow of Richard's right thumb. It was the Order's way of signaling that it was safe to talk of Templar business in the open.

"How the hell did I get here?"

"I take it you don't remember much?"

"About what?" Sinclair coughed, trying to get the strawberry flavor out of his mouth from the mouth swabs the nurse had used to keep his tongue and cheeks moist. Then some of what happened crept back in pieces, slowly.

"There are more questions about that night than any of us have been able to answer. It's amazing anyone got out alive after the site collapsed." Bisol slid a chair over so he could lean closely to Richard above the arm restraints, without sitting on the rail.

"God, don't tell me Mary Beth got—"

"No, she made it out right after she was dragged out by the cop. Then he reached you and pulled you out of the pit. The only reliable witness we have now is the crane operator, but he says he couldn't see that much because the fog was rolling in. By the time he pulled you out of the hole with the crane his view was blocked. There wasn't anything on the security cameras, either. They were both fried for some reason. So, all we've got left is Mary Beth Calvert and the cop. That's not working out so well. She had a mild concussion and the cop is . . . well, sort of crazy."

Sinclair coughed to the side again. He motioned for Bisol to hand him some water. It was then that he realized he couldn't raise his arms. He was tied down with straps. "What is this shit?"

"Easy, Richard," During Sinclair's last initiation ritual the month before, Alex had noted how violent Richard became when he was bound in any way. Bisol raised Sinclair's head so he could sip slowly from the tepid water. He didn't trust Sinclair with more than a small paper cup. The patient might overdo his cravings and end up with a bloated gut. Any kind of swelling or vomiting would only complicate Sinclair's wounds.

Sinclair savored the delicious, clear liquid as if it were the first time water had ever come to his lips. It was heavenly. He could sense how cracked and dry his skin was across his mouth. The water stuck for a moment in his throat where a ventilator had rubbed his tissues raw.

"You've been here almost a month. It's nearly August. We thought you might leave us several times, but you're a fighter. You still have to be restrained to ensure you don't move or scratch at the stitches. Your ribs, a wrist, and one of your legs were torn up pretty bad. When you fell off the crane hook you fractured two vertebrae. We just got you off the backboard and counterweights last week. There are other issues, too. You need to be patient."

Sinclair breathed back heavily, giving out a deep groan. He let out several deep sighs, trying to gain composure. "You said no one can tell you what happened to me, but Mary Beth and a policeman were there. Why can't they tell you anything?"

Bisol hesitated and sat back in the discomfort of the under-stuffed, vomit-green vinyl hospital chair. He couldn't find a comfortable spot that didn't irritate his old war injuries from shrapnel in Desert Storm.

"Hmmm," Bisol muttered, "well, simply, Calvert had to take a leave of absence for, shall we say, counseling. She was on heavy narcotics for a few weeks just to get her to sleep. She couldn't even give a coherent interview. We can't get to her now. One of her relatives has her up in some rehab center in Napa. She comes from old money, you know."

"Yeah, yeah, tell me something I don't know. So, what about the cop?"

"Anything Arnie Johnson might say is mixed with talk of the Devil and the mouth of hell. He's on administrative leave. Even the press won't get close to him. His partner told the San Fran Commissioner that Johnson had been ranting about religion and God for months. So, the cop has been totally discounted. You're the only one who can really tell me what happened. I just hope you know what went down that night."

Sinclair's breathing continued to be deep and regular. He stopped for a few seconds, drawing Alex closer to him. "You gave the hand sign so I will speak the truth. I saw no gold. There was no sign of Sir Francis Drake or any scrolls. There is little that I remember, except being grabbed by something huge and I was also bitten by something small and evil. After that I just remember mist and fear. I can't even remember from what. There's just mist and more mist. Maybe it's a memory of the coastal fog, I don't know. God, just get me the hell out of here."

"It's okay." Alex leaned over and touched Richard's forehead. An invisible circle of energy rolled into Sinclair's mind, giving him peace and wellbeing.

"Why, Alex? Why me? There was nothing there. Nothing from Drake's treasure. Is this search really worth it?"

Alex continued to stroke his head. "More than you can imagine. You have faced the great wall of fear and overcome. Now, Richard, you need to rest and come back to us. To be blunt, you look like death warmed over."

Richard gurgled a little in his dry throat, understanding that humor was not one of Alex's strong points, but he appreciated his attempts.

"There's been another development. There were others down at the pit, sniffing around the next morning. We've gotten some early identification and it's odd. We think they're PRC agents."

"What?" Sinclair's voice was croaky, too dry again to say more.

"Yes, a new player on the stage. The Papists are an issue we've faced forever on this quest for our lost treasure, but we've never crossed the Chinese. It makes no sense. We weren't messing with them. That story we made up about the Tong and lost burial ground was to justify bringing in the archeologists. That gave us the cover of a State seal on the site. Once Calvert was there we could manipulate the Governor and get you reassigned. We've watched that spot for over a hundred years, waiting to see if it matched with the secret Drake maps we've gathered. The last thing we want is the Communists in here plucking at our feathers."

"What about that Christian King, Prestor John? Wasn't he supposed to be somewhere in China, ready to launch a giant army to support the Crusaders when they were losing battle after battle?" Sinclair asked.

"Yeah, that was pure bullshit, just to keep the morale up for the fodder the Papists sent into battle, when the Saracens started kicking our ass out of Jerusalem. Everyone uses propaganda to keep troops at the front, especially when your side is losing. I can't imagine the ChiComs could give two shits about any happy-face rumors from eight hundred years ago. It's just weird, but we'll deal with them later. Maybe then they can explain this other BS we're dealing with."

Sinclair rolled his head to the side for a second, breaking away from the conversation. Something else was bothering him—a terrible burning sensation in his chest. *A heart attack*, he screamed in his head, sure that this is the way it must have felt for his father. He'd died of a massive coronary. The growing fire in his chest was his only reality. It moved around as if it were gnawing through him.

Monitors on the cart to Sinclair's left were beeping wildly. A blue alarm light for the crash cart flashed off and on at the outside wall near the door. Nurse Halleran and two doctors came rushing with a rolling tray packed with emergency medication. Halleran pushed Bisol away from the bed. The fluorescent lights above the bed flickered on and off wildly; sparks shot from the ballasts.

"Get the Epi!" one doctor commanded as he tore the covers off Sinclair. Halleran used a pair of scissors to cut through Sinclair's nightgown. It all stopped. Everyone stood back, gasping, freezing their efforts to stop a coronary arrest.

Alex grabbed the Epi needle from the doctor's hand and drove it into the wriggling form writhing under the muscles over Sinclair's chest.

"What the hell are you doing?" The doctor pushed Alex back away from the bed.

Alex's injection was deft and effective; the writhing shape under Sinclair's skin stopped. Monitors returned to normal. Everyone watched as the head physician poked his fingers at the fresh, swollen scar covering where the infestation ceased crawling over Sinclair's breastbone.

The doctor wrenched his hand back. "It burned me right through my gloves, damn it!" He reached into the crash cart for medication.

The other Crash Team members watched as the ten-inch centipede shape melted away, spreading out flat as it merged into the deep, purple brand. Sinclair's skin remained raised only slightly in the outline of a black centipede. The brand then dissipated and formed a small, red glyph over his sternum.

Sinclair was still. He was not in a coma, but rather in a deep sleep; he snored quietly.

Halleran pushed everyone back and pulled the covers over Sinclair's nakedness. "I think Mr. Sinclair has been through enough, I'll watch over him. If anything changes, I'll call. You, too, Alex. I think we've all seen enough of you for one night."

"Maybe so, Marie." He agreed grudgingly, as she walked outside. "I think my next step is to get a stiff drink."

"Don't expect me to join you. You're the last person I wanted to see where I work. I have to put up with you at some of the initiations of new members, but that's only because of my position as the Keeper of the Doorway."

Bisol nodded, knowing that his real destination was the University of Berkeley Library. Her uncle, Edmund Turner, was another Templar agent, and renowned for his expertise in occult secrets. Turner was the nearest and best source to interpret the glyph—a symbol Alex would never forget. At this point Bisol had no desire to watch over a troublesome acolyte Templar being protected by a woman who wanted Alex Bisol dead.

Chapter 4

Alex ignored the lush hedges, shrubs and rustling trees as he walked across the campus. It was located less than an hour's drive across the Bay Bridge from the clinic. He bit at the corner of his lip nervously as he pushed on the cold, brass crash bar on the ponderous doors of the University of Berkeley Library. Only the most studious and serious would be inside in the late summer. He started to descend quickly down the middle of the broad, marble stairway to the special materials reference desk. Bisol hated touching the stair railings because of the oils from hands of graduate students preceding him. He also avoided the elevator. It had a history of failing in hot weather; a bit of claustrophobia and some horrifying campus urban legends kept him from using it. If not for Edmund Turner's genius, Bisol would never venture to these halls.

An unsuspected sense of vertigo surprised him on the stairs as he grabbed blindly for the handrails. An unfamiliar series of memories rippled through him. He shivered from the fear of falling from some imagined height. Terror of crashing to his death rushed in with no warning. Bisol had exquisitely detailed visions and pains attacking him from someone else's childhood. He'd never fallen as a child, but the memories were clear and persistent. They'd started just weeks before after he had touched the Sinclair's bare hand at the hospital. Vivid impressions of places Bisol never lived in crept into his steel-trap mind. Alex hadn't said a thing about these attacks to others. Oddly enough, the reoccurring nightmares Bisol suffered with since childhood had vanished at the same time—horrific scenes of hand-to-hand fighting in a medieval French city.

Bisol studied the corkboards near the base of the stairs as he wrestled to gather his composure. The board was jammed with last semester's postings for roommates, graduate study assistants, and for anyone who could share travel expenses back home. He noted a series of pink note cards tossed on the floor in front of the mahogany reference kiosk. He picked one up. "Need a brain to help with term papers? Call Jack." The typical 800 number followed, making him chuckle at the same scams he'd seen at Harvard and Duke.

Edmund Turner popped up from behind the kiosk barrier. Bisol faced a middle-aged blonde master of the Berkeley geek squads. His large eyes and small, sharp nose bore a harsh contrast to the chiseled military features of the surprised Templar's Master of Arms.

"Christ's blood," Bisol muttered, "I hate it when you do that crap. Why can't you just sit there like a good librarian and just turn your head like an owl?"

Turner peered over his worn horn-rimmed glasses to give Bisol the eye. "Templars: So proud in battle; so leery in a library."

A flush sizzled up Bisol's neck, rising to his face. "I swear, one of these days, Turner, your smart mouth is going to . . ."

Turner's clothes seemed to be carefully wrinkled into the contours of the Himalayas. He moved in a quirky manner which only Bisol knew was camouflage for the early stages of Parkinson's disease. "Will my smart mouth ever enlighten some of the Brotherhood who would rather chase the tail of the world politic for their own deep, little-known purposes? How I doubt that. I choose to serve the Rose and the Chalice only because of the *great* work. And I don't accost underage women. Thank God Marie became a Templar so you can never touch her again. Even you wouldn't dare the punishment to any Templar raising a hand against another in the Order."

"All right. Let's quit sparring. You enjoy this mental wrestling far too much, and I haven't got time for it. And yes, I like my limbs attached, thank you. You don't have to worry about Marie. You said your piece, as always, so let's get down to it. Did you find anything on the design I sent you?"

"Ah, ah, ah. Aren't we forgetting a little something for my favorite little ponies?" Turner stretched out his long, slender hand, far away from the comfort of the cardigan sweater that covered his bleach-white wrists. Bisol pursed his lips together while grunting and shaking his head in disgust. Bisol reached into his pocket and transferred a sealed, white envelope. Great information always came at a cost, even between members of the Temple.

"You know you're supposed to be serving the community, damn it." Bisol stared hard into Turner's eyes.

"Well," replied the librarian, "when you Harvard boys get smart enough to go to Berkeley, then these little safaris into the library might not cost you. Now, are you ready for a little briefing?"

"I don't like doing business with you, you know that?"

"Well, Master at Arms, I don't like the design of the phone book, either, but I use it every day. You should drop by more often. They miss me at the track." Turner slipped the envelope down to a drawer he had just unlocked, stuck it deep to the back, and then relocked it. He pulled out a green folder from a hidden space under the desktop and put it on the glass-covered kiosk.

"Just get to it," Bisol snapped.

"First, let me get the Gaspard reference out of the way, which you asked about. I'm rather surprised you didn't know the connection. However, these days, it doesn't take as much to be in the Order as it once did."

Bisol clenched his jaw and let his fingers tap on the glass over the worn mahogany surface.

Turner swallowed and cleared his throat, deciding to speed the pace a bit to protect his safety. Bisol's reputation as a field operative for the NSA preceded him. Turner stored his wit as he opened the file, separating notes in a new priority. "Here it is," Turner started, pushing his glasses tight to his face. "One has to go back to sixteenth century France for this reference, which was a crucial date for all Templars at the time. This is just a basic synopsis, as I know you are not a historian by nature." Turner licked his dry lips in preparation for his oration. "On August twenty-fourth, fifteen seventy-two, the zealous French Catholics slaughtered the Protestant Huguenots—*and I am using that term in an exact sense here—slaughtered.* The Huguenots had been blamed for every failing in France, from poor crops to high prices. The typical scapegoat mentality raced through the Catholic communities. There were many famous players on both sides of this genocide, with Catherine de Medici being the royal leader of the Catholic plot. The complexities of the internecine rivalries is a bit tangled for a brief overview, especially relating to political marriages meant to calm the continuing Catholic-Protestant bickering."

CURSE OF THE 8TH BUDDHA 43

"Go on," Bisol interrupted, "And speed it up. I need to know about that design I faxed over." He watched Turner fidget, clearing his throat again, as he pushed his glasses back tight to his forehead. The librarian continued, at an increased pace.

"Catherine invited the primary leaders to a day of celebration and marriage to appease the ongoing tensions. The Huguenots, unsuspecting and unarmed, were easy targets for an early morning raid. Catherine laid waste to the entire leadership of the Huguenots in one deft blow, starting with the primary Huguenot leader, Gaspard de Coligny. The soldiers and Catholic clergy across the countryside then followed her signal to wipe out every Huguenot. The streets flowed in rivers of blood. It became known as the Saint Bartholomew's Day Massacre."

"Good lord," Bisol put his hand over his forehead and eyes as he lowered his chin to his chest. He rocked his head slowly back and forth. "Please tell me we didn't help orchestrate that. I had Huguenot relatives in my family tree, somewhere."

"No, the Templars had long before moved their center of operations to Scotland and Ireland, after that dread day, Friday October thirteenth, thirteen oh-seven."

Both men bowed their heads and made a motion across their hearts, as was required when referencing that day of infamy in the Order's history, when the Pope allowed the attempted destruction of the Templars. That day became the source for the common fear in Western culture of Friday the 13th.

"However, the Templars did support the Huguenot cause."

"So, if someone had memories of this massacre could that be carried through a family line—a sort of inherited memory?"

"I've heard of such things. Some say such memories indicate past lives. I don't know. But if someone is remembering being slaughtered in a French alley, that would be pretty hard to pass along to another generation as an inherited memory."

"I see your point."

Bisol moved his attention away from the pages before him, floating away for a moment. The chance that Sinclair had been there, to have lived and died in such a calamity in France was outside his Templar limits of belief. It was Bisol's nightmare that haunted the coma of his new charge, and Sinclair's fear of falling that troubled Bisol's travel on stairways. Turner's research was the last proof he needed to be sure that traumatic memory transfers were linked to the *thing* buried in Sinclair's chest.

Turner sighed and rotated slowly on the balls of his shoes, evaluating the room to see if anyone was moving towards the kiosk. He took note for the first time of the little islands of students congregated under the glow of the green reading lamps. The women seemed to be so young these days . . . just children. His gaze fell on a particularly buxom brunette with hair flowing like a splash of black velvet over her bare shoulders. Bisol's lip began to lift in a slight smile, until the young woman stretched, relieving hours of stress from reading in one position.

Turner released a low chuckle as he watched Bisol grimaced. "No, Alex, the women here still don't shave. I can see you were thinking about Joanna. I have to admit that girl does bear a likeness."

Bisol spun around, glaring at the man who shrank before his ire. "Listen you little dweeb, don't ever bring up her name again. It was a mistake. Second wives always are. I don't care if she is your sister. Just drop it. Give me the rest of what I asked for and then I'm leaving. If you weren't the best and essential, well..."

Turner knew what it meant to be unessential on Alex Bisol's *list*. "Okay, Alex, but do think about protecting that arm." Turner tapped on his own right shoulder as a reminder. "I apologize. Let's get into the juicy stuff. This was really quite interesting and very, very arcane. I used the drawing you sent over." Turner shuffled the papers again, readying his voice for the masterful diatribe. "That symbol is identical to the glyphs found in some of the Pyramid Texts. In fact, there was a recent tomb opening, near what was once Abydos that had this same symbol featured on the stone used to seal the entrance. I asked Dr. Gerald Camp about this. He's our resident expert in Egyptology. He wasn't sure why this had been used instead of say, Anubis, or the vulture goddess, Mut."

"Just get to the good stuff. I don't give two shits about your staff." This time it was Turner's chance to blush.

"Mut was probably more common in the New Kingdom and had a higher position at that time in the temple worship. Dr. Camp was able to get some inside information from a colleague on the French team that opened the new find. It was the first funerary ever found that had purely decorative columns standing at the foot of the single sarcophagus. There is not enough information about why the columns were carved in a deep, curling relief of a giant centipede. There is just nothing like it in Egyptology. The mummies dated to about twenty-two hundred B.C. Unfortunately, that puts us in a timeframe near the end of the Old Kingdom, where we just don't know enough about the Egyptian's practices and beliefs. It was a very volatile, violent era when dynasties were rising and falling. Dr. Camp was explicit that this symbol did not relate to any Egyptian cult or worship that was highly favored from that period, and there were no giant centipedes natural to Egypt at that time, even in the territories of Punt. Here's the symbol that was traced from the tomb inscriptions."

Turner slid a copy across the glass to Bisol. The Templar gave a slight nod and then returned his gaze to the researcher.

"There must be more than that, although this is pretty amazing, that you got all this in less than an hour."

Turner smirked, giving a slight snort. "Yes, there is a bit more in the record. There was a minor god in the Egyptian pantheon mentioned just briefly. The texts state: 'The two serpents are in the sky. The centipede of Osiris is on earth.'" Turner opened another sheave from the folder: "A minor god, Sepa, whose name means 'centipede,' was worshipped in Heliopolis and was commonly used as a charm against noxious animals and enemies of the gods. Sepa was also associated with Osiris as a protector for guarding the remains of the Pharaohs."

"I don't see how this relates to what I'm looking for right now." Bisol's impatience was leaking into his voice.

"Please, let me continue. There's more to this. So, anyway, that of course made more sense to Dr. Camp, and might explain Sepa's notation in the vault. The reference to Horus, the son of Osiris, is reasonable as there are many demigods that served both of them."

"So nothing about a Templar reference, or Sir Francis Drake and the Templar treasure?" Bisol leaned forward, inspecting Turner's trove of facts, hoping there was another pile of secrets hidden under the man's frail hands.

"I think that's a complete disconnect here. There is another odd side issue, however, which you should be aware of. I can't take all the credit for being an astute researcher. I had a head start on this one."

"What? Are you going psychic on me?" Turner pursed his lips and Bisol enjoyed his moment of superiority.

"Well, Al," Turner replied, knowing how Bisol hated that nickname, "if you'd been here last week I might have been stumped. Someone else was here before you, and she was certainly more pleasant to deal with . . . and certainly better looking."

Turner stepped back, knowing that exchange might bring his ex-brother-in-law over the kiosk. He was right.

"You sniveling little rat bastard. You took my money . . . the Order's money . . . and you'd already done the damn search?" Bisol, furious, grasped the pedestal as if he were ready to turn it over on the marble floor.

"Now, Al . . . if you'd given me just another three thousand I could be done with my artificial intelligence software. I told you my programmer was close to finishing the prototype. I just need to compensate him for a little more tweaking on the algorithm. Bay Meadows has a very interesting race coming up next week. A Preakness winner is coming into town. We could really clean up if this software was fixed."

"You and your damned horse racing. I'm not putting another damn penny into that plot. You promised me a return on my investment five years ago and what have I got to show? I'm ten grand in the hole and I'm not even related to you anymore."

Turner stepped farther back—Bisol was actually rocking the kiosk that was bolted into the concrete floor—and screaming, which gathered a great deal of unwanted attention, even from the furry women of the graduate legions about him. "So who was this bitch that came looking for the symbol?" Bisol clenched his teeth as his jaw muscles rippled back and forth.

Turner had his hands up in front of him, pressing back against the air, building an imaginary wall of protection. "For God's sake, Alexander, control yourself." Turner begged in a strenuous whisper, hoping to dispel some of the rage he had stirred, an aspect of his benefactor he feared, even during Bisol's messy arrest for the statuary rape of his niece, Marie Halleran.

"Out with it, or I'll see you work at a Target store cleaning shelves at night."

"Okay. Okay. She was here about a week ago. She had a drawing of the symbol. Yesterday she came by and I gave her the information, plus this other data about the Asian connections."

"Asian? I thought this was Egyptian."

"Well, originally, yes, but it seems this Sepa worship also persisted and migrated to the Orient, probably through the trade routes. The same symbol was used as a representative of a spirit that protected the Buddha as he came back from the heavens, where he taught the Dharma: the basic laws of truth, so to speak, to his mother. Apparently the Buddhists still fly flags in honor of this heavenly teaching to this day, with the Sepa image on it."

"And this mystery woman wanted this information?"

"Yes. She wanted whatever was the oldest data I could find. That symbol could be an old connection, again, back to Horus, who was the sky god. But the connections are just so old, it's hard to say. There is only one other odd reference to the giant centipede symbol, which was found in the temples at Angkor Wat, in Cambodia. There is some speculation that Sepa was carried there as a sign of a major entity sometime during one of the Chinese invasions from the north. There is only one folk story about this, but it is fairly weird, even by my standards."

CURSE OF THE 8ᵀᴴ BUDDHA

"And this is what you told this person who came here yesterday?"

"Exactly," Turner whispered, leaning forward. "And she wanted to know all of it."

"So who was she, anyway? What did she look like? Who was she representing?"

"Alex, I get hundreds of requests every week. I don't catalogue personal information, especially when they pay on the side for a deep investigation."

"You ass."

"Hey, it was for the software. C'mon. But she was a thing of beauty to behold; that mountain of black hair and those fiery green eyes. You don't see that combination that often in Chinese women. Too bad her voice was rather husky. That set her apart. It was somewhat disquieting, actually."

Bisol snapped upright, as if impaled. "Did you say Chinese?" He was not whispering. Turner saw the stunned, apoplectic Alex Bisol freeze before him, staring off beyond him, lost in blank stare. "What was her name?" Bisol finally asked, breaking an unpleasant silence.

"I never asked for a full name, but she left a first name for reference: Lili."

"Just Lili? Just Lili? I could ask every tenth Chink bitch in Chinatown and she'd answer to that. Christ, you are piece of crap sometimes. What else did you tell her—the rest of the folk tale?"

"Well, she did seem particularly interested in that. The story was that there were eight golden statues of the Buddha protected by this great centipede. No one knows the burial place of the Buddha, but these golden statues were apparently buried with Guatama's ashes. If anyone were to disturb the final resting place, the centipede guardian would overwhelm the invader and possess him with the curse from the statues. Each had a special curse. One would make the tomb-robber see the death of every person around him. One would make everything the robber touch set afire. There was even one that would absorb the memories of horrible events from others, while they absorbed the horrible dreams of the robber. That was the eighth Buddha and its curse. It's quite a story. She seemed to think it was pretty valuable. I got a huge tip from her, and luckily just in time, as we're nearly done with the final tests on the software."

Bisol's face became a flat, open expanse of nothing—no emotion, no life, no meaning. Turner waited, hoping that Alex's heart problem had returned. Perhaps he was on the edge of a stroke.

"Where is the nearest phone?" Bisol demanded.

"In my office," Turner answered, as he gathered up his notes.

"Let's go, now." Bisol walked around the stand and grabbed the slight Turner by an elbow, hustling him back through the stacks to the door under the *Staff Only* sign. Bisol kicked it open with his foot. "There's no time to waste."

Chapter 5

"Whatever you do," Bisol commanded into the worn, fifty-year-old phone set, "Don't let anyone touch Richard. In fact, don't let anyone enter the room. No one."

Marie Halleran's voice was controlled, but quavered slightly. "You've put me in a hell of a mess again, Alex. Why couldn't you just take this problem to a regular goddamned hospital and just leave me alone?"

"No time for that now, Marie. The Elson Center was close to the construction site. You have access as a Templar. You know the situation. We couldn't have *this* go public." Bisol was shooing Turner away with his free hand, even though the librarian was trying to draw his attention to some other drawings from his files.

"Just keep him confined and tranquilized until I can get back over through the Bay Area traffic. Sun sets in an hour. Keep him away from any open windows."

"Sundown. Are you kidding? Now you listen to me," Marie cupped her hand over the receiver, trying to block her conversation from others on the ward, "I just went through some serious shit over here. It was bad enough when that thing crawled all over him and then disappeared under his skin. But twenty minutes ago I walked into his room and fought off a floating black mass of storm clouds hanging over him. Guess it was just a lucky thing I came back. The damn thing formed a face, a woman's face, and shot out the fourth-floor window. Do you hear that, Alex, out into space? Whatever it was it had already shredded the Venetian blinds over the windows and the drapes around his bed. God only knows what it would have done to him if I hadn't come in. So, you want me to keep everyone out? What the hell is going on?"

"Where is he now?"

"Don't take that tone with me," Halleran barked back. "I'm not your tender little ingénue anymore. You tell me what's going on or I'll hide this weirdo so far away the Templars won't even see a trail of dust in the horizon."

"You wouldn't."

"Oh, buddy, you just try me, I'm not some little seventeen-year-old you can charm and take advantage of anymore. I outrank you in the Order. I'm moving up because I've got the blood. You don't, in fact I wonder if you have any at all. I'll be your superior soon enough, so don't press your luck."

Bisol swallowed hard and pulled away from the phone for a second. His heart pounded. The room was beginning to claw at him as his vision reduced to a central focus. His indiscretions were choking the life from him and blocking his work, the only thing he lived for now.

"Well?" Halleran injected, pulling her drifting golden strands away from her eyes.

"Marie, please, this is critical. He may have a curse which we've little experience with, and I have no idea what that *thing* was. You must, if nothing else, find a way to protect him. He's under direct protection from Master Eli."

"Why didn't you say he was under the Master's care? No wonder he's been on the fast track. I figured something

CURSE OF THE 8TH BUDDHA 53

was unusual. Just to let you know, I've already made all the mystical protections. Remember, I have had advanced Templar training. He's safe in the basement with surrounding mirrors in an abandoned operation theater. It's fully equipped with artificial sunlamps, including ultraviolet. I don't think that thing will try anything down there. The room's been properly sealed with magic in all directions from any type of demonic influences. If you'd just told me more at the beginning I might not have had to go through that terror earlier—and I don't mean because of the bug man you stuck me with. Hell, I can still see that bitch's face."

Alex finally gave in to Turner's pawing and looked at the man. Turner pushed forward a sketch of a Chinese woman. Her features were striking and compelling. Bisol noted the powerful depiction of her eyes. Even the rough sketch was haunting.

"We may have a lot of things to worry about, Marie. Can you describe the woman's face you saw in any more detail?"

"Asian, maybe thirty, with a strong jaw and eyes—they were like green coals. It's hard to explain unless you'd seem them. Terrifying."

"Put a guard on the door for now. I don't care what you have to tell the guys to keep people out. We'll have some of our folks over there in about twenty. In the meantime, I want you to do one more thing with the patient. You'll have to be careful so listen closely."

When the conversation was over the nurse unwrapped her hands from around the phone and moved it and the cord back over to the main nursing station desk, which was in the usual distracting bustle and confusion of staff during shift change. Marie straightened her uniform and walked to the security office. Moments later she had a handsome, muscular watchman following her to Sinclair's basement hideaway. They found a comfortable chair from a nearby storage closet. She helped the sentry in the dimly lit corridor just outside Sinclair's room. She touched the guard's shoulder, gently patting it and giving him a warm smile. Then Nurse Halleran went into the brightly illuminated room that held the patient.

She had allocated several ultraviolet light units from the fifth floor operating suite. That was rarely used anymore as most of the Center now focused on alternative treatments for rare illnesses. The way of the knife had lost its glamour. Her choice for Sinclair's placement enhanced the effect of the blue lights. The space was once a rehab center for post-surgical patients. The walls were lined with mirrors for the physical therapists to encourage patients to monitor their progress while working back to some form of normalcy. The room still reeked of sweat and ointments.

She placed the UV lights so their glow would not reach Sinclair's eyes. The fluorescents in the room were low enough to keep everything else in stark exposure. There were no furnishings left in the room except the new lights, wall mirrors and the bed surrounded by a makeshift curtain. A heart rate and blood pressures monitor poked outside the bed shroud like an unsightly extra appendage, hooked by a slender umbilical to the tarnished steel cover plates of the power outlets hanging askew under the mirrored walls.

"Richard," she spoke softly, as she used a spare pillow to push gently against his shoulder. No one had reported any strange effects from touching the patient, except for Alex, but she was taking no chances at this point. She was prepared to withdraw. She kept the drape pulled back away from her side of the bed in case she had to move quickly. "C'mon, Richard. Time to wake up."

His head was still drenched in sweat. She had completely removed his bedding since the incident upstairs. The specter's attack had left him in a soaking mess of his owns fluids.

"Richard, it's okay now. You're safe here, with me. It's me, Marie. Remember me? I met you last month at the initiation up at Lake Tahoe, at the Lodge. C'mon, Richard, try to open your eyes and I'll get you something to drink."

The mention of water stirred him, as he twisted, rolling his tongue over his cracked, parched lips. He was weak and forcing his way out of delirium. "Water . . . a little," he whispered.

Marie brought the Dixie cup with the accordion straw close to his lips. He sipped, slowly, and then eagerly. She pulled it back. "Just a little now. Let it settle a bit first. You've been through a lot. I know." She stroked his forehead with her hand, disregarding what Alex had said. Her training and her caring were too strong to let fear keep her from a patient. All she felt was the need to comfort.

"More," he begged.

"Small sips." She monitored his respiration and color to make sure he was stable.

Within a half hour Richard Sinclair could see clearly again and was able to speak in short, broken sentences. He was confused by his surroundings and the odd light striking the sheets thrown over the poles around his bed. He had no memory of such a place.

"I thought maybe I'd died. Horrible visions. Hell, I was sure . . ." His voice cracked as he struggled with fresh sips of water.

"Yes, we almost lost you. You've had lots of hallucinations. We had to move you to a quiet place where your voice wouldn't bother the other patients. You understand, don't you?" She touched a moist rag to his forehead and cheek.

"Mom said I was a noisy sleeper. So, where is Alex?"

"Oh, he'll be around soon," Marie said, as she lowered the side rail and sat next to her patient, leaning over him. "You mentioned your Mom, so I think we should play a little game my Mom taught me, especially when I was trying to get well. Want to try?"

Her voice was so pleasant and calm. Richard felt a silky relaxation spread over him. She was pure heaven and salve to his pains. Of course he would play, just to hear that voice and those deep, crystal blue eyes. Richard thought someone had cut a piece of the prairie skies and left them in her face, just to remind him of the beauty still left in the world.

"I want you to tell me something from your childhood, but not just anything. I want you to tell me about something you experienced that you've never told anyone else about for many years. It might be a secret that lies deep within you—something that causes you pain. If you tell me, it will be released, and then I'll tell you one of mine. That way we'll both feel better and all the other things bothering you right now will just seem to go away. Can you do that for me?"

Marie touched his hand again, but avoided his chest. She didn't want to think about what might still be under his skin. When she changed his sodden clothes earlier, before the attack by the spirit marauder, there were no marks left: not even a scratch. The entire creature that writhed within Sinclair had just disappeared. *Maybe that bitch took it*, she thought.

"That's a pretty weird game, but my Mom was on the wacky side. "Love kills germs," she would say, until one of my sisters died from a blood infection from a little wood splinter. A splinter. So, sure, let's humor the memory of our moms. I've got nothing else to do until I get back on my feet." With Marie's assistance he pulled himself up to a sitting position on his pillows. Marie scowled a bit at his stubborn insistence to raise himself. "Hey, don't sweat it. I feel pretty darn good, really. Not even that weak. If I'm going to get something off my chest I'd rather sit up and tell it." He noticed how her eyes had dilated when he spoke.

"Did I say something wrong," he asked.

"No, no," Marie said, shakily, "I'm just getting ready for your story."

"Not much to tell, really, just a childhood trauma. Hell, we all have them. I hadn't really thought about it in maybe twenty years. Funny that this situation would bring it up, huh?" He motioned for some water, and this time drank straight up from the cup, emptying it. "Aaaaah, that is so good, Okay, here goes. Where I grew up I lived on the wrong side of the tracks in a small Midwest town. Big Irish-Catholic family, but we had a good sized house for the time . . . but old and not in very good shape. The white clapboards were worn and split. The windows leaked in the cold in the winters, and mosquitoes got through the screens in the summer nights. Home, nonetheless. When you're poor, really dirt poor, you don't even notice stuff like that, especially in a big family with lots of responsibilities.

"Those were days when neighbors knew each other, sometimes for the better. There were disputes of course, but the kids mostly grew up together and became close. There was always someone's house to throw ripe crab apples at in the summer, and snowballs in the winter. There was always someone with a mean-ass dog you had to run from, or an old geezer who'd hose you off if he caught you stealing his apples. Somewhere along the line you started to get older. For me, it was sixth grade. I had a teacher, Miss Davis, who created the first hormone rage in my body. A real blonde bombshell. Of course, she was a goddess and beyond my reach. Becki Halstead wasn't."

"You have a weakness for blondes, Richard?" He could see the slight curl of her lip and he felt his face flush. She reached for his hands and held them comfortably within hers.

"Hey, you aren't making this easy with remarks like that. Did you mean to distract me?"

"No, no. Continue, Richard, you're doing fine."

"Anyway, the Halsteads moved two doors down and kitty-corner from the alley at the end of our backyard. In a small town you know when someone sneezes in his sleep, so it wasn't long before all the neighbors new about her family moving from Nebraska, which at the time seemed like a faraway romantic place. Her father was a railroad man.

"Their daughter, Becky was like the dream girl who haunted my sleep: tall, slender, with yellow hair of a Viking queen. Her blue eyes were not the cutting cold-blue ice of the other Scandinavian girls at school, but ponds of peaceful generosity and hope. They were dulled to almost a violet, which was striking under her highly arched, light brows. She was so perfect I thought at first she might be a mannequin that was really posing as a human. I relished the memory of the day in the school cafeteria when I bumped her elbow while she was reaching for a piece of corn. That sent an electric shock through me, and I was aroused instantly. I couldn't get up from dinner for twenty minutes."

Sinclair stopped, interrupted by Marie's twittering. "Hey, what's so funny? Those were sweet, gentle times when just a slight smile meant a lot. We didn't have to gorge ourselves on porn and filth just to find an emotion under our crust."

Halleran raised her hand and nodded an apology. She assured Sinclair that she was still holding his hand, which calmed him. "No, I just hadn't thought of you as the poet and the romantic. Go on."

"Okay," he continued. "So, with time Becky and I spoke more often and eventually got to be friends over the summer. We played Monopoly and a lot of Scrabble. We read poetry to each other and worked together in my Mom's flower garden.

"Then came the confrontation. It was about two weeks before school was to start for the seventh grade. Her dad walked over to me at the golf course while I was getting ready to caddy. It was a crummy little nine-hole municipal course that let the City use up some of their gray water to keep it green. I hadn't seen him on the course very often, so I was a bit surprised by the visit. He pulled me aside, behind the dinky clubhouse. I can still remember the grip he put on my skinny arm. He was right in my face, and harsh, calling me a little Dago freak, and a no-good fish head. I was to stay away from his daughter. She was a good Lutheran and she didn't need any Papists hanging around her. Then he shook me pretty hard and walked away."

"People actually talked that way?"

"You've lived in California too long. That's the way it was then, and that was the end of us, or whatever us there could have been. I never told my folks. What was the point? That was the rule: Catholics and other Christians didn't date, ever. You could get in a lot of trouble for that. In one small town west of us a Catholic high school kid actually got roughed up by a cop for dating his

Presbyterian daughter. We were fish heads even in public schools because on Fridays they had a special line for the Catholics who had to eat fish. It was pretty brutal and a lot of ugly things were said to us while we stood helpless in those lines, even by teachers. That left scar tissue."

She stroked the back of his hand.

He turned, with a look of resolution, his lips pursed tight as he clenched his hand tighter in hers. "I remember that fall. I was a block ahead of Becky that first day of school. I remember looking back at Becky once more as she hesitated on the bridge going over the railroad tracks. She was wearing just the lightest, white spring dress. There was a lot of lace work around the shoulders. It just floated on her. She held it tightly to her legs as she walked over the cool updrafts, but not enough that I didn't get a little peek. I still had my dreams.

"Olga Muntz was coming out the front door of Mel's Ice Cream store as I went in to get a fruit pie for my bag lunch. Olga was kind of a throwaway in the community. Her father was a bad, mean drunk. They lived in a squalid little shack just off the golf course. She always had worn out clothes and appeared bedraggled. Some of the kids talked about the bruises on her arms from old man Muntz, but we wouldn't say anything to her directly. The rich kids did. They always picked on her. She was skinny, with bad teeth, taped glasses, and smelled a little rank most of the time. Some said she never showered. So, as we passed, I made plenty of room."

"That seems a little harsh, don't you think?" asked Halleran.

"You know how kids are, like chickens; they'll find a weak one in the coop and peck it to death. Anyway, I went in to get my pie, and on the way out the door I heard the jingle and ring of the little brass bell on top of Mel's door

CURSE OF THE 8ᵀᴴ BUDDHA

as I left. I could smell Olga to my right, where she had stopped to pick up some books a bully had knocked out of her hands. I even remembered hearing another noise like a dull thud. Everything after that was so blurry. There was something moving past us—incredibly fast, shiny, and roaring. Then Olga was screaming. I was just looking up at her. She was dripping with red. She was holding one of her bleeding fingers in her hand, but it didn't seem right. There were too many fingers. I couldn't understand why I was on the ground, with her papers flying above me, floating in the air.

"The pain hit me then—so crushing. I looked at my chest. My arm was there, bleeding with great streams of blood, but I couldn't move it. And then it was clear, it wasn't my arm. Not my arm. Her arm. Becky's, with part of a frilly white dress still attached."

"Richard, you need to let go of my hands. I really want to stop this story now. I think we've talked enough." Marie visibly upset. She wasn't just listening to the horror story any longer—she was merging with it and in it. She could smell Olga and feel the warm blood running down her face. She could not pull her hands out of Sinclair's grip.

"That huge Pontiac, driven by a speeding parole, ran through Becky like butter, just up the hill from the ice cream store. She was splattered into dozens of pieces here and there after the collision. She was gone just like that. The elbow that once thrilled me was now pinning me to the ground, bloody and shredded while Olga went into a fit of terror above me. Soon there were people coming from all over. I don't remember much of that. There was just me throwing up again and again and again."

Marie wrestled wildly, trying to pull away. This was just too much—but she couldn't free herself. It was a steel handcuff that would not be broken. She tried to reach for the tray for a needle. He pulled her back.

"So there I was," Richard blurted out, through his tears, "thirteen years old. Forced by some idiot social worker to go to Becky's funeral. 'It will be the best for him,' I can still hear her say. They forced me up there—even my Mom and Dad forced me to go up and see what the funeral home had reconstructed out of someone I cared for, who I saw shredded. All they had to work from was her last school picture.

"When I dragged past that coffin there was no one I knew lying there. No one I recognized. No Viking queen, just a plaque of wax with some bits of tattered hair coming off a grotesquery for a skull. I was petrified. My father never forgave me for 'embarrassing every Catholic in town' that day when I wet myself, right there in the First Lutheran Church. It was just not done. Unheard of, yes, unforgivable, even by our priest. I never took confession again after that. Before I graduated and got out of that rat hole, I had to walk across that goddamned viaduct every day. For the next six years I had to look down at the same tracks Becky had studied before she was butchered by that monster. Everyday. Every goddamned day."

Sinclair still had Marie in his grasp as his body started shaking uncontrollably. A yellow glow began to pulse from his chest and he screamed. He pushed Marie away as a mist of memories flowed back from her, replacing his trauma.

"Marie, open the door!" Bisol yelled. He and four of the Templar guards had arrived just in time to hear the screaming. There was no reply. Bisol motioned for the facility guard to unlock the door. They rushed in. Bisol rushed to Marie, who was rocking in a fetal position against a mirror at the far end of the room. He checked her eyes but her gaze was far away. She did not respond to her name or his touch. She just rocked as she whispered the name Becky over and over again.

"Richard," Bisol called out, "are you all right?" He turned to the bed. Sinclair's head was turned away from Alex. Bisol could hear a low moaning. Sinclair was clutching his groin, buckled in fetal position.

"For God's sake man, what's the matter?"

Sinclair turned slowly, his face set in a twisted, snarling grimace. Spittle ran from his mouth. "You, Al. You killed him! You killed my baby, you bastard! You tried to kill us both." Sinclair was furious with pain and of being tied to a bed, drunk, and seeing Bisol coming at him with wire from a coat hanger. Bisol was the essence of pure, unbridled butchery against him, a pregnant teenage girl.

Bisol ripped the curtains off their rings and swore at Sinclair. He held his hand to strike his student, remembering Marie's grimace as she swore at him a decade ago during a botched abortion. His actions put her in the hospital, ruined his marriage and destroyed his public career. Only his Templar contacts kept him out of prison.

He withdrew his hand and then waved the Templar guard out as he sat on the floor, exhausted, recalling the past.

"God, if I could rid myself of both of you. It would be so easy. Sinclair," he whispered over to the agonized patient, huddling amid the shredded curtains, "if you hadn't already been chosen for something important, for the Master, I would tie you to that cunt and sink you both under the Golden Gate Bridge. You know too much, now, but that won't matter much longer, I promise you."

Marie and Sinclair did not respond, reliving their new traumas over and over, wrapped in a carousel of twirling agonies. They could not hear Alex Bisol's threats.

Chapter 6

The Templar guards took Sinclair to a rejuvenation center deep within Stanford University. The clinic was secretly operated by the Templars since its founding. The finest surgeons and infectious disease specialists were flown in from private clinics in Geneva, Switzerland, from Fort Dietrich, Maryland, and from the CDC in Atlanta. After extensive treatments with EDTA, steroids and interferon, the newest Templar was able to rise out of his hospital bed and walk and exercise normally, after less than a week.

By August ninth, Bisol had prepared Sinclair for a trip to Lake Tahoe. The next morning Bisol aided Richard to his beat up, decrepit black Buick parked in the research center's parking lot. Soon they were traveling through the Bay Area, then through Sacramento, and finally climbing up Highway 50 through El Dorado County.

Sinclair was fatigued by the change in altitude. Even crawling from a near drowning in high school hadn't left him this exhausted—this consumed with heaviness in his head and every limb. He leaned against the car window, feeling the minor shudders of Highway 50 rattle against his forehead. The heat from the southerly sun on the window kept him comfortable against the ravages of cold drafts that Alex demanded from the air conditioner.

Richard hated traveling anywhere with Bisol. No sane or at least normal mammal had the metabolism of a furnace.

"Can't you turn that ice machine down a bit, Alex?"

"Oh, buck up, boy, it's just a few hours up the road. You can take it." Bisol reached for the lighter and pushed it in.

"I'll jump," Richard whimpered. "I'll jump out of this damn Buick if you start up another cigarette. For the love of God, haven't you got any will power?'

"Okay. Guess it can wait."

Richard's head was still swirling from the bitter fumes of the last Marlboro in the ashtray. The smoke reminded him of his stepfather. That man had always risen early, always ready to give all the *bastards in the house* a good whipping first thing to start the day out right, right after he had his cowboy-coffin nails. Being trapped in a roughshod, tatter of a car was made worse by the smoldering butts in the ashtray. As far as Sinclair was concerned it might as well have been a gas chamber, although Bisol claimed it was a classic. He glanced at Bisol, with his black and white Brylcream locks. He wondered where Bisol even got that nasty varnish to slop on his head. Richard wondered why he was stuck with the Templar Master at Arms.

"I see they've completed the bypass around Placerville. Guess that will end P-ville forever."

"I suspect so," Bisol replied, as they drove straight past the once active stop in the road to Lake Tahoe.

"Wonder whatever drove them to do something that stupid?"

"Probably the same old hubris and greed that drove other small towns to do the same. I've seen it a dozen times. Someone thinks it's going to make a big difference and build up more business. In ten years it's damn near a ghost town. Too bad. Neat little town. Lots of really haunted places. I'll have to take you into the old theatre sometime. It was a field hospital when the town first burned down during the Gold Rush. Plenty of horrible deaths from the burn ward in that building. One of the worst haunted places I've ever experienced, next to maybe the old Soda Works, just down the street. At least the coffee shop in there now has a ghost that's a bit friendlier."

"You just live for this shit, don't you?" Sinclair asked.

"Just a side interest. But it has increased my faith in the tenants of the Order. There is more to life than what we see around us. God, if anyone should believe that now, it's you."

"Well, I don't remember half the things people say I should know about. Seems these days I've become an oddity. I'm just damn wore out. I can see going to the cabin for some rest by the lake, but do we really have to go to the Lodge and see the Master?"

"This trip, yes," Bisol responded, slowly, thinking about another Marlboro. "Your recent adventures and new *skills* have piqued the Grand Master's interest. You are commanded to meet him. But as always, we can only trust the most secure locations."

"I'm already queasy enough, Alex. Couldn't we just meet him in a casino for lunch? Damn, I hate rowboats. It's so melodramatic."

"Yes, but it doesn't make much noise, and when it's all wooden, that stupid Coast Guard radar guarding the lake can't pick it up at night."

"And darn near the dark of the moon, too. Just so we won't know to scream if we hit a rock."

"For a man who just faced death twice from who knows what, you sure are picky. Besides, a little sliver of moon will help with the night scopes. Of course, maybe you don't need those anymore since now you apparently can see deep within all the mysteries, including our darkest secrets."

"I have no idea what you all saw or experienced around me, except I know things about you and Marie Halleran that I really, really wish I didn't. I think you two are a screwed-up mess. How the hell any man could become a Templar, after gouging out a baby from a drunken teenager, is beyond me."

"Let's just drop that for now, okay? It's been tough enough this last month begging her for forgiveness again for something she doesn't even know about because that part of her is now in you. Then I have to pull Marie off the ceiling from the trauma she's been going through from something in your childhood you don't even know about anymore. Some girl named Becky and lots of blood. That's about all I can get out of her. This is just frickin' ridiculous."

"Did she say anything else about that thing she saw hanging over me when I was unconscious. What the hell was that all about?"

"Figured you'd get around to that sooner or later," Alex said, tapping on his half-empty Marlboro pack in his shirt pocket. "But you better be ready for a little shock. It's a complication that comes with being part of the Templars. Sort of a curse, you might say, that only shows itself at a critical time in our history. Something really big is near." He lit another cigarette and blew the smoke toward Richard.

"I've seen a lot of terror in men's eyes in my time. In the Gulf, I watched one of the bravest men I ever served with jump up out of a foxhole because a snake crawled over his hand. He was black as night, the Iraqis couldn't see him, but his fears pulled him right into the line of fire rather than face a foe that was in his DNA. Same with our Cherokee scout. He had nerves of iron until we ran into an area in Panama that had a jaguar on the prowl. The idea of a big cat there, in the forest, stalking us—it was too much for his Indian heritage. We had to pull him out of the field. And me, I don't like bears. It's just my thing. Almost shot myself once because of that when I was doing some training up in the Kenai Peninsula in Alaska.

"I saw the same damn fright in that cop Johnson's face when he talked about the monster that went after you in the pit in Frisco. He saw it as a snake or maybe some kind of big bug, which is nonsense. I don't know what it was, but something was on your chest in the clinic, and it wasn't a snake or a bug. And you haven't been the same since. So trust me, there are curses my friend. When I tell you the next story you better listen with an open mind."

"I'm sure about the curse," Sinclair said, muttering a few other expletives under his breath as he tried to straighten up under the twisted seatbelt. "Why else would I be stuck in this rat trap with a stove pipe for a driver?" The conversation, the cold, and the recycled smoke from the air conditioner had Sinclair on his last nerve.

"How long have you been working with me?"

"Far too damn long," Sinclair blurted out, and then hesitated, feeling a wave of nausea welling up. "Stop this goddamn car."

Bisol looked over to see the color running out of Sinclair's face. He looked ahead for a pull off and quickly swerved into the parking lot of a restaurant. He knew the place well as the menu featured his favorite apple pie from the Apple Hill Country near Placerville and Coloma. Alex had just enough time to park the black, beaten-up sedan in a corner of the lot. Long drifts of brown and orange pine needles drifted over the cracked asphalt. Sinclair's door swung out wildly as his stomach emptied on the needles and worn asphalt.

Alex slid out of the car, half in pity and half in disgust. He tossed the burning butt of the Marlboro at Sinclair as he slammed his door on the worn-out '73 Regal and headed inside, leaving Sinclair to his own problems.

The waitress had already taken Bisol's order by the time Sinclair jangled the hanging chain of bells on the restaurant's front door. Bisol got a fresh draft of the pine air before the door banged shut. Sinclair stamped the leaf litter off his shoes before joining his teacher at the counter. Richard preferred a booth for back support, but it was Bisol's preference to sit on the small, round red seats close to the waitresses. It allowed Alex a method for working out his nervous quirks by slowly rotating the squeaky pedestals back and forth. Richard had disliked this inconvenience at first, until he'd sat through a lunch with Alex's bouncing knees constantly hitting a booth's leg. Once was quite enough. He had no patience for ADD patients and their habits.

"Better?" Bisol asked. "I think I'd rather have my dog with me for breakfast."

"Hmm. Some. Still get car sick, and your puffing didn't help. I didn't know you had a dog."

"Nope, I don't. I guess after this stop you can use the heater, if you like. It's getting cooler. Nice air up here. I hate the Bay smog. Nice thing about Frisco, they send all their crap into the Valley and then claim what a clean city they are. What a joke." He continued to sip at the heavy French roast—black, with no additions.

"You must stop here often. Even the waitress seemed to know you."

"Well," Alex continued, "I've been coming up to the main lodge for ten years. Watched some of these kids working in here grow up. No pie like it anywhere around. Of course, the best is in Yakima Valley during the apple festivals. Ah, but the very best—and I *am* an apple connoisseur of sorts—is the German apple pie in the Ohio Valley during the Johnny Apple Seed fairs. Just marvelous."

"You traveled a lot?" Richard asked, after taking deep draughts from his murky glass of ice water. He began eyeing the extra water near Alex wondering if all the foothill water was full of debris.

"Not as much as I'd like. Mostly I traveled other places for the military and feds. Never as much fun when you have to work during travel. I think my best memories are from trips with my parents and my sister, growing up in the sixties. What a time that was." Bisol looked out over the steam rising from his coffee, his focus lost beyond the Bunn coffee machines, stacks of salt, pepper, and sugar shakers and into the dark recesses of the kitchens where hidden elves stood over hot ovens making their masterpiece pies.

Richard had never heard his mentor talk about his own family before, or much in the way of any personal information. Maybe it was the nostalgia of the restaurant, or the surprise interruption. He seemed almost human, but Sinclair's new memories—moments caught from Marie, pushed those thoughts away. He blanched at the idea he was even sitting next to this monster that posed as some kind of religious zealot trying to save the world from darkness. Alex was a hypocrite. *Why even stay with him? Why not just walk out?* Richard was just too weak and confused to come to any reasonable conclusion. There were still so many horrors running around in his head from just the weeks before in the clinic. He could still feel the hot wire driving into his womb and the explosive rage of knowing his baby was being butchered.

Sinclair was grateful for the break when the server asked for his order.

"How's the pie?" Alex asked, as his protégé seemed to suffer over the crust.

"I'm holding it down. I don't care much for burned crust." Alex noticed that Sinclair had pushed a little pile of cremated flour off to one side.

"Yeah, nothing's as good as it once was. Comes with aging. You ready to go on? I promise no smoking." Alex reached over to touch Richard's shoulder, but then in a second thought withdrew quickly. "Better forget the touchy stuff for a while. You seem to transfer intense memories back and forth with people who touch you . . . but not always. Seems like a crapshoot just shaking your hand. I really don't want to know any more things that will keep me up nights. You have any dreams about fighting with swords in France?"

Sinclair pushed the pie away and drained Alex's glass of water. He then pushed it next to his tip on the worn and gouged, brown Lexan counter.

"That's too damn weird, even for me. I can't imagine how you would know about those dreams. They come almost every night. Funny thing, though, I noticed I'm not afraid of heights anymore. I haven't got any idea what happened back in the hospital, but at least I lost one of my worst terrors. All I remember with Marie is that we were just playing a game and then it was like molasses pouring out of me and into her, and then fire pouring into me until we flew apart. I couldn't control any of it. It just happens when it wants to. Well, let's skedaddle out of here before the poor kid at the counter grabs my little pinkies and I have to remember every pie she's served."

CURSE OF THE 8ᵀᴴ BUDDHA

"Skedaddle? Sheer Midwest, Richard. I haven't heard that since a camping trip in Montana, before I went into the Army. You're a bit out of place."

"And aren't we all?"

They were almost to Strawberry on Highway 50 before they started into more serious topics. Alex had already pawned off his old wives' tale about the 39-mile stone and the ghosts of a Mormon wagon train. Sinclair had heard that same story the last two trips up to the Lake. He was in no mood.

"You seem clearer," Bisol said, "so let's get to the heart of the matter before we go over the Summit. I'd like to clear up a few things so I can enjoy that view undistracted."

"Well, hell, I wouldn't want your view disrupted."

"I know it's been tough. You deserve some answers, and I've been pretty hard to pin down. You must have figured I'd wait until the right time. Truthfully, I just didn't want you having any more stress for a while. That's why I've been keeping that stupid cop Johnson from finding you. Maybe a little time would let some of this stuff you've gone through settle a bit. But here goes, anyway." Alex started tympanic tapping on the steering wheel. It was a sign he was in the throws of trying his best peripatetic teaching technique, which most times would have shocked and disturbed Aristotle at its lack of sophistication. It bordered more on interrogation.

"As you've been taught, the Templars have always had three Masters. One is known publicly as the Grand Master. Another is known secretly within the Order. Only the other two Masters knows the third. One Master administers policy and leadership. One controls funds and logistics. Finally, the real Grand Master is of such prophetic and spiritual insight that his wisdom protects and guides the Order. That is why Jacques de Molay—the last outward Grand Master—was arrested with both Hughes de Peyraud and Geoffroi de Charnay in thirteen oh-seven.

"King Philippe IV of France knew they were leaders, but even he did not know the deepest of secrets about their true role in the Order. Unfortunately, some of the most important secrets of the Order were lost in those terrible days of inquisition. If de Molay and de Charnay had not been ordered to be burned in a secret location they might never have escaped. Even then the Templars had insiders paid to support them—just not enough of them to save de Molay. Two of our brothers took de Charnay and de Peyraud's places in those flames. The same was done much later for our Templar Queen, Joan de Arc. Her replacement was burned at the stake, and was also a pure Templar Dame of the Light, whose heart remained untouched."

"Hughes de Peyraud, one of the Grand Masters, protected some of the deepest truths solely within his memory, passed from other great spiritual leaders of the Order. He was isolated in prison, but was able to use symbols on the walls of his cells to pass the secrets to future Grand Masters who would visit those insidious dens for centuries to come.

"One of the great insights deciphered later for the Order was the reason for the blight that fell upon us from the time we opened the great vault of the First Temple of the Jews in May of eleven twenty-one. We had intruded into the Beit HaMikdash: the greatest work of Solomon. Before it fell to the Babylonians in five eighty-six, the High Priests put a curse on anyone who dared touch the treasure of gold and silver they held above ground, or in the vault deep below ground, which featured unbelievable wealth and ancient mysteries.

"Historians claim that the Babylonians sacked the temple and took its treasures away, but that's a myth. They took what the Jews allowed them to think was the 'great treasure.' Truly, it was not. Unfortunately, many of the Jews were taken back as slaves to Babylon. However, just as the great ancient civilizations saved much of Alexander's Library deep in underground cities beneath the Egyptian desert, so did the surviving Jewish priests protect the ancient wonders that the average person today would find astounding. Some were objects so technologically advanced they are still beyond our own current capabilities to fathom. The information about those treasurers, and what became of them, is a story we will discuss another time. What is relevant here are the protections the ancient priests cast upon the booty taken by the invaders."

Bisol stopped for a moment as he began maneuvering through the curves toward the summit. He looked out over the great pass through the Sierra Nevadas. It never failed to thrill him, as if he was seeing it for the first time, but this time fear welled up in his throat—an overwhelming anxiety about the sheer drop-off along Highway 50. When the car passed the breach in the right-hand guardrail, a scar from a less fortunate driver earlier that year, Alex's breathing became constricted. Bisol clenched his hands around the steering wheel, trying to recompose his sense of order.

"Don't stop the story now. Why is this stretch of road whacking you out? You aren't choking on that pie, are you?"

Sinclair leaned forward and looked into his guide's face. He didn't know what to make of Bisol's behavior. It could be another game to mess with his head. Some of the other Templars had warned him about Bisol's time as an intelligence officer. He liked to twist people around like a top and fracture their minds.

"Hey, just sit back and listen. I'll finish the story about the curse." Bisol cleared his throat and popped a lozenge from a package on the dash to ease his dry throat. "Anyway, the great Jewish priests knew of a truth long hidden in rabbinical texts. Apparently the real first wife of Adam, Lilith, spurned his desire to have power over her. She was also a perfect being and she was an immortal with limitless powers. She was, of course, replaced by Eve. Supposedly there was an attempt at reconciliation, but it didn't work. There were no marriage counselors—hah, as if they ever do anyone any good."

Bisol reached for the lighter and Richard pushed his hand back. "You promised."

Bisol pursed his lips as he turned the hard curves overlooking the South Lake Tahoe beaches and splendor of the crystal blue waters from the cloudless day. He began to rock his head back and forth, trying to douse his fears of going off the edge. He clenched his teeth while passing another set of damaged posts on the outside rails. Bisol did not manage fear well.

"Here's the deal," he said, in a cold and crisp tone shooting at Sinclair's head. It froze Sinclair in place. "You don't touch me *ever* again until I say you can. Are we clear?" Bisol was terrified that even more of him, the truly deep secrets, would ooze into this weakling he had inherited, like maple syrup over a pancake.

Richard sat upright, stiff, and perfectly alert. "Yes," he managed to answer, awestruck by the power in the man's voice.

CURSE OF THE 8ᵀᴴ BUDDHA

"Good. Then listen up: I'm going to dumb this down for you, with apologies to historical details. I realize you are no fan of history. What is it you always say? History bores you because it never changes. Well, my friend, real history isn't boring, and it shapes everything you do every day. That is, the real history. Everyone shapes their version of history: the Papists, the Communists, the Nazis, the environmentalists, the Republicans, the Democrats and especially the entertainment industry. Everyone does it— but the real history remains below the radar, always forming our next steps."

Bisol waited until the lighter snapped out of its holder, red hot, before he took a long, drawn-out drag, igniting the tobacco as though it were his last. To his utter embarrassment his hands were still trembling as he held his smoke.

"We're going to get into some pretty heavy shit now, so you better hold onto your panties. You're younger than I was when they brought me into the Order, but I was a lot more prepared for some of the things we're asked to do. I had military discipline and the willingness to take orders from my superiors. You just have that Templar bloodline that you didn't even know about, or in my opinion, deserve. Now sit and listen. This won't be easy."

A wave of psychological concrete flowed over Richard's arms and legs, which petrified him. He was helpless against "the Voice" coming out of Bisol. Bisol's tapping on the steering wheel metal was in synch with Sinclair's heartbeat, slowing it down until it was under Alex's control.

"So, there were the Babylonians, thinking they were rulers of the world. They knew little of Solomon's powers and what info he'd passed to the senior priests. When he talked of calling up the jinn's using rabbinical texts, those were not genies, my friend, or demons. These were the spawn from the line of Lilith, which we so cleverly just call the Liliths. The Liliths are a race apart from mankind—probably living in a parallel dimension that allows them to pop in and out of our three-dimensional reality. That makes them magical to us, but in their own way they are dependent on mankind for mating and apparently for feeding.

"I've never been in their universe, but apparently it is not a robust, healthy environment. Since they slip across for mating and blood feedings, they were probably the basis of the vampire stories we've inherited. The ancient Christians knew about them, but couldn't control or collaborate with them, so the Liliths simply became the stories of the succubus. The were soon the creatures of our night terrors, forcing men to have wet dreams and the reason young babies of human women die in their sleep.

"We know they've been appearing more in recent years, given the blast of reports about dark shadows lingering over beds. Some call them the Shadow People. They are all female. Some have elongated heads that look like stovepipe hats. Some of the females fly like giant birds near storms, which is why Native Americans are seeing the Thunderbirds again. Others see them as moth men, or bat creatures. Marie saw one floating over you in the clinic. It had a Chinese woman's face. That's even more disturbing, considering a recent development in this entire operation." Alex was starting to drop ashes as the Marlboro jumped up and down as he spoke.

"Hey, Alex, slow it down here a bit. Here's where the cops like to put their speed traps. Notice how they changed the speed limit twice within two blocks? It really fills their coffers on the backs of out-of-state tourists."

CURSE OF THE 8TH BUDDHA

Sinclair could feel the Buick Regal slow, but his mind was still rolling with visions from Bisol's tale of the Liliths and their powers. He no longer noticed the cigarette smoke or the cold from the air conditioner.

Bisol started again, taking deep breaths, a sign of his readiness to restart the lecture. "So, the Babylonians blew it. Their greed and lust for the Jews' gold cost them their kingdom. The Jewish priests called on the powers of the Liliths by using ancient symbols of seals developed by Solomon. Let's just say they cut a deal and leave it at that. They knew what would happen and even posted it in prophesy in their texts, some of which became part of the Bible. In Isaiah 14: 22-25, it says: 'For I will rise up against them, says the Lord of Hosts, and cut off from Babylon the name and remnant, and offspring and posterity, says the Lord. I will also make it a possession for the porcupine, and marshes of muddy water; I will sweep it with the broom of destruction, says the Lord of Hosts. The Lord of Hosts has sworn, saying, Surely, as I have thought, so it shall come to pass, and as I have purposed, so it shall stand.'

"The Temple priests also knew another secret that the Babylonians were unprepared to deal with: the Lilith Cycle. Because of the time differences between our dimensions, the Liliths take about forty-seven years to reappear at full strength. Agreements made at the beginning of a cycle are made manifest at the end of that cycle.

"Lo and behold, in five thirty-nine BC, the Persian King Cyrus combined his great army with the Medes and others to totally destroy the power of the Babylonians. The Persians actually diverted the Euphrates River and overwhelmed the Babylonians. We are pretty sure the Liliths helped with all of this, one way or the other.

Babylon was completely wiped out. Persia rose for a while as the dominant world power. What's more, the Jews who had been taken as slaves when Israel fell, were released from bondage and returned to their homeland, and protected by the Liliths.

"The Liliths ravaged the Babylonian population in a feeding frenzy, which went unrecorded except by a few brave Jewish scholars whose works remain hidden. Again, the Jewish priests knew this cycle would return so they predicted it in their holy texts.

"In Isaiah 13:17-22, it says: 'Behold, I will stir up the Medes against them, who will not regard silver; and as for gold, they will not delight in it. Also their bows will dash the young men to pieces, and they will have no pity on the fruit of the womb; their eye will not spare children. And Babylon, the glory of kingdoms, the beauty of the Chaldeans' pride, will be as when God overthrew Sodom and Gomorrah. It will never be inhabited, nor will it be settled from generation to generation; nor will the Arabian pitch tents there, nor will the shepherds make their sheepfolds there. But wild beasts of the desert will lie there, and their houses will be full of owls; ostriches will dwell there, and wild goats will caper there. The hyenas will howl in their citadels, and jackals in their pleasant palaces. Her time is near to come, and her days will not be prolonged.'

"That's another reason the Templars became protectors of the Jews. They shared the secrets of the Temple with us, and in that we are brothers. They later shared their secrets about how to handle money, as well, which helped the Templars set up the banks of Europe."

Bisol drove silently for a few miles through the lines of nondescript businesses along Highway 50 leading into South Lake Tahoe. He passed silently by the environmentally friendly, low visibility squalor of run-down hotels, greasy restaurants, dusty hair salons and oil-stained filling stations. He finally parked near El Dorado Beach so he could look across the adjacent park. An array of tourists, vagrants, and local characters walked under the pines. A stretch of thin, caked sand covered only half the footprints and half the debris from the previous night's partygoers.

"This has a point, Richard. All of this background explains why the Templar warriors who worked in the pits under the Great Temple swore celibacy, unlike the wanton, lusty men of Babylon. The Liliths could not tempt the righteous monks of our Order and could not keep them from the treasures that had been compiled since the time of Abraham.

"There truly were wonders and wealth beyond imagination to be uncovered. Many searched for these later, and some still do, but all of it has long been removed from the Holy Lands. Every bit of that trove of gold, silver, jewels, and the incredible technology carried a price, even to this day. The Liliths still search us out, and about every forty-seven years demand a price—an awful price the Templars must pay or we all perish."

Richard's jaws tightened. His vision narrowed over the sailboats floating over the glassy waters, past the hot-air balloon rising over graceful gulls. None of the charms of the sandy inlet touched him as darkness squeezed at his consciousness. His breathing came hard and shallow.

A bright light exploded into his mind as Bisol made the sign of the cross just above Sinclair's forehead with the tip of his index finger and thumb. Sinclair could feel strength flow through Bisol's fingertips as he traced an ancient sign over Richard's third eye, stilling the acolyte's pineal gland deep within his brain.

"Walk thee in perfected light," Bisol whispered. With that, Sinclair fell into a deep, well-deserved sleep.

Chapter 7

Harsh bands of light cut across Sinclair's eyelids. His forehead wrinkled from the annoyance of the new warmth. His dreams were troubled. He'd had the same visions again and again for weeks: climbing out of a hole only to be pulled back in against his will. It was silent, no feelings of hot or cold, and no smells to guide him out of the darkness. This time was different. *Odd*, he said to himself in his vivid dreaming, *the coffee is ready*. With that revelation, he shuddered in his fearsome visions and began to pull toward awareness. But just before awaking, one last specter manifested, just for a second—a drifting black cloud that piled in filigrees over him as he crawled from the pit, drifting and speeding up in time in a fast-forward film clip of the coastline fog bank rolling over San Francisco. He could see the darkness congeal until it formed *her*. The searing heat from her Asian gaze pierced his sleep.

Sinclair rolled to his right to flatten out on the broad, overstuff leather couch. The living room was designed in homage to the Ponderosa Ranch television series. There were the required open, bare pine beams, the massive fireplace lined in well-appointed river boulders from the Truckee River, the deep, inset windows with fine lace curtains, and the hardwood floors polished to deep amber, sporadically covered in stylish red and blue artificial Navajo rugs made in Afghanistan.

Sinclair cleared away the cobwebs by shaking his head a bit. He awoke staring directly at a pair of massive elk antlers acting as an outcrop over the fireplace mantle. It was all a bit grotesque and too kitsch for his tastes.

"Well, Little Joe, ya' feel like some java this mornin'?" Alex's best impression of Lorne Green sounded like a sappy version of everyone's grumpy uncle.

"Uh," groaned Richard, "how long have I . . .? What the hell did you do to me?" He rubbed his temple, just now noticing tightness around his brow like a belt being slowly twisted.

"Just a blessing, pal," Bisol said, signaling Richard to approach the window to the back area quietly and slowly. "Just a little trick Eli showed me last month. Get your ass over here, but be quiet about it."

"Oh, for Pete's sake, what now?" Richard dragged his socks over the floor, catching them on a loose bit of sliver on the old pine floors. "Shit." He sat down cross-legged to pull out the offending edge.

"Shhh. You'll spook 'em." Alex paid no attention to Richard's complaints.

Sinclair pulled off his white gym sock. Maroon ooze surrounded the wound. The spine of old wood came out with the yank of his sock, leaving a point of pain just under his middle toe near the ball of his foot. He squeezed at the spot a bit until more blood seeped out. "Screw it, Alex, I need some disinfectant. This goddamned floor."

Alex finally turned and paid a little more attention to his tardy guest. "Gotcha again, huh? Haven't I always said lift your feet up, don't drag them? Bad habit, Sinclair. I figured after a couple of visits you'd have learned to walk upright. I'll get you some Neosporin in a second. You ought to drag your sorry butt over here and have a quick look at this before they leave."

"All right. All right." He scrambled up, holding his bare foot up for a second and then tested it slowly. "Guess it'll be okay." He hopped and hobbled over near the window that was recessed above the kitchen sink.

"Take a gander at that," Alex directed. "If there's one thing I fear it's a wild bear, but at this distance they can be almost amusing."

Richard watched as a small mother black bear and her two large cubs rustled through the cabin's empty garbage cans. Alex hadn't tied down the metal bins since he wasn't expecting to be back for several months. The bears seemed perplexed at the lack of goodies. One of the cubs took a bit of fun throwing a watering can about like a toy. Soon they moved on to other properties and the continual search of an easy meal.

"Better than at the zoo, eh?"

"I suppose," Richard replied. He held back any enthusiasm until he had his foot tended to, but quietly admitted to himself that indeed, seeing large wildlife outdoors nearby, without restraints, was a bit exhilarating.

"If only I had my .30-.30 right now. Pop, one for mama. Pop-pop, one for each baby. Just like that."

"C'mon, Alex, you wouldn't shoot them and you know it. Besides, they're protected up here."

"I don't give a rat's ass. Right behind the eye on the cubs, and for mama, a clear shot right up her ass. They have a name for a shot like that in Texas, you know."

"Don't care and I don't want to hear any more of this. I just want to get my foot fixed up. You and your damn bear fixation."

"Yeah, well a shrink told me it comes from some kind of weirdness with a teddy bear my parents gave me when I was growing up, right before my father committed suicide. Who knows?"

They turned away from the window. Richard shook his head with his eyes tilted upward. He sighed as he continued to hop on one foot.

Alex walked ahead of Richard to the single large bathroom in the cabin. Its walls were decorated in a wainscot style in two sections, the lower half in earth-tone tiles, and the upper covered in a multi-toned texture paint of mixed soft blues and whites, giving the interior an impression of being outdoors. Skylights provided natural lighting over the shower and the sinks. The room was three times the size needed for most lodges, but with the numerous Templar gatherings it was a design necessity.

Alex started digging through his assigned drawer. He plundered through foot powders, long-discarded combs and deodorants, and several brands of hair restoration sprays that all failed to raise even an ingrown sprout. Eventually he found the Neosporyn tube and tossed it to Richard. Sinclair stopped immediately and rested on an orange upholstered stool.

"So, the blessing—walk thee in perfected light—you wondered about that?"

"You pick the weirdest times to start up a conversation."

"Just when it suits me," Alex replied, with a bit of a smirk. "It's something rather new, actually. The Grand Master has asked us to use that prayer to calm the spirit of the agitated. Apparently with some training it allows us to move upset people directly in balance with the new spectrum of light coming from the Sun. I followed up on that finding last year about the new shift toward the blue spectrum in sunlight, with the ultraviolet becoming more intense. It has far-reaching effects, including this quickening that the airy-fairy mystical types keep throwing out. Strangely enough, they are right this time. It makes finding Drake's hiding place even more important than ever for the Order."

"If I didn't know you and the Order better, I'd swear you make half of this crap up just to keep me confused. Of course, after all the training I've been through here, London, Malta, Scotland, and Egypt I guess I should have learned to keep an open mind. Maybe this is all to help us shift to a new consciousness—the thing that never happened in twenty-twelve."

"That was an odd remark, Richard. You might be closer to the truth than you think. We'll have to explore that sometime, indeed." Alex looked into the mirror and rubbed his face, remembering he hadn't shaved yet. He pursed his lips, angry at his forgetting the important little hygiene requirements as he began to stretch past sixty. His Halloween birthday the year before had shaken his Scorpionic self-confidence. Sixty had gotten him to wondering intently about death, renewal, and his life path, and about the final judgment for his life of evil deeds.

"Checking for mushrooms growing on your north side?" Richard chided.

"Hmmm—only moss. Keeps my compass updated. You take a hot shower and I'll have breakfast waiting for you. No smoking. You know I only smoke in Mary Anne."

"That's a deal. Why do you always have to smoke in that old jalopy, anyway? And why name that rattle trap Mary Anne?"

"Why?" Alex asked, somewhat taken back by the question. "Well," he paused, "there's forty years of my life in that museum on wheels. I smoke to remember the times I once had. And Mary Anne, that's really none of your business." Alex pulled the bathroom door shut tight behind him and moved on to the morning menu.

Sinclair finally emerged wearing a deep-blue flannel shirt tucked tightly into his jeans.

"Smells great," Richard began, sniffing deeply over the plate set for him on the long, mahogany dining room table. "We could have just eaten in the alcove. That little sun room is fancy enough for me."

"Yes, but not for me." Bisol poured fresh coffee into the blue-willow china cup. "I think it's time to be a little more formal for breakfast, and I like being the host."

Richard knew what that meant. He was about to either sit through another pontification or get his ass chewed. Alex didn't like serving anyone, and Sinclair knew it. What he did like was bringing his livestock in for a meal while he sharpened his butcher knife. Richard had identified that unappealing characteristic weeks ago as one of Alex's worst character flaws.

"Coffee's great, and you actually made fresh corn bread. One of my favorites." Richard tried to keep it light in hopes that when he hit the iceberg there might be time for life boats.

"Mine, too. Learned it from my great-granny. She was a Kansas homesteader back in the eighteen-hundreds. Tough and sweet. Totally devoted to her family without a second thought. Which leads to a discussion we should have." Alex didn't look up, but continued to sip his coffee between slicing his scrambled eggs.

Here it comes, Richard thought, trying to actually enjoy the feast of bacon, eggs, cornbread, fresh fruit, and a bowl of strawberry yogurt topped with granola.

"Do you remember how you first met me?" Alex stopped eating for a moment, put his utensils on his plate, and folded his hands up over his mouth, his elbows in support on the lace tablecloth.

Sinclair could feel the burning, probing glare from his teacher, from those black pits of interrogation most would call eyes—but on Bisol they were long tongues of hungry dragons resting in his skull. There would be no iceberg today. This was going to be one of the hellfire sermons that Bisol had only "shared" with Richard on one other occasion following his particularly embarrassing faux pas when Richard first met the Grand Master.

"I thought we agreed never to speak about the initiation up here. I didn't particularly care for being tied up naked in front of all those people and flailed," Sinclair replied, hoping to deflect the energy now surrounding his side of the long table.

"Perhaps, but this occasion requires unusual actions so we can be sure of our bearings. I, as your instructor and mentor, have a vested interest in your future, and mine."

The eggs seemed to be cold and greasy, even with steam coming from their middle. Richard was having a hard time feigning hunger.

"When the Templars found you drifting toward Catalina Island in March, off the Coast in that ridiculous old lateen, did you think we weren't aware what you wanted to do? You had no water on board. No food. No compass or maps. You'd been out three days and you were delirious. And you knew. You *knew* there was a squall coming. Was that your idea of a Viking ceremony?" Alex's voice was higher-pitched than normal, exposing a sense of rage out of his typical control. "We took your sad sorry ass in and awakened you to a new life. You still don't fully appreciate what has been done for you. It is time for you to buck up and leave all the excuses and pains behind. A

Templar does not back down, and a Templar does not whine. Are you getting this?"

Richard felt naked again, just like in the final initiation ritual before his Templar brethren, and helpless before the questions. The blood was welling up around his neck. His vision blurred a bit and then refocused to a fine pinpoint within a tunnel of darkness.

"Okay, so what is your point?" Richard said, feeling his own anger rising to meet his teacher's words.

"We didn't pull you off that dingy because you were a victim of depression, or a lost sailor, or even because we particularly liked you. You've been watched over, at a distance, since childhood. It's about blood, Richard, blood. You have a damn important responsibility you can't even imagine yet. Did you think all these initiations and the training was just Templar benevolence? Did you ask yourself even once why you got saved?"

Richard began to breathe harder, wondering how hard it would be to pick up a knife and tear open Bisol's throat. Of course, he had no training and Bisol did. Why even try?

Bisol sat back, closed his eyes, and folded his arms over each other, making the sign of the crook and flail of the ancient Egyptian Pharaohs. *"Hamset unte Re,"* Bisol intoned.

The room stilled as if they had entered the eye of the hurricane within Sinclair's deeper soul. Richard's on-edge emotions went quiet and he felt light, peaceful, balanced, and without stress. There was no burning in his chest, no twisting headache, and no roaring anger welling up from his guts. Alex Bisol's dark soul had been replaced with a greater spirit that had been allowed to come through the imperfect host.

Richard recognized immediately that a different being would now address him, whether Alex Bisol allowed it or not. He first learned about this practice in his training in Egypt where he'd seen one student allow an ancient seer of Egypt's past to enter into him and speak.

Bisol brought his arms down and rested them, palms flat, around his plate. "Forgive my actions, my friend. It is my human host who speaks to you so poorly, not those of us acting as the Templar guides from the higher realms. We knew of your loss, of your wife and child passing in the flu epidemic in San Francisco. We have wished only success and growth for you, ever since your birth. However, no one could have foreseen the massive loss of life from that strain of disease. Many of our Templar families were harmed in that outbreak, but you particularly. You were established with your education, a new career and a young, lovely family. It was all so perfect. To lose all of that in just a week is more than most will ever face."

There was a pause for a moment as Bisol drew his head back and a deep, long breath forged from his lungs.

"We wait for a time in a chosen one's life when he is ready for the raiment of our Maltese Cross. It cannot be offered lightly, or denied more than once. You were ready for a new road after an absolute catastrophe, and we offered that. You earned the right by birth, and you were bestowed the honor through rites of pain. There is nothing noble about suffering the loss of a family, but there is nobility in rising above the darkness. It is no small feat. You must remember that."

Bisol closed his eyes as his head nodded down, chin to his chest, as the powerful presence stepped back away from the host body.

"Who . . . ?" Richard began to ask.

"Richard," Alex's voice was returning, "You have heard from the guides, the souls beyond our souls. Every

Templar must be open to let the wisdom from the ageless ones come through us as needed. I, this humble servant, was uncontrolled and irresponsible with you, my student. That will not happen again. I will explain what brought me to the Templars, and why, at times, I have a loss of—shall we say, perspective?"

Richard was still floating in a calm sea of relaxed confidence. The previous being had left him filled with comfort and caring, as though his own mother had held him in her arms and rocked him with a lullaby. He was fully open to whatever Bisol had to offer, but still cautious knowing that Bisol was capable of almost anything.

"I was just like you, once, so cocky and sure of myself, no matter what the challenge. And just like you, I had a wonderful family. My first wife led a law firm in Frisco. My daughter was an honors student at that new online high school that Stanford started. Of course, since we run Stanford, we had a straight shot inside the door. She was headed for a bright career, and she was pretty as her mom. Then one day, after a volley ball tournament, she collapsed after showering. The coach said she was exhausted from the semi-final match and all her homework. So, we let her rest a few days, but she still couldn't get up. We took her to the docs. What the hell do they know?

"We went for weeks until they told us she had some kind of germ cell tumor—that she had advanced ovarian cancer. If she hadn't been so athletic and disciplined she might have complained much earlier, but she had a high pain tolerance. Her mother knew Mary Anne had painful periods for months, but just wrote it off as stress and the final six months of high school. So, there I am, a top operative for the NSA, and I can't find anyone—not a damn soul who can do anything. Sure, they tried," Bisol hesitated for a minute, looking for cigarettes in his shirt that he didn't have, and then he caught himself. "Shit, I didn't know this was going to be so hard to talk about . . . goddamn it." He pushed away from the table and then reached forward to take a deep drink from his glass of water as an afterthought.

"So things got pretty awful shortly after that. It seemed like a runaway train. Every day was a treasure, but Mary Anne was in a hell of a lot of pain by then. Even the painkillers weren't giving relief. Brenda, my wife, was opposed to the morphine pump, but I signed for it. That caused a lot of issues, and just made dormant garbage rise up—you know, 'Why weren't you home more often?' and 'You were never involved with raising her.' On and on. When we weren't fighting each other we were at Mary Anne's side. Toward the end she begged me to pull her off the machines. I couldn't do it. Me, a trained killer, but I couldn't do that. My brother Bill, a firefighter over in Daly City, he was there a lot, too. He and Mary Anne were real close, especially since he'd been a jock in school, and an honor student. Even in her pain they were close and shared a lot of things I'm sure Brenda and I never heard. I'm sure of it now."

Bisol got up from his chair and moved over to the dark New Zealand pile carpets to the cherry veneer bookcase that towered over the south wall of the dining room. He opened the bottom glass doors and quickly pulled out a single sheaf of paper stuck between two volumes.

"Anyway, Brenda calls me down to the hospital one morning—we were staying with Mary Anne in shifts. She had left the room for a short break and when she came back the life support was unplugged and the monitors were off. My kid was just lying there, smiling, with her eyes closed. She hadn't smiled like that in months. Brenda just went crazy. She just lost it. There were lots of fingers pointed at her, but witnesses had her in the restroom when this all happened. When they finally ran the security footage for me, there was Bill, walking out to the parking lot. He was in his dress fire uniform, with his award ribbons and white hat, the whole number. We could see the flash from the car windows. By the time we realized what had happened it was too late to do anything; hours too late. So, in one day I lost my daughter and my only brother. Within a week Brenda served me papers."

Alex straightened out the crinkled edges of the paper on the linen table cloth as he paused.

"For weeks I rotted, blind drunk in a flophouse off Turk Street. It was really tough. NSA was going nuts looking for me, but I knew how to disappear. All I did, between the drinking, was read Mary Anne's poem over and over again. Let me ask you, does this sound like someone who wanted to die?" Bisol cleared his throat, and read through the short poem with a desperate tremble in his voice.

EBULLIENT

I do not long for the distant ocean's shore,
Nor do I dream of the deeper water's roar,
For here beneath the sunshine do I stand,
Below the hand of God in the midst of man.
With joy I race the sands upon the strand,
Within my soul I bless the time bestowed,
For surely greater wills than mine prevail,
Until my soul shall on that great tide sail.

"I don't ever remember being pulled out of the room. I guess I'd fallen asleep when I was smoking. The place was filled with smoke. I just didn't care. Four days later I woke up in Stanford, and there were the Brothers, waiting. They offered me some new hope, new direction, and a renewed faith that, to be honest, I had lost to the bone. I was human wreckage and they pulled me up—and why? Because, dear Richard, it is our blood. I owed my honor and my life to the bloodline we both share. It is a sacred trust we must never waiver from serving."

"So none of this is about who we are as individuals? Our souls? Our free will? We have to suffer and almost die to be what—resurrected by this society of history freaks and secret mongers?"

"No. Now calm down," Bisol said assertively, but not with anger this time. "Our DNA has something most humans will never have, and that is a gene that transcends all others. I had enough from my mother's line to bring me into the fold. You, however, have it in spades from both sides of your lineage. You just didn't know. Sometimes the Templars skip entire generations to bring in a new initiate. The subtleties of recessive genes and the Templar gene escape me, but apparently it has been tracked for many generations.

"Whatever we opened in that hidden chamber of the First Temple awakened an awareness hidden to all but the highest priests of Israel. It revealed the truth behind Abraham, Jesus, Moses, John the Baptist and other great avatars; it showed who they really were and their connection to the blood, and of course the curse of the Liliths. It has taken a long time for a complete survey to find out where all of us are located. Did you think it was a coincidence that the Genome Project was founded over at Lawrence Livermore Labs, under the control of the University of California? Why did you think Berkeley sought you out for a scholarship? You aren't a woman or a minority, Richard, so just stretch your brain a bit. The Order never forces, but it aids and assists, hoping they can be there when the time is right."

"So it's my bloodline that put me in this nightmare?"

"Well, yes and no. There's more going on here than the Order was aware of, especially what was inside that pit. Your newfound skill of transferring memories is a bit unsettling for all of us, as is that beast buried in your chest. Eli has commanded me to bring you up here in the mountains to meet with him as soon as possible. The Liliths don't enjoy the energies of Lake Tahoe. That's beyond me. As long as they stay away, we can focus on what to do next and maybe bring your new powers to bear on this quest."

"The Drake Treasure?"

"Exactly," Bisol replied. He headed back to the bookcase, and after a short sigh he carefully stuck the poem back between *Ivanhoe* and *The Tempest*.

"So, why haven't the Templars found a way to placate these ancient demons, or whatever they are? I mean surely, with all the Order's wisdom and insight, there must be some way to stop all this nonsense." Richard regained his appetite and began to consume what was remaining of the breakfast that had gone cold.

"You must never bring that up, again, Richard, ever. The Liliths are monsters, truly in every sense. What they have done these many centuries is blasphemy against the blood. The only way to release them is for our priesthood to forgive them, and that will *never, never happen*."

Bisol left the room like a cloud of ignited gases. Richard shook it off, seeing it as all part of the weirdness that seemed to ooze through Alex; unlike most of the Templars he'd met worldwide. It was true he had met some Templars with quirky behaviors or outlooks that made them particularly eccentric. If they had all gone through the traumas the he and Alex had experienced, that would explain much. Post-traumatic stress alone could make anyone eccentric or perhaps excessively peculiar.

Richard decided on practicality for the moment. He was hungry. He wasn't about to deter his need to feed even in the presence of highly bizarre behavior from Bisol. At least the breakfast remains were normal. He continued to eat.

Chapter 8

After Alex disappeared into his study, following his amazing expurgation about the Liliths, Richard decided on a modest constitutional to work off the heavy grease of breakfast. His wounds seemed to be in complete retreat. He dressed warmly in a red Macintosh coat and went out to the backyard. The weather was unusually cool for August, even for Lake Tahoe.

The bears created more damage during their light exploration of the rusted, green and white garbage bins than Sinclair had expected. He pushed the rolling bins back in place with his knee and then thought better of it. The old arthritis and questionable surgery on his torn meniscus always let him know when he was exceeding his limits. After a few expletives he had the cans back in order and tied down with the crusted chain. Alex had let it become part of the leaf litter long enough for pine roots to seek through the eroding links. Richard had little confidence that the cheap, rusty safety chain could even hold a Pekinese from breaking into the cans.

The faultless skies made the morning one that Sierra residents savor. Tourists just expect them. At a mile high it wasn't hard to imagine reaching up on tiptoe to pierce the darkness of space. The far horizons were close to a blue-violet over the dark, jagged crests, carpeted with the Ponderosa Pines and the occasional patches of scrub cedars near the snowline. The lake had a blend of light and dark blues that were edged with the turquoise. They didn't call it the Gem of the Sierras without cause. Richard was enjoying the light roll of the dock next to the Templar's speed boat, a covered canoe, and a weathered black rowboat. He stared at the rowboat's cracked and dilapidated varnish.

He barely noticed Alex walking up behind him. "Can't buy a day like this. Notice the color in the lake?"

"Just spectacular," Sinclair agreed.

"Yeah, beats most days of the year. You only get that color when you hit the 'tween season."

"The what?"

"It's between the summer and fall lookie-lous and the winter ski bum stampede. For about three weeks they quit flushing their toilets and their grandfathered, leaking septic tanks, so they don't send their crap down to build up the algae. This is the way it used to look before all these stinkin' La-La-Landers came up here and built their summer cabins and casinos. Who needs 'em?"

"Yeah, I kinda think the Miwok feel just about the same."

"Fuck 'em. Goddamned Indians never owned this land. They weren't here when this lake was formed. They came across it like everyone else. They were just looking for food like all the other teepee-creepers, and killing any other tribe that interfered with 'em along the way."

"Screw you, too, white boy." Sinclair looked away from Bisol, feeling the flush in his neck again. There was an unfamiliar pulsing in his chest . . . something foreign and disturbing.

"Oh, hell," Bisol returned, "I keep forgetting about your little bit of Sioux blood. Sorry. Didn't mean to get personal."

"Hmmm, you never do, it's just getting a bit old. You should know better."

"You really are different, kid. You never had that much spine after we took your dying remains out of the water. Maybe there are more changes going on in there than I suspected. Hey, look, the trout are jumping."

They looked north away from the dock up the east shore of the lake to Logan Shoals and Vista Point.

"You know how I stare at the shoals every time we come out here; the ones they call the Dragon's Backbone? Ever wonder why I watch those piles of granite popping out of the water just off the shore like a sea serpent?"

"Not a clue. Worried about your safety when you're water-skiing?"

"That's pretty funny for a guy with no sense of humor. Think a little deeper."

"Deeper? You mean like . . . wetter?"

"Exactly." Bisol held his hand up in front of his face. "Remember the three points of the fleur-de-lis?" Richard shook his head, recalling the lesson.

"Well," continued Bisol, "it's one of the basic symbols used to train the Order's initiates. Here's my wrist, the stem of the flower. Above are the three holy points of the sacred trinity. Then there are these two extra points, the thumb and index finger. Together they are the backbone of the Dragon. And that pile of stones on the shoal is one of the points of the hand. A petal for our Order to bloom. And what keeps our garden growing and healthy? Simple: Power. And what is the basis of all power?"

"Great wealth. I've heard that over and over. The reason we have to find the rest of the treasure that Francis Drake buried somewhere in the Bay Area. So what have those rocks got to do with it?"

"Simple enough. The best place to hide things is in plain sight. Just below each of those spines of granite on the shoals is part of the pinky finger. Beneath each of those granite fingers is a box. Each box has a treasure worth over ten million in gold bars and jewels. In all, one hundred boxes, all hidden and tied to the bed of the Lake, right in front of the Park Service, the Tahoe Regional Planning Association, and the fuckin' Mafia bosses. A billion dollars in gold, silver, and raw diamonds, all setting there in a watery bank. No one dives there. It's off limits for fishing. The really funny thing is that about four hundred people a year use it as a backdrop for their wedding photos. What irony, huh? So that's one of the fingers on the hand, but the thumb is the treasure that Drake took from Scotland to bring to the New World where it would be safe once the Templars began to establish their powers within the government."

"So that's the reason for that goofy, useless lodge? It's just an outpost watching over Templar treasure. My God, I thought it was weird enough to meet the Grand Master in those secret caves under Vikingsholm in Emerald Bay. This is just too much. How long did the Order take to set all this up in California?"

"The first efforts picked up in the early eighteen-hundreds. The last Grand Spanish Inquisitor, Jerónimo Castellón y Salas, sent a team out to investigate us and eliminate the California contingent. The Papists tried to find Drake's cache for centuries. So, we helped agitate and organize a little rebellion and *voila*, the Bear Republic comes to be, kicking the Spanish clear out of the State along with the Church's power. Ah, ain't it lovely when a plan comes together?"

"Is there anything the Order doesn't tamper with, I mean, really?"

"Only the unimportant ones. Anything else is fair game."

"So why did you bring me up here this time, besides keeping the Liliths off my back? You never have just one reason for doing anything."

"Richard, you do know me well. Seems the Grand Master wants to meet you again since your mishap in the pit. If that's what the Master wants that's all we have to know. We're going to Fannette Island."

"Please tell me we don't have to row all the way across this damn lake again in that piece of shit rowboat." Richard looked over at the long boat with trepidation.

"That's the deal. Consider it a little aerobic exercise."

"Well, it's a hell of a lot colder now than the last time we rowed over. I'm wearing a wet suit this time and a stocking cap, not to mention a better set of gloves. I've still got splinters from the last time."

"You catch splinters like a sponge, and you whine like an old woman." Bisol grabbed Richard by his shoulders and squeezed hard, pinching his muscles until Sinclair winced. "I just love that. Better than a Vulcan death grip."

Sinclair used a smooth one-handed motion to whisk Bisol's grip away and twisted Bisol completely around.

Bisol was caught off guard and visibly upset at his student's capability to dismiss his aging prowess. "You and that kung-fu stuff they taught you in Malta . . . just keep it to yourself. I don't care what they taught you in Europe. You're here now. Better show some respect."

"You should find a better hobby then, old man." Laughing, Sinclair ran up the wobbly dock toward the lodge, ignoring the cries of agony from his knees. He knew Bisol's corroded lungs would fail him, leaving him far

CURSE OF THE 8TH BUDDHA

behind, cursing and spitting up his lungs' cigarette mélange.

It was 11:30 when they dropped oars quietly into the water. Bisol pushed the boat away from the dock mooring as Sinclair pulled at the oars. The initial resistance from the oarlock on the gunwale warned him of the night ahead. He had to take some care, as even the rowlocks were made of wood. Even though the rowboat had a wide, shallow draft for stability, it could still be damaged easily if it struck a rock. Everything made of metal had been removed during the boat's design. On this voyage there were no nails, no coins, and no metal zippers.

Before they launched, each covered their last remaining exposed skin on their heads with matching black balaclavas, leaving only their eyes showing and a small slit for mouth breathing. It would be cold. The water in the middle of Lake Tahoe was only forty-five degrees Fahrenheit, even in August. Any remaining exposed skin was covered in black camouflage paint. Soon they were both donning unique generation-three night vision goggles, allowing full visibility even in the middle of the lake under a moonless sky, but designed without a single metal part in any of the goggle construction. Sinclair was told these special goggles were worth a small fortune and specially made for the NSA by DARPA. It gave them a major advantage in the midnight gloom.

The bobbing dot moved slowly over the inky water, slowly, silently, and without detection. There were no words, just measured breathing and coordination of rowing. Bisol used his navigation skills from the aft to ensure the boat would meet its mark. Sinclair wondered if the Coast Guard crews stationed on the lake would be taking their rounds tonight, scanning the waters with their radar. The row boat and its cargo would leave no pings on the screen—not without metal to bounce off from such a small craft.

It was after one AM when Bisol signaled for a rest by tapping on Richard's wrist with his oar. Alex took his bearings. Sugar Pine Point was just a dim glow in comparison to a single bright cabin light on Rubicon Point almost dead ahead. It was time to head southwest and make for Emerald Point. Alex knew if he overshot a bit that the glare off the granite on Eagle Point would lead him back to the mouth of Emerald Bay.

The journey was uneventful, which was more than a relief for Sinclair. The muscles in his arms and back were burning. He'd been laid up in a hospital bed too long to attempt this labor. Just the thought of having to repeat the whole exercise again, after a break of an hour or less, seemed insane. He had come to expect little that made sense in the way that Templars held their meetings. With all of the technology available, and the many incredible toys Alex kept showing up with for their field operations, it seemed likely they could find some way to meet at the Marriott or the Hilton, and not in crypts, abandoned mines, mothballed ships and old fortresses. Maybe it added a bit of mystery and intrigue, but he felt a man in his forties should refrain from tromping around like a teenage super hero.

They finally reached the south point of Fannette Island. Sinclair tied the prow of the boat to the rocks. From there they would be unseen by any of the Park staff that might be staying late at the Vikingsholm residence. Fannette Island was just a small outcropping jutting out to the east from the main mansion on the shore.

The stench of years of goose droppings rose off the wet granite. The lack of predators on the Island allowed huge flocks of Canadian honkers to survive comfortably through much of the year. The two men struggled up the steep talus below the Tea House that was nestled atop the tiny outcrop above the Lake. Even with the goggles it was precarious, especially with the rattlesnakes that sometimes slithered through the century-old building debris.

Richard wondered if the general public would ever imagine the real purpose of Vikingsholm, or the irony of Mrs. Knight, the original builder, leading the construction work for this Knights Templar stronghold. Even in the 1920s there must have been many eyes watching, but with the depression on the country, workers were just excited to have honest work. Why no one ever saw the side excavations into Fannette Island, just east of the Vikingsholm, remained a mystery to Richard. He'd heard the local rumors of master masons being brought from Europe and then disappearing, along with hundreds of workman. Now all that remained was the State-owned main residence jutting out to Emerald Bay, and the shell of the fine summer mini-castle on Fannette Island, once the site for high teas during pleasant afternoons with the wealthy escaping from the Sacramento Valley heat. Those memories languished now in the circle of eroding stone walls of the Tea House, its ruined flooring vandalized by bored delinquents, the offspring of bankers and lawyers from Southern California.

Bisol did not worry about such lost glories as he entered into the broken fortress. His goal was the block of stone behind the façade of a dragon's head frieze on the west wall of the Tea House, now chipped and hammered by memorabilia thieves. Bisol pushed hard against two of the smaller stones until there was an audible click. Richard then pushed a third stone. The combination of stone release points freed a half-dozen steel pins that would have otherwise held back a major explosion. The system was made specifically to prevent a single, dedicated robber from finding the combination. After the clicks there was a slight rolling and grinding. The fireplace mantle slipped forward just enough from the pressure of a hidden lynch spring so the two men could push it out along its ball-bearing track. Richard could feel the warm air rise up from the cave below. After they squeezed through the narrow entry the two intruders pulled the mantle doorway closed behind them. Soon the wall bolts reengaged. They took off the goggles and their wet suits. Bisol threw a switch that lighted the stone stairway down into the grotto below.

It was difficult to maneuver the underground descent to meet Eli. Richard remembered his first time. He thought he might be headed to some cannibal cult and he was on the menu. In the first visit he'd forced himself to focus on the stairwell ahead and not to freeze in fear from the precipitous drop-off just to the edge of the walkway. Now there was no fear. Sinclair didn't even have a memory of such a concern as he managed the steep decline with ease. Bisol looked shaky during the entire process. Sinclair could see the sweat beading up on Bisol's eyelids and forehead.

They worked their way down eighty feet. The walls were smooth from the years of visitors coming to build and expand the chambers. At the bottom the stairs opened up into an unobstructed entryway. It was a wide expanse with white sand on the floor. Mrs. Knight obviously picked her artisans carefully. The grand gallery divided into a dozen passages each guarded with museum-quality statues and friezes set in the Greco-Roman style. These depicted the many gods and goddesses of history. Recessed lighting washed over them in a breathtaking display, adding dramatic swathes across the statue

CURSE OF THE 8ᵀᴴ BUDDHA 107

musculature. Running marble draperies disappeared away from the fine carvings into the walls of the cavern.

Richard again wondered at the planning and exquisite taste in the design, but also about who maintained all of this glorious work, who provided the electricity, and who kept the place clean; practical considerations for which he never expected an answer.

"Which route tonight?" Richard asked.

"Follow Aphrodite's invitation." Bisol pointed at the goddess of beauty and sensuality. Her arms were open and beckoning with her round breasts exposed, offering a frozen moment of pleasant enterprise. The men moved through the entry under the inscription: Beauty, Charm, Grace.

The passageway was new to both men. Parts of the tunnel shrank, requiring them to stoop and feel their way along the rough walls while following the electric wires strung along the ceiling for the fluorescent lighting. The tunnel took a sudden sharp turn to the right, where they first felt the change in temperature and humidity—a sure sign of a pool nearby where air vents from the surface moved clean air and water vapor into the maze of the subterranean hideout. Too much moisture encouraged molds, which would make the environment unbearable. Too little moisture and people's skin cracked and dried in a few days. Mrs. Knight had the best engineers from Germany crafting this den before they returned to be bound to the Nazi war machine.

The tight entry path finally opened into a vast gallery. The back of the vault was dark and undefined, seemingly endless. Directly before them rested a serene pool held in place by a terraced, limestone lip. The water shimmered from underneath as recessed lighting made the surface sparkle and flicker like a fan dancer's skin covered in glitter and rhinestones. The lip of the rim circled to the front where it melded into a limestone throne, white as alabaster and regal as any made for a great monarchy. It was here that the Grand Master waited for his followers' arrival.

Bisol approached first, bowing his bared head as he knelt to kiss the ruby cross on the Master's ring finger. After a blessing on his forehead, Bisol stepped aside and Sinclair attempted to repeat the same actions. This time, however, the Master did not allow the required hand-blessing. He gestured for Richard to simply kneel, without touching any part of the Master's person. Instead, he leaned forward and whispered in the acolyte's ear. "You are the lantern."

Bisol could not hear what the Master said, even though he was just a few feet to the side. He noted that the bearded Master's wizened countenance was growing frail. The gray, straggly hairs had gone to silver and were less cared for than usual. The Master's vitality was declining a bit more at each visit. Eli moved back to the throne in a few stutter-steps to take his seat on the limestone chair.

"You are late," the Master said sternly. "There is no time for tardiness now. We must move with haste because of the new situation before us. You, Alexander, had the responsibility to protect your ward. I am led to understand that our oldest, most fearsome foe almost overtook him in his weakened state. Can you explain how this was allowed to happen? You know very well that it could have created a complete interruption of our most important preparations."

"An oversight, Master, truly. I have always acted in the interest of the Order. I admit I was lax in my defenses. It is my fault and mine alone." Bisol bowed to one knee again and bent his head down.

"Spoken honestly and openly. We have to guard against repeating such errors in judgment. We have many reasons to protect young Sinclair. But now, even more, since we must put to use the gift that he has been given. Richard, come forward."

Richard rose and stepped so he could kneel just below the reach of the Master's hands. He bowed forward, saying, "How may I serve the circle and the square?"

"It is your insight and skill that might now open the path we have sought for hundreds of years. You can bring new vision that would otherwise be withheld. Do you know the name of Sir Edwin Brummel?"

Richard thought for a moment and then remembered some pictures in *People* Magazine he'd come across lately on a flight to Denver. "You mean that adventurer from England? The one who developed that software empire in the 'nineties? And . . . an entertainment conglomerate throughout Europe?"

"The same," the Master replied, stroking his beard while looking off into space for a moment. "There are, Richard, many discoveries being made about our DNA, and who we really are. As you know, the Order believes that Jesus, our spiritual father, taught us about the blood and the line who must protect the true Temple. We have known about Sir Brummel's true birthright and bloodline for some time now, but he is totally unaware of the secrets his body may hold. Until now there was no way to reach those secrets, but you may now offer a pathway."

"I don't understand. I don't know a thing about this DNA stuff. That's not my field of expertise. I'm honored, but—"

"Silence." The cavern went still. Richard felt as if his heart had stopped beating. Even the water glimmered less after the command. "Wait to speak when I ask for your words. Now, this is what must be done: You will meet Sir Brummel in Sacramento at the Hyatt Regency Hotel during the coming conference on Global Warming Tuesday evening. He will be in the lobby meeting dignitaries and those attending the conference. Alexander will introduce you to him. Your handshake will allow a transfer of information, at least we hope. Alexander will help you focus your abilities before the time of the meeting.

"You have the opportunity here to find the true vision we need about our treasure that Drake hid for the Order in Oak Island and somewhere here in Northern California. It is imperative that we retrieve this memory from the soul of one who was in the line of Sir Francis Drake. You can do this, Richard, with whatever creature or energy now lies within you. My informants have kept me fully aware of what you have endured, and this odd new power bestowed to you. The Liliths may have, by their own foolishness, given us the very tool we need to overcome them at last."

Richard then realized what the whisper in his ear, "You are the lantern," meant.

Richard could see the blood rising up Alex's neck. He was sure there was something he had done that was now infuriating Bisol.

"And one last thing, Acolyte Sinclair. I am led to understand you do not agree with the secrecy of our meetings or the strange, dark places we choose to gather. In these times that may seem a relic of the past, from a time when we were hunted down and butchered by the French Papists. However, those who hate us have not ended the Inquisition. We still have a silent war of which few are aware. Alex, for all his faults, is still responsible for removing those who have tried to destroy the Grand

Masters and others of the Order. He may have failed in some of his recent duties, but his efforts to rid us of *Opus Dei* pests have proved most helpful, especially their *Patrius Unum* hit men. Even now they have agents in the U.S. government in the highest positions, trying to use intelligence systems to find us. That, Richard, is why we are still so secretive. What we have to say must only be spoken in person and only in the safest locations. If the Papists found out about your newest gift, well, you might be in dire straits."

"Master, I believe your informants may have been too quick to judge Sinclair's new ability. Richard has no power over it and it is irregular in its outcomes. Perhaps Marie overstated the situation."

"That will be enough, Alexander. There will be no further discussion. Where, when, and from whom I receive my information is none of your business. Your task is simply that of Master of Arms, nothing more. Is that clear?"

"Yes, Master."

"Then this meeting is over. What has been spoken here is not to be repeated to any others either inside or outside of the Order. Now go."

Having completed his directions, the Master offered his ring finger again to Bisol alone for a final departure ceremony. Richard and Bisol completed their act of piety through genuflection. After rising and leaving the throne room, they backtracked through the labyrinth and out of the Fannette Island Tea House to the waiting rowboat. It was close to three o'clock. They knew that there was no time to squander if they were to return undetected. Just before pushing off, Richard heard a disturbance across the face of steep rocks to the west of the Island, as pieces of talus tumbled to the water. He motioned wildly to Bisol.

With their night vision they could detect a large black object swimming toward them, with something in its mouth.

"Christ, the bears are hunting the geese," Bisol blurted. Richard could hear the fear and concern in his voice. "That's an angry hunter and we're in his territory. He's not scavenging. It's a big, male black bear. They can swim damn fast. We better row like hell. God, I hate bears."

Richard didn't need any prompting. Bisol had never broken silence during their secret jaunts to the island. They were only twenty feet offshore when the massive marauder jumped into the dark waters behind them with a noisy *whomp*. His head was gaining on them as the men strained with their all, pounding their fear into the strokes. The bear slowed and turned back as the boat made its escape into deep waters.

Bisol made a mental note to bring a plastic tranquilizer gun next time.

Sinclair's thoughts were much closer, wondering about the predator sharing the oars in the row boat.

Chapter 9

Bisol stopped at the curve outside Richard's Sacramento condo. The beige-and-brown exteriors made the condos as indistinct as all the rest in the community: another tastefully bland adventure in mediocrity so that no one was pleased to come home at night but the resale market prices would remain stable. The carefully aligned sweet gum trees along the streets of Sacramento led into the cloistered parking area and boringly standard swimming pool. The pool was abandoned by busy government professionals populating the trendy quarters. There would be no renaissance of Vietnamese homes with pink doors and azure siding. There would be no Frank Lloyd Wright ventures into modernism or sharp angles. Everything in the "Sacred Tomato" would be subtly nondescript and without disturbing indications of taste. There were just wooden walls of the same flavor stretching for miles in Natomas along the American River and Sacramento River confluence. Richard was anxious to return to the bland display as he wrestled with the wobbly handle on the inside door of the Buick.

"Well, no matter what you said coming home, I'll always wonder if that bear might have really eaten us."

Richard laughed, preparing to close the door hard so he could see the rust fall off the under panel.

"Ah, not likely. It scared the hell out of me, too, but we probably just looked like two smaller bears invading his hunting turf. With my luck, I'll die coughing up a lung in a nursing home while Nurse Ratchet is giving me an enema." That was followed by a hollow, sardonic laugh.

Richard could feel a sense of the fear that was behind the black humor. Maybe the fear that the nurse might be Marie Halleran.

Richard looked back at the taillights of the eroding hulk as it pulled away. Every speed bump rattled little flecks of steel erosion from the heap. It was a sickened animal leaving its spore behind as it sought a place to die in the jungle. Richard trudged to his dwelling.

There were twenty-three voice messages on the answering machine, all loaded to rip into any sense of peace he had before taking a well-deserved nap. The Governor's Office was enraged at his unexplained absence without supervisory approval. One of the messages threatened the loss of his state job and pension for abandoning his post—a state version of AWOL. Mary Beth also left several concerned messages. She sounded on the verge of hysteria. There was even a nice medical follow up from Marie Halleran. Her voice was hypnotic, but after just a few sentences the waves of anger over the abortion rocked through him again—a hideous body memory to which he was now forcefully bound. His bowels erupted in burning agony. He discarded the message quickly and moved on, trying to bury the new trauma that washed over him.

Then, for the very last message, a powerful, quiet voice rolled through the speakers and surged through him, leaving him dazed and paralyzed. "This is Lili," the voice stated in a deep, barroom growl. "I believe it is time we met and talked about your recent discovery in San Francisco. I will be at the old torpedo docks at Crissy Field, near the Golden Gate Bridge at four o'clock in the afternoon on Tuesday. Don't tell your friends or your Brothers, cuz this is between us'ns, just you'n me."

The intonation was definitely Asian, but that "us'ns" revealed a touch of dear old Dixie. It was perplexing. Richard had developed a strong sense of linguistic identification over the years, but this one baffled him. Chinese, maybe . . . but something very strange and subtle was behind the added Southern drawl, like a layer of silt. He looked for the caller's identification but it was simply "withheld." And oddly enough, as he prepared to play it back again, the entire record of his messages self-erased. All of his messages disappeared right in front of him, without a trace. He shook his head, wondering in his fatigue what stupid-ass wrong button he'd pushed.

An immediate realization of the Lilith's manifestation set him in action. Richard picked up the handset and hit the #1 autodial selection. He heard one ring to Alex before the phone went dead. Richard pulled the handset away from his head to redial, but there was no light behind the keys. Then the keys recessed. The plastic molding quickly pulled back as the handset fell apart in his hands into its integral pieces like spaghetti strands drifting through his grip. The base set also crumbled into its unique units to become a pile of drifting components. The pile crashed like marbles across the tile floor, soon to be followed by the wooden coffee table beneath it, as the screws and nails fell out of the legs and top. He watched as the power connection to the phone sucked back into the wall socket like the Wicked Witch of the West's stockings disappearing under Dorothy Gale's house. The message was stark and clear: *Don't call his Templar Brothers.*

"Okay," Richard whispered, "I got the message. I'll be there ... by myself."

Richard pulled off his deeply wrinkled and smoke-tainted green cardigan, his worn blue jeans, and dilapidated high-top tennis shoes. He dragged himself half asleep back to the bedroom, leaning against the walls for support as exhaustion began to set in, overcoming his adrenaline. He hoped the other magical protections around his condo would hold back any other of the Lilith's manifestation. Sleep clawed away at his reason. He felt he might not even make it to the feather mattress before he slammed into unconsciousness. The mission in Tahoe, on top of the last month of trials, simply left him spent.

It was noon the next day before he felt rested enough to roll out of bed. His bladder drove him like a mad charioteer. After relieving his driver, and scratching the lint from his eyes, he walked toward the kitchen to start some coffee. He'd run out of the pre-bottled Starbuck swill. Since his family's death he'd become lazy about housekeeping, like keeping groceries on hand. There was just too much travel from one disaster to another across the wide Pacific span of California. California's disaster seasons were callously called shake-and-bakes. The devastating fires in San Bernardino County two months earlier had killed almost two hundred people. The floods in the spring, including the failure of the Questa Dam, had killed thirty-five and left five billion dollars in damages. Of course none of these touched the Daly City quake last year that left a thousand dead, and ten thousand seriously injured. It was always something, year after year. And for all of that, here he was, standing in his tighty whities, exposing his love handles to the open refrigerator door.

The front door buzzer made him wince and think about his next moves, both for safety and dignity.

The buzzer was practically worn out by the time he had on his stolen Hilton terrycloth bathrobe. "Okay. Hold your damn horses," he yelled at the closed door. There was only one way to see the culprit. He risked looking through the peephole. At first he thought it must be a hallucination, but no, it was Mary Beth Calvert dressed in a long black gown.

"Mary Beth, is that you?" he asked.

"Oh, please," she replied, putting her hands to her hips, steadying her posture in her Vigotti Jolissa pumps.

"Hey, I'm not really ready for visitors. Can you give me a minute?"

"You forget, I've seen you—" A neighbor exiting his condo across the adjoining hallway interrupted her conversation, giving her a quick once over. He sneered, and then gave her a knowing smile as he pulled in his middle-aged gut. "Oh, go on," she continued, yelling at the door, "I can't wait out here all day." She tried standing elegantly so that she wouldn't appear to be a call girl making a visit. *Oh hell*, she thought, *it's Sunday. Does that schmuck really think a whore would be out here on their Lord's Day, already?*

Richard opened the door. He was disheveled, draped in the remnants from the Tahoe Lake journey. The dirty attire was thrown on in haste. There was a waft of a manly scent from a Rugby Team locker topped with stale cigarettes.

"C'mon in. What's the honor of this visit? Hell, you really look great."

"Wish I could say the same. Rich, have you been on a bender or something? You look like dried dog shit. Smell pretty close to it, too."

That mouth, Richard remembered, and a professional woman using it.

"Hey, love you, too, Mary Beth. So what's the occasion? Somebody important *and* wealthy die in the family?"

"Hey, you know not all wealthy people are Jews, and most Jews aren't wealthy, so cap the crap. You can be such a putz."

"Yeah, well, I believe it was the *putz* you were looking for the last time you were here." Richard turned and went back to the kitchen, hoping she'd cut this short and quit nagging. He could never win in a verbal match with her. They'd had a tumultuous affair six months before, but they were just too far apart about most of life and how things really worked.

"Oh, the little Catholic *goy* picked up some new words. Just don't sing about a *dradle* again, okay. That wasn't so pleasant the last time I heard it."

"I can always put on Ave Maria. I'm sure you'd love to hear the Country-Western version."

"*A chorbn!*" she cried out.

"I guess that's a no." He snickered.

She clacked across the floor sounding like two peg-legged sailors rambling over the poop deck of a pirate ship. "Now listen, Richard, I've got to speak to the Council of Jewish Women in an hour. I don't have time to waste here and this is important. Besides the fact I've been worried half out of my mind about you." She waited for him to turn and share a moment, but he didn't as he kept stirring his instant coffee for the microwave. "Okay, so I see your deep concern. *Ver dershtikt.* You can't imagine what it did to me, thinking about you down in that cave in with something trying to get you. Are you hearing me? It took me two weeks with my shrink to get through this, goddamn it."

CURSE OF THE 8ᵀᴴ BUDDHA

Richard could tell she was near tears. He put down his cup, turned and walked to her, giving her a big warm hug.

"Not the hair," she warned, pulling away. "You know what this cost? *Ahcck*, and that smell, it better not be on this dress. My lesbian friends would turn on me."

They both laughed for a moment. Mary Beth had a tear in her eye and she tried to dry it with a nearby napkin from the kitchen counter. It streaked her masquera and eyeliner.

"You better see to that before you go, Mary Beth," Richard suggested, trying to dry some of the streaks. "There just a lot that's been going on. I've been through hell and back myself and it's not over yet."

"Oh, it's worse than you can imagine. The Governor is personally blaming you for that mess in the pit and all the negative press. It's going to cost an additional twelve mil just to fix the underground damage. I guess the pylons hit a gas main and partially destroyed a main water line from the Embarcadero. The whole tunnel system in that part of Chinatown is flooding and full of gas. You're dog meat in Sacramento right now."

"Least of my worries now, really." He gave her a light pat on the shoulder, remembering his new curse, and turned around to put his coffee in the microwave. Even the taste of that bitter brew would be better than the halitosis rolling out of his face after sleep. He was surprised it hadn't melted Mary Beth.

"Look," she continued, "I brought something for you. I know it may not mean anything, but I've been having these horrible dreams since the accident. This keeps coming up in my nightmares. I just think it was meant for you." She reached into her sequined shoulder bag and pulled out a small, deeply oiled leather pouch.

Mary Beth offered it, holding it out an appropriate distance away from Richard's crust and odors. He pulled the leather ties open and extracted an odd ring. At first glance it appeared to be a simple double band with the stone missing from the head of the setting. Then Richard turned it slightly to reveal the setting was clearly a snake's head on a double winding of a serpent's body, with the tail ending in the snake's mouth. It was a clear representation of the Ouroboros, the ancient sign for infinity. He'd never seen anything quite like it in all the antiquities centers he'd visited.

"Where on earth did you get this? I don't know what to say. It's simply fabulous." Richard tried it on the middle finger of his right hand. It was a perfect fit. A sense of electrical force rushed through him and his vision cleared immediately. He shook his head in surprise.

"That is not a story I am proud to tell. Three years ago I was working through some of the debris piles from the Temple of the Mount that the Arabs threw away in the Kidron Valley. Dr. Barkay and I had worked together for years trying to gather up enough evidence to start a case for returning Mount Moriah back to the Jews, to whom it rightfully belongs. During one of the sifting operations I came across this ring. I recognized right away that it was unique, but it has nothing whatsoever to do with the Temple or Jewish tradition. Jews don't allow symbols of snakes in their temples. Not ever.

"What I did next is reprehensible. I pocketed the ring. I mean, I could have lost my job, my degree, and even been jailed for two years for doing such a thing. Why I did it, I can't explain. I just knew I had to have it for some reason. That goes against everything I believe and was trained to do in archaeology. Hell, I've handled gold works that were priceless and never thought twice, and an emerald the size of my thumb. No interest. But not this one."

She paused for a moment while digging through her bag for her makeup kit. She bobbed her head back and forth in frustration.

"So I took it home and had a friend of mine over at Lawrence Labs run a spectrographic analysis. I wanted to check out what kind of silver alloys were in it so I could date it. My friend Henry did runs like this for me once and a while, during the occasional standardization tests they did at the Labs on their systems. He came back absolutely pissed. This time it wasn't silver, gold, or brass—it was platinum, iridium, and something Henry said he couldn't even tell me about because of research going on in the Labs. Alarms went off all over the place when the little piece I gave him went through the processor. Apparently some of these alloys are only found in accelerators and from some hush-hush work being done on organo-metallics in the space program. So who knew?"

"Are you telling me this is, well, alien?"

"I'm not telling you anything. I don't know anything. Like Sergeant Schultz, 'I know nothhink.'"

"Wow, I really like this." He pulled on it with a twisting motion without success. "But it doesn't seem to want to come off."

"Hey, keep it. In my dreams, my grandmother first points at the ring and then shows me giving it to you while saying, *A leben ahf dein kepele*. She always said this to me as a kid because I was a really smarty pants, but I know she meant I should do this. She's telling me this from wherever she is in heaven, bless her soul. So here I am. Here you are, and I'm late. I'm going to use your bathroom mirror to clean up this mess. *Oi, gevald*. It took me two hours to do all this makeup and hair."

"I wouldn't use my can if I were you," Richard warned, with no effect on the clacking feet moving across the room to the hallway. There was no sound as she turned on the light and closed the bathroom door except one yelp of *mieskeit, Chas v'cholileh.*

Richard wasn't sure if he'd left the lid up or not, but he was pretty sure he had flushed—well, sort of sure. The real issue at hand was that the ring stuck to him like glue. He reached under the sink for some Pam and sprayed that around the finger. That always worked. Not this time. He took the ring to the window to examine it and then noticed a very disturbing characteristic in the metal: It made the snake appear to breathe; it actually inhaled and exhaled. The synthetic coffee smell drifted to him as the bell on the microwave went off. "This is too much, I need some fuckin' coffee."

He'd almost finished the entire cup, black and hot, when Mary Beth came back out, fully restored and clicking across the oak inlay flooring like a race car heading in the victory lap.

"Hey, how about a hug goodbye? And by the way, thank you for everything. I mean it."

She turned for one quick retort as her hand opened the front door, "Mr. Sinclair, it has been a pleasure, but I assure you, I am very orthodox, and Jews don't like pork, remember?"

"Yeah," he said, stringing out his word into a full breath. "And your point, *Miss* Calvert?"

"You, sir, are a pig. An incredible pig. If it weren't for my grandmother, I don't think I would have ever come back here. *Oi*, how I had forgotten. I'll probably get a *makeh* on my ass just from being in there. *Shalom*, Mr. Piggie. *Oi!*" And with that she slammed the door behind her and marched, with the echo of Taiko drummers from her heels as she reached the shared condo stairwell.

Yeah, you, too, he thought. *Queen for a Day, but a Princess for life.*

Even a hot shower didn't bring back all his awareness. At one o'clock he was still drowsy. The coffee just wasn't kicking in. "Gotta go, gotta go," he whispered. He already had his route planned out in his mind down the I-80 corridor to the Marina area in Frisco. There would be some remorse in going back to the shoreline in that park, where he and his family loved to play on their free weekends. He recalled their dog Alfie charging for Frisbee tosses and the joy of flying kites with his daughter while gazing out over the beautiful San Francisco Bay. It was a folder for memories of joy and laughter, sunshine, happy barking and smiling faces getting sun and wind burn. He shook his head and rubbed his eyes dry.

His faithful Volvo sedan was waiting under the corrugated metal of the covered parking area. Even with the covering it was clear that the car had not moved in some time as it was under a glaze of heavy pollen and other grime. Sinclair checked the tires, especially the front right since it had a bad valve stem that he just hadn't had the time or interest to replace. All seemed well except for the finger writing across the back window that read, *Wash Me, Asshole.* Richard made a mental note of that as he retrieved a rag from the trunk to clear the graffiti. He realized whose kids in the area were constantly trashing the condos. "Maybe it's time to let Alex take an ear or two."

Traffic was heavy, especially on a stretch near the I-680 split going to San Jose. A big rig had turned over in the fog earlier that morning. There was still clean-up continuing in the outside lane in the afternoon. Richard had listened to the news to check for delays. Apparently there had been two fatalities. Morning traffic for churchgoers had been backed up for hours.

His concerns increased by the time he reached Pinole. It was already almost three. This would be tight. It was one of his failings. Some subconscious urge always drove him to be just a bit tardy, no matter how early he started a journey. This created stress constantly at work; he was forever missing a meeting's start by just a few minutes, and he'd always have to apologize. This had become an art form through his days as a professor at San Jose State. After three years he'd come to hate his work as a teacher.

He constantly told his wife how he didn't want to be in class until the bell rang so he didn't have to hear the sniveling and rusty excuses for tardy work or past absences, or even offers of sex to bring up a grade. It was inane and insane. She understood, but then his habits slipped over into his private life, which sometimes meant his family waited outside the mall for him in the rain, or missed planes, and there was the forgotten wedding anniversary party.

Richard and watches were definitely at odds. It was one of the battles the Order had brought to his attention in sterling clarity for it was absolutely inexcusable in their precepts. You were prompt or you were punished. There were no exceptions. He had almost missed his own initiation at the Lodge at Lake Tahoe. Master Eli was not amused.

Traffic over the Bay Bridge was a mess because of a minor fender-bender. By the time he pulled into the parking lot for Crissy Field it was ten to four. He could see the old Naval Center buildings several blocks to the west. There was only one solution, and it gave him some difficulty accepting it—his inline skates. He thought about them on the Bridge, but kept hoping he could make up the time. His knees didn't care for the stress of the skates. They were also a relic left over from family outings almost a decade earlier. Regardless, he popped the trunk, slipped them on and applied their Velcro straps. He then hurried west down the bike path toward the jetty, as fast as his tired, aching knees would let him.

A scattering of tourists and locals enjoyed the sights. The light breeze meant clear skies and just the normal light haze to the other side of the Bay. The marine layer was holding off the coast like an anxious puppy, barely drifting off the harbor. Alcatraz sat like a fat mushroom on the horizon. The points of color on the far side, in Sausalito, were just reminders of the homes poised in the hills, pondering their eventual slippage into the waters below.

His muscles strained as he breathed heavily, avoiding a sporadic, light number of visitors including a two-seater perambulator, a few bicyclists, and a handful of runners with latex suits belted with their typical Frisco emergency pullovers for the sudden temperature shifts. A chill was rising from the ocean while the sun peeked in and out of the approaching marine layer. With all his efforts he was still ten minutes late reaching the tan, nondescript billets that were once a core of naval warfare research and development in WWII.

Richard searched around the sides of the buildings, which were sealed shut for tourism on a Sunday. There was no access to the piers, so there was no need to venture out by the water. There were plenty of places to sit. All the food vendors had left for the day and families were abandoning the site for their warm cars. Richard finally rested at a picnic table still exposed to the lingering rays of the declining sun. He could stay warm for a while and try to calm his racing pulse. *She'll just have to find me*, he thought. He noted the sunlight closing off as the fog started to make a break for shore.

The urge to rest his head led to micro-sleep. The sunshine felt so comforting. He could usually refresh himself with just three or four minutes of dozing. He sat up at the table, looking ahead at the concrete tiers gracing the top of the old weapons bunkers under the green mounds dotting the park. The concrete markers were installed to give the public a sense of scaled architectural context that was pleasant to the eye. He felt warm and comfortable, fully aware of the sounds and activities around him, including the pesky seagull that was standing on his picnic bench, staring at him. It flapped its gray, splotched, grungy wings and swept backward, away from him. Richard spun around to see an Asian woman standing behind him.

There are those rare moments in a life when a single instant is so starkly important and striking that few other experiences will meet its measure. There was his marriage ceremony, the birth of his baby girl, the death of his father and mother, and now . . . Lili. He had wild expectations that she might be an axe-wielding assassin. Maybe she would have a band of hired thugs from the Tong surrounding her, prepared to pull his arms and legs back while she disemboweled him with a Jian sword. But no, she was a demure Chinese fountain of beauty and grace with a sea of black, drifting hair tossed over a shiny Lakers warm-up jacket. She wore comfortable jeans over Pink Pony tennis shoes. He noticed her hands were in her pockets, so maybe, just maybe, she had a pistol hidden away, or maybe a grenade. He had no idea what to expect from these monsters Alex had warned him about. But no monster he had ever met had green eyes like these—deep, sea-green eyes that did not reflect light.

"Hello, Richard," she said, slowly, in a sweet Southern drawl.

He was nonplussed. Her face was a translucent moon rising over the Bay, interrupted in the middle with two glistening emeralds, shimmering and beguiling. Her mouth was the red of a sliced tomato, fresh from the garden. It was all overwhelming him. And who the hell, he pondered, gave a southern accent to this Chinese goddess?

"Y'all mind if I sit next to you for a spell?"

He moved immediately like a compliant schoolboy sitting next to his seventh-grade teacher. Richard's subconscious was pounding at his Id, reminding him of his fantasies of forbidden Asian love as a high school student, slobbering over the Jade East cologne ads. His father had served in the Pacific in WWII and often told stories of almost marrying a Japanese woman. Those stories always fascinated Richard until he had dated a Japanese student in Berkeley one summer, while taking a geophysics course. It was clear it was just a means for her to learn more about Americans, but not about American men. There was no kissing, fondling, or even hugging. It didn't matter how many dates. She explained it very clearly, eventually, that it was part of her study to understand the American mind. He was just a convenient lab rat. One did not consider cohabitation with a zoo animal. Shortly after that he'd met his wife and all the biting memories about Miko were put in the deep freeze. The fears boiled up now as they rushed out of cold storage.

"Well," she continued. "cat got your . . ." and she paused, coyly, "whatever?"

Richard grunted, trying to look away from her—trying to get a grip. He wasn't a teenager. He was a mature man in his forties with a world of experience. She was obviously younger, in her late twenties, and not a match for a man of the world.

"You first," he said with a flat, even, controlled tone. "This is your game."

"You're late as well as rude. That won't do, honey." The sweet tones covered an icicle that jabbed hard at the right side of his head. He could have sworn he was having an ice cream headache.

"I'll bet that didn't feel very good, huh, darlin'?" Again, the deep drawl caught him off guard and made him forget to put up his magical defenses. His right hand felt like it was on fire. His middle finger was burning and itching under pressure of the new ring.

"Okay, Lili, or whatever your name is. Let's get to the point. You obviously have powers and influence. You also owe me for another goddamn phone by the way." She giggled, making him even less sure of himself. This isn't fair, he argued within, it's like wrestling against your favorite teddy bear when it's armed with a commando knife. "You tell me why we're here and then maybe we can leave these nice people around us alone and not make a scene. How's that?" He turned sideways on the bench to look directly at her. That proved disastrous in some ways as she did the same. He was helpless in her presence. He was a bee thrown into a honey jar . . . stuck and filling himself with her nectar, disregarding that he would be drowned alive.

"Oh now, darlin' Richard, you shouldn't be so bothered by little 'ol me."

She smiled broadly and her perfect, pearly teeth shone brightly, becoming a new set of bars over his soul. He was by now completely intoxicated, yet using every power he had not to show it.

"Actually, I'm having a bit of a problem with you, which is a real bother. Let me introduce myself, if that is proper."

Richard nodded.

"Well," she said, drawing the well out in a long, soft breath, "I'm Lili Zhang. My father was a half-Cherokee American diplomat in the Far East and my mother was from Hong Kong. However, I lived most of my life in Atlanta. I've never really been to China. I'm here finishing my doctoral program at Berkeley. I've got two years to go in Native American studies. I got a pretty good deal on a scholarship all the way around. Plus, I'm kinda' special, too, don't you think so, Richard?"

Richard began rubbing the sweat off his forehead. He was sure it was from the last rays of the direct sunlight and the skating. Whenever she said "Richard," it took every bit of will he had not to get on his knees in front of her and grovel like a puppy. He found his lack of will terrifying, electrifying, and totally mystifying all at once. No one, ever, had taken such a hold over him in just a few moments. Not even the Master during the initiation. Looking in Lili's eyes was like manna. He just couldn't look away as he saw his own image in her verdant seaweed pools. He also began feeling blood rushing where he hadn't felt anything since Mary Beth walked out on him in the middle of a moment of intimacy.

She looked down at his pants and then back up, smiling briefly. "Umm, I see you aren't quite as dead as you try to appear. All because of this poor little girl on her own?" She smiled broadly, exposing two dimples under her high, perfect cheekbones. She put a finger in one and twisted her head back while doing a flapper batting of her eyelids in a Betty Boop routine.

It was just too much for Richard. Every button had been pushed. Every desire. Every weakness. "Look, lady, if you want to fuckin' torture me, you've had your fun, but this has got to stop. Maybe I can't get up without embarrassing myself right now"—at which she broke out in a twitter—"but hey, gimme a damn break here, I don't know what kind of game this is, but I'm serious and so are my Brothers, if you get my drift. So either get down to business or I'm out of here."

Lili's posture changed and Richard could feel the bench vibrate and the wood began to crackle. He could see black twisting tendrils forming from her hands as they lay flat, palms down on the bench. It was very sobering.

"You dared to intrude on our holy ground." A deep, gravely voice ground out of her. It was artificial and forced, lacking enunciation and human qualities. Lili buckled a bit under her jacket. Richard wondered if she was going to vomit or explode.

"I don't know what you're talking about," he replied, again reflecting her coldness by degree, hoping not to expose his terror.

"We were called to protect that treasure from all but the rightful owners. You are not the rightful or the just. You are an intruder. You have the spirit of our pet within you now. You must return it or face the penalty of death."

"First, whoever you are in there, the Order is the rightful owner and it is you who have intruded. Sir Francis Drake left it there for us hundreds of years ago. How dare you make any other claim? And as for your pet—you can have it back. It's a pain in the ass and I never wanted it." Richard thought of pulling back that offer, remembering his next duty assignment at the Hyatt. He wouldn't be able to perform without this thing in his chest. Perhaps he had been hasty in battle.

The black mist wove farther from Lili's hands. He could see it start to permeate out of her sports coat and through her hair. Thankfully the sun had begun to dip down below the hills, providing a gathering gloom; otherwise the strange darkness exuding from this Chinese beauty would have attracted too much attention.

"You are wrong, young Templar. That was not your treasure. It is for the People—the People of Han."

"The Chinese? Oh, please. What treasure would they have buried here? That's preposterous."

"No, Richard Sinclair. Almost a thousand years of history lies between your Order and the People. Remember the work of one of your agents who is now known as Marco Polo? That is actually a false name, like Moses, to cover the adventures of many wrapped into one person. You sent many people to the Orient for centuries. You Templars always claimed it was a search for your silly concoction about the kingdom of Prester John—a total figment of the European mind. Through all those travels, your Order really learned nothing of the People. All you wanted were more secrets, more treasure, and more power.

"And here you and Lili sit: the emotional debris of those sojourns for power. You are pawns in an eternal war of blood. She is our tool and you are theirs. How odd for two old souls, tied together in history, to unite as puppets for two warring factions."

"I'm aware of the legends of Prester John. It's no secret that we have sought out such a person in our history. Some are still waiting for a new messiah, too. That does not make them intruders or enemies. You have no authority over Templar matters or Templar treasure. Why are you using us—or me at least, to stir up your battles?"

Lili heaved and rocked a bit this time. It was clear the energy of the Lilith was taking a toll. "For centuries the People of China visited this land of California, long before the Europeans came. There were plans to one day build a great empire here. We came with many trade goods for the gold ores the natives brought openly. This building of trust was a slow process. Then the invaders came: the Russians, the Spanish, and the English all trying to control and destroy what they found—all men bent on conquest. Over the years the Han brought their people here for seemingly other purposes like the Gold Rush and the building of rail lines, but what did your people do? You isolated the Han. Chinese men could not bring their wives, could not worship without fear, and could not walk among the streets without bowing their heads. They mined the ores for your people under nothing less than slavery, both under the whip and the rifle. Your histories don't tell much of that, no.

"The gold from your California mountains filled the great coffers and built the great cities of greed and lust. San Francisco was the center of that depravity. It was also the location of the mint where the tears and blood of Chinese labor gold were turned into currency. The evil and inequity had reached such a level by nineteen oh-six that we were able to call upon the Earth to turn this City upside down. In the midst of all the turmoil the mint was partially destroyed. Our tunnels below were ready and the People took back some of what was rightfully theirs to be someday used to restore the great empire here, on this land, as it was meant to be.

"The government, and the family of Frank Leach, who was the mint director at the time, to this day claim the huge treasury was saved, but that was a cover story to save their pride and their lives. Leach and the troops that were sent to save the mint's vault knew the truth. They were all silenced by bribes, threats, and by unprecedented promotions, including the elevation of Leach as the new

CURSE OF THE 8ᵀᴴ BUDDHA 133

Director of the Mint in Washington. If the First World War had not followed shortly thereafter, the United States would have been a laughing stock as two hundred million dollars in gold bullion would have been reported missing. It was not all of the gold stored in the mint, but enough to require your President Roosevelt to secretly replace much of it by train over several weeks. To this day there is a secret unit of Treasury agents still seeking the treasure that was lost without a clue. They still don't know how or why it happened. They actually think Southern Rebels did it."

A light whistling sound came from Richard's mouth. This was all news to him. He turned his head in puzzlement, looking hard at the visage before him, hoping that no panhandler or idle passerby would disturb them now in the depth of this revelation. The history he was hearing was completely opposed to his understanding about the San Francisco Mint during the Great Quake of nineteen o'six.

"So, you want me to believe that what was in the pit I entered was a hidden cache from the o'six mint."

"I do," the gravelly voice continued.

The drifting veins of darkness continued to stretch out from her hands like an inky jellyfish. Richard looked up just for a moment to notice the fog bank recovering its night position over the Bay. A roll of furry cotton was already swallowing the Golden Gate Bridge. The marine breeze was stilled. The park was emptying as a bone-chilling ground draft crawled through Crissy Field. Remaining runners and walkers wore sweaters and jackets as they headed toward the park exits to home and hot tea. He realized he would soon be alone with the Lilith, unable to cry for help, as if that would ever have been of any use.

"So this whole mess is about you protecting the U.S. Mint's treasure? That's a bunch of bologna." Richard tried to stand, but couldn't straighten up. His knees just wouldn't obey him at the moment. It wasn't magic, this time, just arthritis and floating pieces of cartilage stirred up from the hard skating.

"No." she stated. "No, not *your* treasure. It is the People's. They died for it. They dug it out of the ground. They suffered and fell for that yellow pain. No, it is not yours, and we are charged to guard it for them at all costs. Are you willing to be a cost?"

Richard struggled to rise. He felt the acid coming up from his stomach. He couldn't gain any advantage by staying here but his own faltering limbs paralyzed him.

"We were called upon by the People of Chinatown to keep this treasure safe. *We*, who have protected and guarded secrets, treasures, and the precious heritage of this planet for all of time, back even before your myths tell you giants roamed the Earth. Only two of our honors have ever been broken. Both because of Templar dogs."

A terrifying, gut-wrenching scream came out of Lili Zhang's body. It was death and the voice of the world's tribulations combined. It was lost in the fog covering the park grounds. No one was nearby to join Sinclair in his panic. The shriek unlocked his limbs, but he found now he could not speak as the black fungus tendrils from Lili's body lingered across the nape of his neck. The two of them sat alone with the edge of the fog nearing them. Richard forced himself to take an act of desperation, one that was counter to his training. He reached with his right hand and placed it over Lili's left wrist onto the black tendrils, praying that the new thing within him, whatever it was, might return through him to the Lilith.

Richard was flung off the side of the bench onto the ground. A new shriek resonated through the fog, but this time it was one of deep, fresh pain, and not just a haunting, vindictive cry of the Banshee. This was a startled scream from unexpected injury. He looked back to see Lili Zhang spring up from the table, and turn her head to face him with a set of glowing, yellow cat eyes shining through the pressing fog. Another shriek followed. Lili flew straight backward and up into the air, transported by an invisible strings far above him and out of his vision. She vaporized into the mists as if she had never existed.

Richard's heart was near bursting and pressing against his chest. He had trouble catching his breath. He stood, ready to flee and realized his left knee would only allow him to hobble back to the car. He pulled at his leg and made the best time he could across the pathway on his skates, with each movement searing through his ligaments.

The sporadic lamps in the parking lot provided markers for his escape. There were no other lights except for a few safety bulbs draped here and there on the masts of vessels in the marina slips. He could hear the foghorns going off in the Channel and out near Alcatraz. He finally felt the first sense of safety with the dull thud of the Volvo door, but even the Volvo offered no protection from the terror still racing in his head. There would be nothing but anxiety feeding him as he drove back to Sacramento, slowly, past the ocean's pillow.

Chapter 10

The sound of the service buzzer was muffled in the back room of the Berkeley Reference Library, but still loud enough to agitate some first semester students stuck under green reading lamps. Richard was willing to wear the buzzer out if Edmund Turner did not get his tired butt up to the counter. He also felt the kiosk rock unsteadily. It wasn't as secure as usual, as if some force had dislodged it from its foundation. Sinclair had visited the Research Center in the Library for years and never noted that before. As he waited, he studied the base of the kiosk to inspect why it was off kilter.

The door to the back area behind the stacks finally creaked open. The musty and unshaved librarian dragged his demure frame and a stack of books up to the kiosk tabletop and rested them with a thud. Turner grunted as he released the burden.

"I'm ready for you, young fella," he drawled, rubbing his hands off against his tattered green plaid shirt. His pants were covered with various shades of dust, splotches of paste and some ancient grease stains visible between the many wrinkles and crusted creases. Edmund was not fastidious in his appearance or lifestyle. Only horse racing and research interested him for any span of time.

"You are a bit of a wonder, Edmund. Who else could find so much material in such a short time? I only called yesterday."

"Hmm," Edmund muttered, pulling his glasses off and then trying to clean them with a threadbare blue handkerchief he popped out of his back pocket. "Anything for the cause. I figured you'd be looking for more of this stuff after your visit up to the Lodge."

"So, you have the inside track on everything I do?" Sinclair asked, somewhat perplexed.

"Oh, no, Marie kind of filled me in. She's my niece."

"Really," Sinclair replied, stroking his chin, while looking over the titles on the spines of some of the tomes. "Gosh, Edmund, I had no idea about what had happened to Marie until . . . well, it's hard to explain, really."

"Oh, no," Turner interrupted, "I believe I understand some of what is going on, but not all of it. I spent three days with Marie in the psych ward after that transfer between you two, trying to get her through one of your traumas. This new capability of yours is nothing less than frightful. It's a damned inconvenience, if you ask me. And there's Alex, right in the middle of it. I hope the bastard is really worried, but that's pretty hard when you haven't got a conscience."

"Yeah, he's a piece of work sometimes." Sinclair stopped and bit his lip, realizing he was talking before thinking, again. "I apologize. I didn't mean it that way. I think I know what makes him tick, though, now that I know what he went through with his first wife and daughter. That must have been awful. I know how tough it is watching your kid die a little bit every day like that."

"What?" Turner asked, looking up through his freshly smudged glasses.

"You know, his daughter dying from that odd cancer. It sounded pretty horrific." Richard looked down, remembering his own losses.

"Oh, Lord," Turner spoke slowly, "is that what it is now, cancer? Gee, the last Templar trainee he brought up through the ranks was told she died from falling off a cliff on the Pacific Coast Highway. Hell, Richard, he never had any kids by his first wife. My sister couldn't get pregnant by him either. When Marie came back from boarding school, after Alex had been on a long mission in Turkey, well, it just got crazy. I guess you know about that part of the story. Damn, there's days I'd kill the bastard myself if Joanna hadn't told me to let him go. She said he'd live out his life a sad, broken piece of crap. Think she might have been right on that account. Sorry he pulled that old story to get your goat. He can be such an ass. Did I tell you he owes me money, too?"

Sinclair could feel his vision narrowing again as his pulse raced. His hands shook as he steadied them on the kiosk. He used his training to lower his breathing rate again and release some endorphins into his system. Bisol wasn't here, so what was the point? He couldn't let that monster control the situation. Every day it seemed there was another reason to distrust his teacher. It was becoming obvious that the Templars were riddled with lies, conspiracies, and deceptions. Anything to get the desired result.

"And the poem, the one he read that he said his daughter wrote?"

"*Ebullient*, you mean? He stole that from a little known poet from Texas. Unbelievable he would use that again. He's been warned."

"Warned by whom?" asked Richard.

CURSE OF THE 8TH BUDDHA

"Don't judge everyone in the Order by Alex, or even the people he works for these days. Most of us are really here to do the work and we mean it. Ah, enough of the personal garbage. Let's just move on, okay?" Turner began fidgeting with the books. "I put some markers in here and there to pick out what is known about the Liliths, but you really won't find too much before the Sumerian clay tablets, about twenty-five hundred B.C. There is a bit of new research, however, coming out of the Indus Valley. I included a paper in there. No matter how you look at it, the stories of the origins of the Liliths are confusing at best.

"I'm not sure you'll find what you need, but good hunting. I also put the information about the San Francisco Mint on the bottom. Funny thing, when I was pulling some of that up from the archived electronic files I got a call from the Treasury Department. I just told them I was doing some research for a student writing a brief history on the disruption of commerce after the Great Quake. We left it at that. I have no idea how they could know what I was looking for within the university's own archives. Have we got something else going on here, Sinclair, that I should know about?"

"Nah, I just want to tie up some loose ends for my real job. You know I have to make a living, too. Right now I'm in the shitter for being gone so long with no contact. Guess I might be looking at early retirement."

"Oh, phooey, you know you'll be taken care of by the boys. Hell, there isn't a governor been elected in any state in a hundred years that isn't owned by us."

"Well, I suppose we can forgive them for their actions, then. Might just as well forgive the Liliths as well. Somebody probably pulls their chains, too."

Turner stood rigid for a moment, resting against the kiosk podium while staring Richard directly in the face.

"Son, you can joke around about a few things, but if I were you, I'd never say something like that again, especially not in front of the Master. If you do, I'd bet fifty to one that you'd come away with fewer limbs than you brought. There is a reason you had to kiss his balls when you were initiated."

Richard stood transfixed. He didn't really like thinking about the Templar rites, but he knew the bigger meaning of their symbolism. However, he was completely caught off guard by the strength of resolve in Turner's voice. In the last two months he had worked with him, gathering information for Alex, he had never heard such conviction.

Turner looked down, finally, breaking his icy glare. "Man has a complicated duality about him, Richard. On one hand he has the overwhelming compulsion, an integrated desire, to learn new things. That inherited capacity for curiosity is so great that he will forgo almost all comfort and even his life to learn even one new thing. Yet, at the same time, he has almost as strong a predilection to forget what he has learned in the past, like a snake that is constantly shedding, leaving behind piles of himself as dry, twisted essences to blow away in the wind. That is why there are librarians. We gather up the remains and help those who follow to remember what those who preceded them discarded, and the price that was paid for those lost memories."

Turner slid back from the kiosk. He turned and slowly ambled back to his den like a crippled armadillo, pulling out his handkerchief again to give another useless swipe at his soiled glasses.

It took Sinclair a half hour to reach his Volvo. He'd found his secret parking spot years before behind a small coffee shop just off campus. Another Templar owned the café and allowed Sinclair to use the spot. It was designated with a special red sign that read, "Tow Away Zone—For Fire Officials Only." No fire official ever asked a question about the sign, and most students had enough sense to avoid the potential wrath of people who wielded axes.

Hauling the thirty pounds of books across the campus was a bit trying and winded Sinclair considerably. His arms and shoulders were still sore from the rowing. He reminded himself it was time to do something about his knees—really get them fixed this time. The arthritis was crying out at him in nail-sharp outbursts. Damage from the escape at Crissy Field was a constant reminder of his growing disability.

He remembered his wife's words when she'd look at him, smiling. "I wanted a man I could make better. You'll be a lifetime of labor." He shuddered a bit and moved on.

Getting the haul up the stairs of the condo and into his office area was also a pain-filled sojourn. The elevator didn't relieve any of the stress. He finally settled into his apartment and readied his work space for an afternoon of study. Before he started his investigation, Richard donned another ice pack from the freezer and used his roll of bandaging material to secure it to the worst of the offending joints. "Just ten minutes each side. Don't freeze your dumb ass." He talked to himself as he looked for a light snack to munch on and a cold beer. It was finally time to get into the mountain of wonder the aging archivist had exhumed.

The texts ran the gamut of ancient cultural philosophies, mythologies, legends, and the religious rumors of the ages. There were specialty papers on Sumerian cult legends, Babylonian stories, and Jewish traditions. Most of the stories led back no earlier than 2500 B.C., as Turner said.

They all tied the dark spirit, Lilith, to a magical Hullupu Tree and other ancient references. In almost all cases Lilith was associated with a snake, or to snake-like beings, and the stories typically referred to Lilith as a demon. It was practically universal, but Richard knew from his studies that the term "demon" had, strangely enough, been demonized through the ages to mean almost anything—from an enemy, to a force of nature that was little understood.

The few exceptions to these references to demons came from fringe archeology which included claims that the source of the Lilith legend came from Atlantis, or from references from native peoples about the effects of their exposure to upwelling natural gas pockets. The vapors from the deposits asphyxiated the unwary sleeper. There were even tales that Liliths were remnants of racial memories left from visits by aliens with past human ancestors.

The alien concept amused Richard until he considered how the ancient, untrained peasant might have reacted to a woman being sucked into a black cloud, disappearing straight up into thin air. Some surprises came in newer references to Jewish women who regarded Lilith as a misinterpretation of female power that had to be subjugated by male-driven theocracies. Richard couldn't imagine the Lilith he'd encountered as being so easily subjugated.

Richard sighed as he came to the final paper, a recently unpublished draft about a site in the Indus Valley near Mohenjo-Daro. Sinclair wondered how Turner had even accessed documents that were not even through the peer review process. The draft had references to Lilith that were quite different from all he had read. The text on one ancient vase described not one but many creatures that protected the crops such as wheat, olives, and dates, ensuring the land's fecundity. Their powers were represented as a snake circling a date palm. Inscriptions described an Earth energy being transmitted from the ground up to the dates in the trees. There was nothing evil at all associated with Liliths. Instead, they were often depicted as a bird flying over the homes of families, carrying a suckling infant under their protection. The idea prompted the suggested interpretation that Liliths were also the bringer of fecundity to humans, like the stork legends of Europe. The Indus writings predated the Sumerian by at least a thousand years. Her image had been maliciously degraded and evilly redefined sometime during the bridge millennia.

Richard looked at the reconstructed shard paintings and observed that in a few there was a nude woman standing over what the Indus text referred to as "great treasure." She stood with her hand on the head of a beast that was, indeed, snake-like, but rather more like a dragon from the European and Asian legends. Sinclair began to see a picture that had been terribly misreported: The Liliths were originally the protectors of the greatest treasure of all . . . the ability to continue both the human race and its food supply. What treasure could be greater than the basic understanding of sexual reproduction and agriculture?

He began integrating his understanding of history from the Templar training with his new insights. It became obvious that as the male dominance for authority of worship was increasing some of the patriarchs reversed the original role of Liliths as the protectors of the young of mankind. They perverted the Lilith image to one of being a horrible beast that ate children. The patriarchs had bastardized the truth in a most foul and devious way while they sent their peasant offspring off on Children's Crusades or to private horrible deaths from institutional abuses provided through the twisted practices of their own clergy. Richard now had a much different picture of the way the truth was manipulated by the Templars and other organized religions striving to unseat and repress the matriarchal balance of nature.

He stood up to remove the ice bag from his aching joints for the third time. It was a nuisance to keep replacing them. They weren't even all that cold anymore. Sinclair filled a glass of water from the tap and hobbled over to the window overlooking the pool. The afternoon sun was too low to generate a glare off the heavily chlorinated water. There were no middle-class sunbathers and waders flopping around on the sticky plastic deck loungers. Only the leaves from the sweet gum trees and the fire bush swam today, and many lay drowned on the bottom, unattended by the illegals that primped and snipped at the landscape. *The Mexican elves must be on holiday today*, he mused; the pool was a mess.

He tried to take a break from his reading by putting a cold cloth over his eyes as he listened to the latest CNN drivel, just to make sure he hadn't missed an important disaster. There were another fifteen calls on his brand new answering machine but he was wary in trying them again. Why waste another fifty bucks just to have the machine disassemble? Instead, he ignored what might be there, threatening him, from Alex, to the Gov, to, well—her.

His curiosity for the next piece of information eventually drew him up from his nest on the overstuffed couch. It was the one remaining luxury he allowed himself these last two years after the loss of his family. It had been a wedding gift from his wife's uncle, a furniture wholesaler in Santa Cruz. Richard never cared for the tough, strong appointment of real leather. For Richard the feel of micro fiber was heaven. The body of the sofa was really king-sized, which allowed him to stretch out. It hugged and

CURSE OF THE 8ᵀᴴ BUDDHA   145

caressed him. He could sleep, eat, and think there, just drifting away as the cushions swallowed him in the quicksand of comfort.

But the cat's curiosity was now overwhelming and it pulled him back to the work desk. The lure of the secrets Turner had offered pulled him up from the quicksand, grudgingly, across the wooden inlays to his waiting reading. He took a deep breath and began to dig in again.

The histories about the San Francisco Mint were far less interesting than the ancient texts. He found the reports from local observers to be particularly dry, including excerpts from a fireman's diary describing his service with the military as they fought the fires at the Mint. Only a few comments were made anywhere about the loss of the treasury. In one tome there was a chapter titled, "Myths and Legends about the Great Quake." There was more political wrangling than fact, especially about who directed the military to destroy some of the poorest sections of the City, including areas that had resisted the onslaughts of major investors who wanted to rebuild San Francisco in their image. There were stories about cannibalism, about sexual assaults, and about . . . of all things . . . the selling of children who were orphaned after the disaster.

There were two brief notes about rumors that interested him: A secret society of Confederate sympathizers attempting to infiltrate the treasury that may have made off with hundreds of thousands in gold; and the second that the Chinese had taken some catastrophic losses of their property and homes following the military demolition, perhaps in an act to drive them out, especially those who were becoming successful business owners.

It was a bit baffling. The Lilith boondoggle was easy to verify, but there was no validation for the story he'd been given about the millions hidden in the pit. It was possible the Lilith was lying and they really wanted the Drake treasure, the Templar cache, as compensation for whatever transpired between the Liliths and the Order.

Richard shrugged while reflecting on some flashbacks about horrifying little statue. He suffered intensely from visions of a monstrous face and teeth in his dreams. He would wake holding his wrist, frantically pulling away the searing jaws ripping at his flesh. There were, however, only fuzzy memories of the gold statue exuding a green glow as it assaulted him in a psychedelic drama. It was just another puzzle piece from the last month of missing time.

He shrugged, clearing the tightness in his shoulders from his intense hours of reading, and the continued aches from rowing. "Time to get a drink and some painkillers," he said aloud. He pulled out the backup supply of Ibuprofens from the second drawer. The lid almost fell off. Richard hated the child-safety lids so he left them half closed to speed access. There were a variety of vitamin and supplement tablets here and there on the floor under the dusty cupboards and under the refrigerator, proving that more than a few had escaped because of this habit. His paranoia about germs, after the pandemic, kept him from following the three-second rule.

Sinclair wrinkled his nose at a whiff of jasmine coming from behind him. It was compelling and one of those fragrances that made his libido fire up. His heart fluttered for a second and the warmth began to fill his loins. There was no explanation. Maybe he had once been a lover of Marie Leveaux in New Orleans in another life. He liked to fantasize . . . but then he realized this was not just a memory. The smell was now very strong. He twirled around to face Lili just a foot behind him. She wore only a white string bikini and red high heels.

"Oh Jesus," he muttered. He reached back behind him trying to find the knife drawer.

The weak, sweet voice stopped him. "No, Richard, no need to defend yourself, sweetie pie. You have the ring. Do you know what it is?" Lili reached to him, even as he pulled back, dragging her long nails over his chest and down to his belt.

"Not a clue. Just go away. I have no issue with you." He couldn't get the drawer to open.

She still moved forward, pressing herself against him until he was arching over the sink. "You wear the Ring of the Veil. Only those who are truly our masters may wear that object. Only those who have seen the snake and the dimensions beyond may bear its mark." The tender, slow Southern drawl began to pull away bit by bit, revealing the hidden presence within Lili, the voice from the gravel quarry. It had more of a resonance, but with a slight mechanical echo. It gave the impression of a transmission being received through this Chinese bombshell receiver.

Sinclair pulled his right hand around and placed the serpent ring on Lili's face, hoping it would drive her away. It had the opposite effect. She did not fear his powers of transference. The Liliths' beast within him apparently provided no threat to them, and the visitor had already found some way to fend off any pain from Mary Beth's jewelry gift. Now he knew what must have saved him in the park…the surprise of his touch to her hand with the ring.

"Oh, how long we have waited for the right consort to come to our arms. A companion. An equal. A bridge that could balance the forces of two worlds and bring the rush of the essence of life back into the soil, the trees, and the air."

Sinclair tried to move away from Lili's slithering over his chest and crotch. The jasmine was overwhelming. He was infested with his own desires. She pulled him back when he rushed for the door. The demure maiden nymph threw him on his beloved sofa like a rag doll. She was on him, writhing and groaning. Her lips pressed on his. He did not resist. Their heat began to melt them together in a single motion.

His training awoke. Startled, and angered, he pushed her away again, holding her at bay with his hands on her bare shoulders. "Lili, wake up. Fight this. Don't let this thing use you like this." He made the sign of the cross over her forehead with his right hand, touching the ring to her pure, radiant skin, while intoning, "Walk thee in perfected light."

She collapsed on top of him. She inhaled with some discomfort and then began heaving with tears and remorse. "Please, please forgive me. Oh, I am so ashamed." She tried to cover herself.

"Wait," he said, as he slid from under her and worked past his knee pain to the bedroom. He returned quickly with his white hotel robe. "Put this on." He handed her the wrinkled terry cloth.

She slipped it on quickly and then pulled herself into a ball on the couch.

"Lili, we really need to talk. Let's just chill for a minute here. Let me get you some coffee and we'll work this out, okay?" She said nothing but bobbed her head a little. He couldn't help but be transfixed with her now that he wasn't in defense mode. She really was quite attractive and yet so vulnerable. The Lilith had added nothing but venomous sexuality to what was a pure and gentle flower. Richard could feel a real sense of purity and peace coming from Lili, even in this moment of exposure and shock. He kept an eye on her, just in case it was an act, as he put the coffee makings together, making sure it was the decaf. The last thing she needed now was a nerve jolt. By the time the microwave beeped, Lili was beginning to stretch out a little. She was not as protective as she had been just minutes before. He reached in the cupboard for a small bottle of whisky to add a little relaxation to the brew. Richard brought the fresh mix over to her and sat next to her.

"Here, drink this straight. It will help. It has a little kick, but it does help settle the nerves."

"Thanks. I'm glad y'all didn't do the tea thing. It's so predictable. I hate it."

"Now, don't hold back. You can tell me what you really think." He smiled broadly, finally comfortable that he wasn't dealing with a fury from hell.

That broke the tension a bit. She smiled, slowly, sipping at the concoction. He spent more time just looking at her and her lustrous eyes. Their magnetism was compelling. He sat closer than he should, but he couldn't convince himself to move back away out of chivalry.

"Are you here, Lili?" he asked, hesitating, "I mean, is this just you? Christ, I sound like a friggin' amateur exorcist." He leaned back against his comfort zone in the couch, hesitating to look at her directly.

"Yes. I think so. I never meant to be like this. This isn't me. My family would be so humiliated." She raised her left hand to cover her face as she reached out to set the coffee on a nearby stand.

"You haven't hurt anyone, and you haven't shamed yourself, either. Look at me. C'mon, pull the hand away and look straight at me. Do I look damaged?" Richard set his coffee on the floor and faced her.

She turned toward him, moving her hands to her sides and then put them beneath her legs in a protective motion. Her innocence and sincerity melted away whatever control he had left.

"Not on the outside, but I know I hurt you inside, deep down. There is so much in your face. There is so much pain there, but also wisdom. You do understand what has happened. I can feel it." She freed her hands and reached out to stroke his face. She did not pull away as he moved to kiss her. She cupped his face in her hands.

"No," he warned, pulling back with a jerk, "don't touch me, it's not safe."

"Oh, poor Richard, that silly parasite can't harm us. It can only make us closer. Come back here." She wriggled her index finger at him, beckoning him to continue.

He reached up to join her by supporting her wrists, showing his sense of relief and ardor. By the time he felt the syrupy energy flowing between their hands it was too late to disengage.

Sinclair was acutely aware of being within a dusty, squat building in a remote environment far from Sacramento. He could still feel Lili's gentle warmth on his face while he was experiencing a totally different reality directly in front of him. His children—their children—were next to him as he passed the simple wooden bowls of rice to each of them. The brown rice was topped with small pieces of fish and some fresh herbs. Cups of a warm tea were set before each one at the rugged, roughly hewn table. Words came from his mouth that Richard could not understand; yet he did understand. The meanings were clear to him. He was blessing the food and each child. He was blessing his wife, who was far away. Then he blessed his ancestors for the richness of the harvest to come.

He was living out a life in another body while feeling his own still sitting in California on his comfy micro-fiber reality. He turned the head of his "other" body and found the surroundings very simple except for some wall paintings scribbled on the rough pine, and scrolls of paper hanging with black, stark Chinese characters. This made sense; the children were Chinese. He looked at his own hands as he swirled his tea: the cuticles were yellowed with cracks running through the nails. There was dirt under some of the fingernails and rough calluses on the palms. He was a farmer: a hard-working coolie farmer.

The farmer whispered into the air, "Where are you, my Fuchun?"

Richard understood each word and the deep sorrow of separation.

Bright light burst through the doorway of the hut and filled everything in the room with a blinding radiance. The children did not react at all. Only the farmer bowed his head.

A voice emanated from the light. "My beloved Ma Yu, I am with you always. Let me touch your heart." Richard felt a roaring inferno erupt in his chest. It was an energy he had not felt in this lifetime. He feared he might be set ablaze. In his vision the farmer was simply bowing his head while his hungry children ate. He breathed deeply as the voice grew deeper within him. "Always, my spring wind, will I come to you, the jasmine flower of your soul."

Richard was pulled back and away from the scene, as if he were looking through the wrong end of a spyglass. The tunnel got longer and the tableau of Chinese life, long ago, drifted away beyond his vision, into the darkness. His hands fell away from Lili's wrists and broke off their kiss. He dared to open his eyes and found her jade pools overflowing down her face. Her face revealed both a sense of shock and fulfillment.

"Richard, do you know what I saw? Do you have any idea what just happened to us?"

"Don't tell me you saw the man in the hovel, feeding his children, with the angel appearing?" he asked, barely able to get the words out fast enough.

"Yes, yes. And you were the beloved Ma Yu, and I . . . I was Fuchun. Yes, it was me coming to you, so long ago. How can this be? Oh, my. I must have been Sun Bu'er. I was one of the Seven Masters of Quanzhen in the Taoist faith: one of only a few women in the Taoist faith to reach that attainment."

"Whoa a minute here." Richard pulled back a bit. "You think you were a god or something and I was your deep love left to tend the brats? This makes no sense. Turner never said anything about any of this Taoist stuff or a Sun Bear. Where are you getting all this?" He didn't move far away but he showed his discomfort by slouching.

"There is so much for you to learn, my dear heart. Oh, it is meant to be. I feel so clean and whole again. You rescued me. My heart, soul, and body are all yours. And yours to mine."

Richard could not deny any of what he felt, or the vision he had experienced, but this was real life. Sitting next to him was a young woman almost half his age who'd tried to kill him at least twice, and was now prepared to spend a lifetime or more with him. That wasn't setting well in his Templar mindscape or his self-imposed semi-chastity as part of the Order's restrictions.

"That's just about enough for today," he snapped. He stood up, gathering up her coffee cup and heading to the sink. "I don't need any more stress and you are obviously in shock." He looked at her again, letting out a puffy exhale as he sized her up. "Lili, there is a blue denim shirt and a pair of jeans in that closet"—he pointed to the far wall—"that should fit you. I'd suggest you protect your dignity and put them on so you can leave here with some discretion. Oh, and don't worry, they've been dry-cleaned. They're still in the bags." *No, he thought, I won't need them any more. Mary Beth was tasty . . . but toxic.*

"No, please Richard. Let me explain." She held her hands out in a praying posture, rocking in the white bathrobe. "This is bigger than you can imagine. The evil forces here have tried to keep us apart for centuries— maybe longer. Can't you see? You can't just . . ."

"I sure the hell can." He walked quickly to the closet, ripped the clothes out of their flimsy plastic draping, and threw them at her. His patience was at its limit. "This is all a game to you Liliths. It's the Templar's treasure, not yours. Get these on and get out."

He turned, wondering if his actions were wise. She might just revert again and try to eat his head off. He was relieved to hear the familiar zipper closing on the pants, followed by the tapping of her heels over the hardwood floor.

"Oh, dear Richard, my love, there is so much we must learn. I am the Priestess of the Taoist Temple in San Francisco. I am sworn to know no man. Love was never to be a part of my life. You have won me. I am your jasmine."

The "my love" rattled him like the clapper in a cathedral bell. He could hardly stand as he heard her pull the door shut.

Moments later, while trying to find relief for nausea from his bathroom cabinet, Richard found himself struggling on his knees retching up clear bile. The water and Ibuprofen stayed down but something both solid and unseen was trying to leave him. He struggled to contain himself as he rocked in agony on the hard wood floor of the front room. The phone interrupted his groaning. Alex's stern voice came onto the answering machine. The suffering Templar decided to answer the phone as Bisol started to leave a message.

"Sinclair, is that you? Why the hell haven't you called? Do you know what time it is? What day it is?"

"I'm in a bad way, Alex. I don't think I can make it tonight. The Liliths just kicked my ass. " Richard got a few words out but his stomach was still cramping.

"I don't care if you're fucking legs are both cut off! You've got two hours to get your suit and tie on and get your beat-up ass down here to the Hyatt. Don't make me wait for you on this one, buddy. I mean it. We're getting damn tired of you showing up late."

Richard's eyes swelled in excruciating pain from his pounding headache. "Okay. Okay, I'll be there."

"Damn straight." Alex slammed the phone down, sending a crescendo of shrill pain knifing through Richard's head.

"Why me?" He rolled to his knees, feeling them creak back in protest. He crawled to the bathroom to clean up for his meeting with English gentry.

Chapter 11

As Sinclair eased his Volvo north on 9th Street in downtown Sacramento, he was thankful there wasn't the usual parade of protestors on L Street near the Capitol grounds. Sinclair remembered being tied up in an abortion protest years before when *Roe v. Wade* was under challenge by the Supreme Court. The Governor had come out in favor of overturning the law. The furor was a groundswell from every angry ego on both sides of the issue.

Sinclair was comforted that no protestors were throwing eggs and rocks as he drove past the angry lines of sign wavers from both side of the abortion battle.

He was still on the edge of his typical tardiness. It was fortunate for him that the parking garage at 12th and L was owned by the Templars. The garage's strategic placement ensured guaranteed ease of access to the Legislature and the Governor whenever a quick meeting was needed to straighten out the elected power-hungry, should they forgot they were not the elite.

The parked Volvo's radiator snapped and popped from overheating as Richard ran to the elevator. Once at street level he headed at a steady clip to the Hyatt Regency Plaza at 12th and K. While the once politically powerful met at Frank Fat's downtown, the new shakers preferred the clean, open spaces of the Hyatt. It was a slick production for the downtrodden capital's center that had still not risen from its dark past. The K-Street Mall remained a haven for panhandlers and petty thieves in the wee hours. Even the Capitol grounds weren't all that safe after dark, unless one had a badge and a Rottweiler.

Sinclair took a quick look at his watch; this was going to be close. He walked past the western edge of the hotel grounds that were lined by odd topiaries. The bushes were shaped into the outlines of families, animals, and obscene characters. As Sinclair hobbled up the steps to the main entry he noticed Alex's head above the rest of the guests in the foyer. Sinclair did a final tie-straightening and hair-flattening before reaching the top, hoping he didn't look too much like one of the homeless hiding in the shadows.

"If you were a fetus I'd have tongs around your head, pulling your ass out just to get you to be born on time. Christ, when are you going to grow up?" Alex whispered, holding a fake smile so it appeared a cordial meeting.

"This probably isn't the best day to do this, Alex. Really. I'm a fuckin' mess. I don't even know if this will work. This Lilith thing is—"

"Not here," Alex said as he pressed hard on Sinclair's shoulder. "Here he comes. Just keep your yap shut and let me do the talking. When I introduce you, shake hands, but use both hands, with one on the outside of his wrist. From the one example I've experienced it should only take a second to pick out his deep memory. Don't settle for something personal. We want the genetic memory."

Sinclair looked around the festive room. It glimmered with golden world globes of brass and gold filigree that twinkled from dozens of carefully situated high-intensity spot lamps. The polished reflections off the marble flooring and pillars created a shimmer on some of the women's

CURSE OF THE 8TH BUDDHA 157

hose and off a few faces sprayed with cosmetic glitter. There were hundreds of Sacramento's finest gathered in the main hall, in full gala array. They all waited in anticipation under the massive chandelier, which seemed poised to snap from its suspension from a fine golden chain. The support was so thin that the ball appeared to float in midair.

"There he is. Now pay attention. Remember, both hands."

All Sinclair could see at the moment were the crowds of onlookers pushing up front, hoping they could get close to the celebrity. The security teams were busy chatting into their plastic ear pieces tied to gray communications umbilical cords drifting down the back of their ears and under their shirts.

A path began to clearing in front of them as Sir Edwin Brummel's entourage entered. It amazed Sinclair how this ne'er-do-well rose up in the 1980s. He'd somehow manipulated his minute software firm in Great Britain to become a billionaire raconteur, famous for his cruise ships and investments in the racing team chasing after the America's Cup. Brummel was very popular with the press and the public, which was clear from all the hoity-toity sycophants trying to get just a touch of his hand. Sinclair felt uncomfortable in this mix.

Richard could hear two men whispering to each other behind him.

"Can you believe this show? Christ, he's about to be investigated for killing off his partner, Giles Edwards."

"Yeah," replied the other man. "Edwards goes missing on a simple one-man sailing trip in the Channel, right after becoming the fifty-one percent owner of Brummel's software company. And this by a guy who sailed around the world single-handedly and set several one-man sailing records."

"The billionaire wasn't crazy about the fifty-one percent thing. My broker told me that his sources heard that Edwards had the goods on Brummel's fudging the corporate books and was about to—"

Bisol whispered directly into Richard's ear. "Okay, start making your move over towards Brummel."

Just then a man—or a short wall impersonating a man—confronted Alex and pushed against his chest with one hand. "You'll have to move back, sir. You need to clear the way."

"Like hell I do," Alex snapped. "You're with Ferguson Security, right?"

"Sir, you need to move back or I'll have to remove you," the guard snapped right back.

Richard could read the security agent's badge: *Stinson*.

Alex popped open his cell phone in a flash, surprising the guard, and pressed a single number for speed dial. There was a brief exchange on the phone and then Alex handed it to Stinson. "Better talk to the voice on the other side of this, kid, if you don't want to be cleaning bath houses in San Francisco with your tongue for the next twenty."

The color went out of Stinson's face. He stood pole straight as he listened to the person Alex had called. He kept bobbing his head up and down while repeating "Yes, sir," over and over again. He finally handed the phone back to Alex, did a snap salute, and then turned to work on other members of the crowd.

Richard's knees went weak; his daring failing him. Maybe it was just dehydration from the vomiting. He breathed deeply and tried using one of the techniques he'd been taught in the caves in Malta back in May, before coming back to the States. Al Zhighar, the second-level hierophant in the Templar training center burned the words into him: "You can't be frightened or faint from pain if you repeat a palindrome. Since it reads the same way backward or forward it takes your focus off the fear and engages the subconscious in what is called overt overload. "Do geese see God?" Richard asked aloud.

"What are you talking about?" Alex asked, angrily, still trying to push through the evening gowns and tuxedos.

"Nothing, nothing at all," Richard replied, reminding himself to speak within, not without. The mantra kept rolling through his mind, easing him.

"Sir Edwin, if you please, may I introduce you to my colleague, Richard Sinclair? He works with the State of California to protect business and the public during disasters." Alex bowed lightly as he motioned toward Sinclair with his left hand.

"Of course, Alex. It is my pleasure to meet civil servants who do such outstanding jobs for their country." He extended his hand outward.

Richard couldn't help but notice the Thirty-Three Degree Masonic ring. Apparently Brummel had some level of achievement in the hidden societies.

The photos Richard had seen of Sir Brummel were simply not adequate to prepare him for his powerful presence. The energy from his sparkling blue eyes overwhelmed him; it made Richard's energy dull by comparison. A true sense of magnetic flow came off Brummel's body. His hair glowed like the mane of a lion king. *So this is charisma*, Richard thought, as he reached with both of his hands for the lord's wrist.

Whether it was immediate or not didn't matter, that first wave of intensity was a blast of explosive force in Richard's mind. It was not like molasses this time, but more of a freight train of images rushing through him in a mad rush. The room opened into a holographic movie. It was the everlasting impression of all things that ever were, are or will be: the string of timelines and all the little nodes on that eternal string; he was in the Akashic Record.

Sinclair walked next to the actors in every scene of history, hearing every word and every thought and sensing the heat, cold, drafts, and the smells. The first scene was of Brummel bludgeoning Giles Edwards on the back of his head before tying the corpse to a drift line, and then setting Edward's sloop sailing off toward wave-pounded reefs. Sinclair felt the urge to vomit again but the scene disappeared as though a hand had whisked it away.

A bit of cloudiness washed over the view and then a rolled back to reveal a new diorama. Sinclair stood next to Brummel, who had morphed into his ancestor Sir Francis Drake. He stood on the deck of the *Pelican*, Drake's lead ship, which was bearing northward parallel to a coastline. The captain was tired and gray around his face. It was clear he was in a troubled mood. Although Brummel's eyes and energy were there, the scruffy sailor before Sinclair was ill-bred in manner, character, and hygiene.

Sinclair's stomach churned again from the odor of pine tar and human waste as it rolled up from the lower decks and spilled onto the foc'sle. He heard the slaves wailing from below while the crew grunted and strained to pull in the sheets to the yardarms and drop the anchor. The captain checked aft to make certain his companion ships were following the same actions in order and staying abaft his position.

As the flotilla of vessels aligned, a French ship approached on the port bow. Drake, or Brummel, ordered the galleon's cannons out of their gun decks and through the firing ports. The English red cross fluttered clearly

CURSE OF THE 8ᵀᴴ BUDDHA 161

above the *Pelican*. A white cross floated above the encroaching galleon as it came to rest two points off the *Pelican*'s bow. The flag clearly identified it as a French ship of war. Unlike the *Pelican*, it sat high in the water, with its empty hold.

A longboat left the French ship, headed toward the *Pelican*. Eventually the two captains met and solidified their greeting by spitting on clerical raiment from the Catholic Church. Sinclair followed them down the gangways of rough-hewn oak and pine to the officer's quarters in the stern. He was surprised at how cramped and dirty the quarters were—certainly not like the Hollywood versions of seafaring men. Even here the smell of the rot and filth in the bilges was nearly unbearable.

Sinclair could understand the gist of the conversation between the two men. The French captain opened a wax-sealed letter impressed with the royal insignia of France. What Sinclair could gather was that they were making some kind of exchange and that King Henri III had agreed to secretly support the rising ranks of Protestants in France. The two men signed the two copies. Drake placed one in a sea chest behind him.

There were no comforts in this captain's cabin. The Frenchman made a note of it, stating that even at sea the head of a fleet of ships should have better accommodations. Drake laughed and said something about his men following him for his hard hands and not his soft back. This brought a flush to the visitor. Drake slapped him on the back and bid him to share a glass of wine.

The scene flash-forwarded in time when two other French ships were floating astern the *Pelican*. Slaves had been set to work at moving heavy troves of chests and irregular forms covered in oil clothes and protective bumpers made of twine-drawn straw. The *Pelican* was now much higher in the water. There were other boats arriving from the rest of Drake's fleet with additional goods to transfer to the French.

The vision disappeared.

Sinclair stood in the present, still shaking Brummel's hand and arm. It was a firm and friendly exchange, but some of the light in Brummel's eyes withdrew as he pulled away from Richard's hand. "You filthy, fucking swine!" he screamed at Alex. "How could you do that to me? That was our baby! My child!"

Richard snatched his hand back, realizing he'd swapped memories, and no longer remembered Marie Halleran's experience, except through conversations with Alex. He was horrified by the burden he'd just delivered, but after all, Brummel was unlikely to care; he was a heartless murderer, just like Alex. It was time to make a quick exit.

The crowd curled back in shock as security guards rushed to Brummel's aid. The Britain was highly agitated and throwing back the hands of anyone trying to give him assistance.

Alex pulled Sinclair farther back in the crowd and out of the Hyatt's marble palisade. He already planned to change clothes in his car and get to the crowds on the K-Street Mall, then blend in with the tourists. There were expectations of some memory transfer, but not *that* one. From now on, his insider value would be found wanting at the Brummel Mansion, should he ever decide to visit when passing through London on Templar business. Brummel had always been a puppet for the Templars.

"Do geese see God? Do geese see God?"

"*Quit* that nonsense." Alex pulled hard on the Buick's crusty door handle and pushed Sinclair into the back seat. "I brought some of your old clothes. Get them out of the

CURSE OF THE 8ᵀᴴ BUDDHA 163

bag and put your suit and tie in it; you can pick those up later. We're going to see the Master tonight underneath Old Sacramento. You know the site."

Alex began undressing in the front seat. Richard began thinking about the 'dungeon,' as he dubbed it. He truly loathed the confines of tunnels, caves, and abandoned spaces that might collapse or flood at any moment. Old Sacramento's underground was dangerous enough from cave-ins, but there were plenty of other reasons to avoid it, including the violent, homeless vagrants that sometimes lived there, the street gangs that used it for organizing dope deals, and the local cops who thought it was a great place to run their idea of war games. It was hard to tell which of them one might be lurking in the dungeon.

The two men walked through K-Street among the crowds gathered late for dinner at some of the newly renovated restaurants. There was a small crowd gathering for the opening of the new Lucas 3-D blockbuster film at the IMAX Theatre. It wasn't difficult to blend in with their simple blue pullover turtlenecks and blue jeans. They looked like two middle-aged friends, maybe even gay lovers, passing along the streets of the Capital. Alex broke their pace now and then to stop to catch his breath.

While he waited for Alex to gather his energy at one spot, Richard picked up a free copy of the SNR newspaper out of a corner box. He turned to the back to read his horoscope for that week. It warned of avoiding meetings with superiors and keeping information secret. *Just what I need*, he thought, sticking the paper back in the rack.

The men then walked west for several miles to the heart of Old Sacramento. Many of the stores were beginning to close along the rickety wooden frontage. The Kettleman's T-Shirt shop was still open. A few tourists were still ambling in from the boardwalk outside and setting off the noisy electronic guard frogs set at the entry. Alex bent down to slip his hands past the head of the frog and set the amphibians croaking in a pattern that was known by the owner of the shop. Richard was glad Alex could bend as his own knees were locking.

Cicero Jennings was a lumbering tub of jelly strapped into oversized pants and a globular T-shirt with a widespread graphic of the earth emblazoned around it, and under the folds of his flabby chest and arms. His red, wiry hair topped a wide, pig face. He had no chin left to speak of and only a whisper of a voice came out of his rotund hide. Why Cicero thought a sparse and poorly manicured handlebar mustache would add to his appeal was truly unimaginable. Still, he was prompt to serve the Order and had protected the underground entrance with vigor, as had his father and his grandfather.

"Evening, gentlemen. We're going to close soon. Anything I could help you with?" Cicero waddled toward them, barely audible over the background music piped into the store over the racks of tie-dye shirts and '60s paraphernalia.

"Just here to pass the time, like the three leaves on a flower." Alex let the passwords flow smoothly.

"Right this way. I have a little something to take the weight off the cross you bear." The owner rocked back and forth on his broken-down tennis shoes while leading them to the back office and the private staircase.

The passage to the dungeon was even more precipitous than the entry into the underground at Fannette Island. A double set of metal doors slid back to allow the exhale of must, river mud, and rot from below. The lights came on for the stairs, but their dim illumination and the smells didn't make the occasion festive.

The *Pelican*'s odors had been friendlier, Richard thought.

CURSE OF THE 8TH BUDDHA

Sinclair no longer had to fight his life-long terror of falling as he stared down through spaces on the dilapidated wooden steps hanging over the forty feet of molding pylons that supported the Old Sacramento buildings and streets. He was perfectly comfortable and confident on the stairway. Richard noticed how unsettled Alex was, though; as they descended, Bisol practically clung to the walls.

After two flights, they were down in the stone-lined passage that led into the main streets and alleys of the eighteen-hundreds' underground. There was no point in using night goggles here as there was no source of light whatsoever in this part of Old Town. Alex used a flashlight intermittently to avoid the largest barriers. They had both been trained to remember details between flashes.

Much had been closed off in the underground for decades, at least officially, until the City had opened certain parts for the tourist dollars. Even that had stopped after the disappearance, rape, and death of a woman from a tour group last summer. The crime was still unsolved. The old Gold-Rush-Days' vampire stories came bubbling up because the woman's body had been drained of blood. After that, the cops had stopped their underground paintball games, which now made the dungeon undoubtedly the spookiest and least protected territory in the City.

The City had worked diligently to seal off every known entrance after the woman's murder—but the Templar entrances remained undiscovered. The homeless living below had to exit as their lifelines to the surface were cut off. There was now little likelihood of encountering anything larger than a rat in the abandoned sections of Old Sacramento's underground.

Richard remembered Cicero in the shirt shop telling him two months back of how he'd discovered a dead vagrant huddled next to the hidden Templar entrance door. The poor fool had died of dehydration. It was ironic since the Sacramento River bubbled just sixty feet away through the eroding walls of the downtown levees. There was hardly a doubt this sojourn to a Templar sanctuary would soon be empty of human residents, but interrupted flashlight use was just a reasonable precaution for now.

Alex came to a corroded metal sign that said, "4th Street." He tapped against the wall three times, waited, and then tapped three more times. A place in the wall slipped backward and then opened into a lighted alcove. The Grand Master motioned them in. The wall closed quickly and quietly, leaving no sign behind that anyone had been swallowed up from the dark remains of a once prosperous river city buried below the scurrying 21st century residents above.

Sinclair had found in his research that the Keyhole Grotto was once the meeting place for gangsters, rum-runners and various nefarious characters from the eighteen-seventies up through the nineteen-twenties. It was only part of the local folklore now. Only a few knew its occult entrance—a secret that once required criminals to give a blood oath followed by a small branding of the left ear. Sinclair didn't know how the Grand Master came by the possession of this secret, but there was certainly no brand on his ear. That was one initiation Sinclair had been grateful to avoid.

After walking carefully through a short span of a candlelit passages, the three men encountered a heavy oak door. The Master released the lock with a gigantic brass key shaped like a death's head skull. Behind the doorway was an open circular space with a single table and a rickety

CURSE OF THE 8TH BUDDHA

wooden chair. This section was not musty or dank, but distinctly dry and crisp. A hint of fresh air wafted from a shaft above them. The slight ventilation made the cobwebs covering the vent drift back and forth like billowing smoke over the air shaft grating.

The setting was harsh. There were six rooms circling the central hub like spokes. Each had once held prize merchandise and robbery loot but now only stored imprints from sea chests, barrels, and bales. A few pallets were still stacked in the room nearest the table. The single chair in the center well was splintering from its age and disrepair.

The Master rocked on the creaky oak tines of the aging furnishing. He moved with agitation and mumbled like a grumpy troll. Alex and Richard both knelt before him, each kissing a separate knee.

"Rise and report. You first, Alexander."

"We had the meeting as you requested. There were some unforeseen difficulties. I believe an exchange was made. There has been little time since then. As you requested I have not spoken more than was necessary, as you wished, to keep the memories fresh."

"And you have not done any interrogation, as you were told?"

"No, Master, I have not, nor has he offered."

"Hmm, that shows some wisdom from you both of you for a change. I'll speak to young Sinclair alone now, Alex. Please step outside the door and close it tight."

"But—?"

"Now, Alexander."

Alex turned smartly and exited with mechanical coldness. The Master waited to speak until after the oak door was closed tight. "So, your gift did, indeed, bring us a plum. I hope it is one worth the time we've spent tending the tree."

"I don't think so, Master." Sinclair looked away, knowing the news he was bringing was not what the Templars had expected.

"And why not? What did you see in your visions?"

"It was incredible. It's still all in my mind as if it happened just now. Some were so dark that I dare only mention them here within our Order. First, before we speak about Drake, you must know that I saw Brummel kill Giles Edwards. There was no accident at sea. It was a brutal murder meant to cover Brummel's own crimes." Sinclair looked down, still kneeling before the wizened elder.

"Don't let that bother you, young Sinclair. Sometimes there are actions that must be taken. The failure of the Brummel companies would have led to a cascade of collapses and might have exposed the Order's involvement in the manipulation of cyberspace through our control of Brummel's products. With Brummel's software being used so universally, by so many governments—well, we have an open doorway into the great secrets of the world. Do not judge the man so harshly. He did as he was ordered."

A ball of phlegm formed in Richard's throat. '*Ordered*' clanged inside him. His heart beat like a freight train. *Do geese see God? Do geese see God? Do geese see God?*

"Come now; let us get to the matter of Drake and our inheritance. Did you see the burial place of the trove?"

There was no point in delaying the inevitable. It was just how to talk around the truth without being too close to the explosion that would follow.

"Not exactly. In fact, no. Drake did not bring the Templar treasure to the California Coast. That is a piece of fiction we have been told. I expect that lie was handed down by the Scots to put us off the trail."

"What?" The empty alcoves acted as echo chambers to enhance the retort like a concert hall. It rattled Sinclair to the bone. The Master rose quickly, kicking the chair behind him, leaving Sinclair far below, still in a position of submission.

"It is true. I saw it all. It had to be early in Drake's travels to circumnavigate the Earth looking for the passage to the Orient. He did have treasure with him. I'm sure it was from the Templars. But he gave it to the care of the French to—"

"The what? French? Blast you to hell if this is a lie!"

"It is clearly what I saw." Sinclair raised his right hand above his head while still looking down. "I recognized the colors of the flags and the period. Remember, I was an historian of sorts. It was Drake. The treasure was meant to support the fall of Catholicism in France under King Henri III. Drake hated the Catholics. We all know that. What we didn't know was that he hated them enough to cheat the Order and support his own personal vendetta against the Pope. Brummel carries the same trait today, playing with someone else's money and expecting never to be caught because of his daring. I'm sorry. There is nothing for us to find here."

"You're sorry? That is all you have to say?"

"Yes, Master. I have reported the truth as to our code, 'three points to the square and circle round, by my heart and by my blood.'"

The oath of truth settled the Master's fury. He righted the chair, sat hard, and this time rocked back on two legs, with disdain, almost daring it to fail under his weight. He stretched his right hand forward with ring exposed.

Sinclair kissed it, head bent. "Go to your mentor. Have him come back to me, alone. You wait outside this time."

Sinclair rose and followed the command verbatim. He couldn't help but notice a change in the timber of the Master's voice. His demeanor was that of a broken spirit—a child who had been abandoned.

There was no exchange between Alex and Richard. Richard directed him back to the waiting Master with a jerk of his thumb. Sinclair's hope sank into the murky sands of the underground as the door pulled shut. He had the death's head key in his hand, still warm from Alex. He thought of just putting it back in the lock and snapping it off. He'd brought devastating news back to the Order. Giles Edwards was just one more bellwether of the dangers posed by continuing to work within the mindless intrigues the Templars led or invented. The positive he had seen in his whirlwind training was now fading away to disgust.

Alex pushed the door open after only a few minutes. He had a sallow appearance. This was a new look; a look Sinclair could not read. Alex raised a finger to his mouth to indicate silence. And so it was that the two visitors backtracked, without a word, through the tunnels, up the stairs, and past Cicero Jennings' watchful eyes. The rotund clown trundled to the front door, opening it just long enough for the Templar travelers to leave. Jennings then flipped the sign to "closed" and turned off the front lights.

"Take the road north up Main and then across G Street. Don't cut south until you've passed the Hyatt and then double back around to your car. They may still be watching."

"Alex, for once I'll tell you I don't like this. You're acting stranger than your normally weird self. You know I just walked more than my knees can handle. I'm beat up from the damn Liliths and you're just tossing me out here to walk home? And what about the Master? Was he pissed or just in shock?"

"Later. Just do as you're told. I'll see you in three days up at the Lake. We can discuss it then. The Master wants to meet with the Council and then with you at your favorite rowing spot." He finished coldly, without a smile, grin or hint of a smirk. He turned his back on Sinclair and walked directly east under the I-80 Bridge, traveling back on their entry route. Sinclair didn't see the fairness in his having to take a more circuitous route, with aching joints, but since he was the one that apparently set off Brummel he might well be the culprit being sought.

The walk was lonely—few ventured north near the tracks after dark, and the mid-August evening changed as a brisk chill flew in with the Delta breeze; the street lighting was random. There was little comfort from passing the city police outpost: the former county sheriff's offices. This part of Sacramento was a depot for assorted denizens who came in and out of the police station, before and after arrest. Sinclair walked with a purpose to ensure he would not be stopped as a vagrant by a lazy cop having a slow night. His knees ached in response.

As he turned east, he calmed down. He was soon walking past the old Victorians being restored in central Sacramento. He passed under the pleasant glow from a Presbyterian church's stained-glass windows far above its graveyard. It was still functioning as a final resting place within the heart of the city, maintaining the remains of those who came with the '49ers and those who came later to settle the land with orchards and fat livestock. There were fewer new gravesites now as most of the parishioners opted for cremation or the fancier cemeteries on the outskirts of town with a view over the city lights. He walked on, stopping frequently to rub some fresh blood into his calves, trying to massage some of the pain out of his knees. He was in no rush to return to his car or the condo. Once at the Volvo, he sat for a half hour just looking at the concrete wall of the garage, contemplating escaping somewhere else from all of this, like Maui or Tahiti. After withdrawing a tube of ointment from the glove compartment, he raised his pants legs and rubbed the fragrant treatment over his agony.

Finally home, Richard tossed his keys next to the barely functioning remains of an old answering machine he'd excavated from the back of the closet. Even with its poor sound quality and marred surfaces it was still in one functional piece, unlike the last device he'd watched deconstruct in his hands. He was reluctant to push the flashing light on it, but when he tapped at it lightly, he saw only two messages, so how bad could it be? He turned his head away from the coffee table hoping it would reduce the impact from whatever he heard.

"First message," squawked the mechanical voice. "Richard. I'm so sorry I was so rude to you. Truly, I am. It is your place. I was the one who intruded. I wasn't thinking. What can I say? Please call me. Are we still friends?"

Mary Beth, he thought. *Must have been dumped by another new boyfriend. She looks at me like I look at my couch. Mental note: Don't call.*

"Second message."

"Sinclair I found some new references for you on that topic you asked about regarding the Mint. Pretty odd, really. Also, just as a passing note, I came across a bit of your family history I thought you'd find interesting. Apparently, you had a very distant relative, through your father's line, who signed the Flushing Remonstrance in sixteen fifty-seven. That's quite a claim to fame. I realize you may not know about it, but it was the first written agreement in the New World formed by citizens against government restrictions on the people's freedom of worship. The people of that time craved religious tolerance as their birthright. You apparently have a deep-seated bloodline of Quaker pacifism and civil rights running deep through your veins. I'm sure 'ol Alex won't find that delightful. I'll be in my office tomorrow. Come by and we'll exchange documents. You bring back the stuff I loaned out and you get these new files. Deal?"

Sinclair raked his fingers through his thinning hair, shook his head, and then made a beeline to the bed. No time for flossing or tongue-scraping tonight. No tweaking hair from the ears. No moisturizers. His tossed his walking clothes on top of the growing mound of dirty laundry in the corner. The fabric collision elevated a few dust bunnies but he didn't notice. The king-size foam-comfort bed was all he wanted. It was piled high with enough comforters to asphyxiate him. The bed was already a vast, sprawling mountain chain of pillows, covers, and sheets that had been through a melee of disturbing dreams, rude awakenings, and simply bad housekeeping. His eyes were sealed instantly as sleep seeped through him. Sinclair had just enough awareness left to push the switch on the black metal gooseneck reading lamp next to the bed. The carpet-thick curtains provided absolute darkness for his cocooning, but also provided a means of seclusion for someone else.

"Sorry to do this to you again, honey . . ." Lili's voice hit him like a hot iron.

"Holy fucking Christ almighty!" He screamed, kicking the lamp over as he fought against his own down comforter in his state of combined catatonia and terror.

She pulled him back down to the bed with incredible strength. A pinch hold on his neck near his carotid artery stopped his movement, but he was still aware. He couldn't throw off this grip like he had with Alex.

"I . . . we . . . those here in Lili's body will not harm you. It is time you know what you have within you and what has happened to you. You bear the wound from the curse of the Eighth Buddha. Now rest your body and listen to the story. We will show you pictures as we touch your forehead. There will be no pain, but you will learn. We see that you are open, there, in your third eye. You have the power of the vision of the gods."

He shuddered throughout his body as Lili's warm hands stroked his brow and then pressed hard between his eyes. There was no pain, just clouds and an eternal rush of vistas far from his reach.

Chapter 12

Lili's smooth, delicate fingers flitted across Sinclair's wrinkled forehead. He had all the appearances of a man deep at rest, asleep in pure comfort, but underneath that stillness was a soul struggling to find his way out. His whirlwind Templar training abroad prepared him to release his fears of being lost in the eternal gray ethers that separated the three-dimensional world from the astral world of the unseen. With patience, the seeker in this void could drift away until the visions and the clarity of "being" returned in focus.

His mind's intruder used her deft manipulation of delicate energies to drag him forward. He was tugged about by the pulsing surges emanating from her fingertips. It was quite different than the 'Walk Thee in Perfected Light' blessing Alex had provided. Sinclair was compelled to move on a specific path through the Matrix, which is what remote viewers called the great pool of time and space woven together on the other side. Lili was pulling his consciousness, guiding it like a ferry boat tugging a freighter into port.

As the clouds parted, Sinclair could sense the presence of a planet below him. He was in deep space, thousands of miles above its curving surface. The colors were familiar but the landmasses and oceans left no reasonable guideposts. It certainly wasn't the Earth as he knew it. Rolling below him was a sphere with just one gigantic continent surrounded by broken sections of several seas and one single great ocean. There were also no polar icecaps. The most surprising revelation was the presence of two small satellite moons, but not the moon Richard had looked at in this lifetime. The ancient vision was hundreds of millions of years past, perhaps as old as the Permian period. The vista below him was the fused super-continent of Pangea.

The guide pulled him harder, bringing his elevated view closer over the central plains below. There were no modern cities, power lines, ports, or any sense of human developments. Instead, there were clearly hundreds of well-defined pathways that reminded Richard of the NASA photos he'd see of the channels on Mars. The scope of the interlinking spider webs was vast. As Richard came within a few thousand feet above the surface, he could see the routes splitting up the landscape in defined sectors. The precision of the lines rivaled the Nasca Plain in Peru. Here, however, there were no clear entities defined in the sprawling web of connections.

The flora surrounding the pathways was very tropical, but not as developed as a tropical rainforest by height or variance in the ecotypes. There was no overhang from a giant forest canopy. Instead, there were palm-like shrubs ten and fifteen feet high over a ground cover of heavy vines blocking access off the mysterious trails.

Richard wondered at the great resources expended to keep such a trail system cleared down to the bedrock. His answer came quickly as he descended farther to view the works from ground level.

CURSE OF THE 8TH BUDDHA

He did not scream. He did not falter or try to run. Sinclair knew he could not actually be harmed by anything in these visions, but the sight of the giant centipede approaching him at full speed was dreadfully disturbing. The centipede's plate coloring blended with the soil and the surrounding plants so well that even this large specimen was completely camouflaged from above. It was not detectable until there was a direct confrontation at ground level.

Sinclair estimated the colossal specimens were at least nine to ten feet high, with a width of six or seven feet, extending over a body length of some fifty feet. The beast's compound eyes were black and shiny, with the wet sheen of fresh asphalt. The beasts moved forward at a rapid, steady pace while their front segment snapped back and forth, clipping away and consuming any stray foliage, while its appendages perforated and rototilled the soil.

Sinclair could see small amounts of light flickering fluorescent blue and yellow as the centipede's segmented plates occasionally touched when crossing over each other. A strong static charge surged from the plates to the shrubbery as the centipedes moved forward, shocking to death any new foliage it contacted. These amazing arthropods were simply efficient excavators and maintenance engineers.

Richard floated up again to view the constant caravans of the arthropods trekking the lines in all directions, as if building an eternal maze. There was no great central thought behind it all, no controlling direction, nor any restriction or guidance as far as he could tell. This was just an amazing natural adaptation that didn't need a divine intervention for its existence.

"Richard, relax a little more. We are now going to the origin of my people here on Earth. Prepare yourself. Just listen to my voice. Do you understand?"

He thought *Yes*, very clearly, but realized he was not really talking. The mind was one with all things. There was no reason for guttural, wasteful speech. Communication was instant and perfectly understood.

The reverberations of Lili's gentle tones flowed through him. Her guidance was a slow, wrapping coil pulling around his consciousness until it was protected from shock or dismay. He knew, deep within, that he was comforted and within the circle of protection that the Liliths were providing.

His body flew forward like a comet over the plains and flat swamplands of the vast continent. Extensive green and brown rivers flowed from the land into a few land-locked lakes, but those were hardly more than estuaries and savannahs. There were herds of small reptilian forms and surging swarms of insects. This was not the age of great dinosaurs or large mammals; it was much earlier than that.

As his cosmic sleigh ride raced north the land began to rise, slowly, until he saw some gentle hills. Here and there a quiet volcanic cinder cone was visible like a black pockmark amid the sparse, ancient palms and saw-toothed ferns. Directly ahead was a giant shaft of yellow and green light shooting straight to the heavens. There was no evident source, at first, until he traveled directly over the center of a huge, stone labyrinth, the entryway to a city carved directly out of the remains of a massive volcanic cone.

A dozen Lilith priests stood at the center of the labyrinth, calling upon some unfamiliar power. As Richard came closer the nature of the light was more profound, for it was not rising out of the ground to the sky, but from the sky downward. The light pulsed and swirled in and around the priesthood as they held their hands together and looked up in deep meditation.

Richard began to evaluate the rest of the community design. At least a third of the cone was excavated completely away, leaving the inner face totally exposed. The walls were carved and reformed throughout the core into a vast nest of interconnected living areas. Richard reflected that the shapes of the living spaces were similar to Native American cliff dwellings. The excavation technique gave the red-and-black walls a sense of splendor against the sharp color contrasts of the cone walls. Here and there were streaks of a blue fluorescence in the formations.

The walls were alive with entities walking in and around the scoria. They wore nothing more than modest white robes. The color was identical to the white clay of the pathways cut by the centipede herds. He estimated that at least a quarter million lives were present in the concentrated hive. He was drawn to the gathering circle within the center of the base of the cone. A crowd of thousands surrounded a stupendous stone face.

The facial monument was captivating. It stood sixty feet high with a base circumference of several city blocks. Its composition of gleaming alabaster was finished as smooth as glass. Although the features were slightly Asian, they were also quite alien. The head's shape was too wide, like the Olmec ruins of Central America.

"What is that incredible figure? I have never seen anything quite like it. It looks almost like . . ."

"A Buddha?" Lili whispered.

"Yes, and yet somehow very different. The face is so much wider and the cheekbones stronger. I can't be sure but I could swear I've seen a face like this before."

"You have, in your very ancient bloodline. But it wasn't here."

"Of course not," he replied, "we're in modern-day California. We'd have to go to the Orient to see Buddha works of this proportion."

"It is not the statue of Siddhartha Gotama, your Buddha, but of the founding Buddhas. The Eight Great Founders."

"I don't understand. There is only one Buddha."

"No, Richard. The Buddha is just a term of recognition of an enlightened one. Here, in this place of harmony, we were in perfect balance with the forces of enlightenment, peace, and joy. The energy of what you call ley lines were kept clear and uncluttered across the land so that the energy we balanced from the cosmic center of the universe could flow and bring life and growth to this planet. It was all set in place by the Founders. We, the Lilith, were the first sentient beings placed here by the Founders. We were to draw other higher forms of life here to help settle the planet from its primordial angry seas and toxic atmospheres. Our only reason to live was to bring harmony and evolution to the Earth. It was to be an oasis for weary interstellar colonists."

"To the Earth? I'm lost here. How could such a civilization rise out of this primordial environment?"

"The Founders came here with the mission of love and growth. They were the wisest and kindest from what you now call Mars. The Earth was ready to colonize after it had been through two terrible destructions from heavy bombardments of asteroids. Some losses also occurred on Mars, your sister planet, but not like the extinctions that occurred on Earth's surface. Before those two events your planet rotated evenly, without a twenty-three-degree wobbling axis.

"The earlier, pre-strike conditions had been very stable and fairly unchanged for hundreds of millions of years. The Martian civilization could not enhance that natural cycle of development. The primary reason was that the atmospheric gases were just not conducive to colonization. However, there are cycles in asteroid activity. After the Earth recovered a second time, the Founders felt it might be safe enough to help rebuild the ecology using our advance metaphysics and technology. They designed and implemented a selective terraforming process. You have just seen the results of those efforts. We were here for hundreds of millions of years, guiding the life of the Gaia, as you call her, along on a measured, balanced pace."

"So what changed? Why do we know nothing of your kind and your accomplishments?"

"Part of this drape of darkness is our own fault. Our lack of humility led to unrealistic assumptions about the motives of the new visitors who might come to this jewel of light and life. Many visitors did explore and exchange their cultural values over the eons. Most were friendly and most moved on to other worlds. There was nothing to conquer, destroy, or rule here. The environment also had such a healing, peaceful effect on those entering the atmosphere that the more vicious races simply didn't want to land as it reversed the militancy of their armed forces. One race, from what you call the Crab Nebulae, was particularly affected to the point that it caused an overthrow of their mighty galactic empire."

"And you were never threatened or disrupted?"

"Not in the beginning. As you can tell, as you look more intently, we were barely in this physical world. We were close to the 'shift' to the ethereal realms. We were almost beyond the need for corporeal form. This was most disturbing to the physical space travelers. The Earth was known by many as the 'spirit planet,' or the place of the soul. The concept of Eden or Heaven actually came from these ancient ideas. Here was a place of eternal peace, complete harmony and a paradise for all to share. It was watched over by beings that most visitors could walk through without interaction.

"What we didn't realize was that the Earth would be struck again. At the same time, two of Earth's greatest resources became incredibly valuable in this part of the Milky Way: inter-dimensional gateways caused by a unique magnetic field and the growing abundance of free water."

The drape of clouds grew over the scene. The Earth slowly reappeared through the haze as if a curtain was being pulling back for the second act. However, the stage was completely reset. There were no visible ley lines. The centipedes were gone. Gigantic beasts roamed the lands within vast, towering rainforests. Volcanoes were releasing gases on every horizon. The air was heavy with sulfur and ash. The humidity and temperature were cloying. The Eden had become a tropical hell.

"Where is the Lilith city?" he asked.

"Gone forever, I'm afraid. This scene finds us a hundred of million years later. Our powers had weakened after the third gigantic asteroid strike. The two moons were driven from the Earth's orbit and sent circling around Jupiter, while a small inner planet was captured by the Earth's gravitational field. Another larger planet between Mars and Jupiter was completely destroyed and became the new asteroid belt. The land had split apart into new plates and was drifting into the new continents. Only a few thousand of us survived and those that continued became marginalized.

"Mars was stripped of its glory as the battles of the new planets and asteroid showers ripped her grace and beauty completely away. Some strikes were so violent that entire sections of crust were thrust into space. Those remaining on Earth were forever abandoned and separated from all other conscious life in this solar system.

"The Eight Founders became a dull memory as we began to decline into madness and revert slowly into a more physical form of existence. Some of us were able to resist and we became completely ethereal. The voices of those living in that other land of silver light could still reach us, guide us, and give us support on the physical plane of existence. However, ever so slowly, those who had been the highest order of our evolution became quiet memories as we descended into a flesh-born, angry, lustful and war-driven race battling in a world of darkness. We grew as vicious and degenerated as the giant reptiles you now call dinosaurs. We ruled over them like you rule over cattle. Instead of the cosmic gifts of spiritual balance and growth, we developed technology and sciences to accomplish our desires. We grew tired of working for light and love.

"In the midst of all these changes, we made alliances with physical beings from other worlds. The alliances allowed us to protect the Earth's resources and protect the gateways used for trans-dimensional space travel. That became our new role: guardians. Our Founders, our Buddhas, had represented many aspects of the highest orders of existence, but the least of these was the responsibility of stewardship. The Eighth Buddha, the role of maintenance and protection, became our bondage."

"So, the giant heads you once worshipped were not real people? Just concepts?"

"Worship is not the word we would have used. The Founders did exist, but the concepts of the great path were the precepts of life. The statues were of people, but rather of the *ideas* of the ancients. The eighth concept was all we had left to caress and accept. It became our last trace of faith and hope."

"We would not do that," Sinclair replied.

"Oh," Lili paused as they watched the carnage of the dinosaurs feeding on each other in the haze of the jungles. "You have no accurate statue of your Jesus, your Moses, Abraham, your Zoroaster, your Mohammed, Siddhartha, or even Confucius. All of your icons and paintings are assumptions. In the end, you crave for their images and forget their teachings. That is an error many civilizations before yours, and after yours, will make. There is, of course, a price for that error."

"So this is your history: Your curse is to hold and protect. I do not see why any of this is relevant to the work of the Templars or the monster inside my body."

"It is more complex than that. Watch what happens in what is now your Africa."

Lili's hand swept away the scene again to reveal a city of glass and stone floating over the land beyond clouds and mist. It was an amazing scene of high civilization hovering a mile above the dry plains below. The castle of crystal circled slowly as the light twisted within its high-flying buttresses. The city drifted gently, leaving only a momentary imprint of shade and a play of rainbows over any one location beneath its silent path. The residents in the sky palace flitted in and out of the twinkling structure in small shuttles. The pilots dove down to the surface as other teams returned from their study of wildlife and sample gathering.

"Here, again, our people rose to a level of high technical sophistication that could have led them back to their rightful development. The work was hard and grueling on the surface.

"So," she continued slowly, as she pulled Richard deep into the inner structures of the sparkling cities aloft in the puffy cumulus clouds, "our leaders were lured by their own ego to begin manipulation of the genetics of the lesser creatures under their care. Yes, we still watched over the Earth's resources, making sure that other aliens did not ravage what had now become our permanent home. Yes, we still guarded the gateways to ensure that they were not opened for marauding armies. We forgot that to live is to serve. We wanted someone or something else to do the menial work. We came to believe that labor was below our station.

"We began gene manipulation of the native primates that were developing at their own rates. There were hundreds to choose from. The sizes ranged from almost forty feet tall to the most miniature beings just a foot high. Some believed that the division of labors would require just such a variety of minions. The giants could build massive edifices to act as capacitors to gather the Earth's energies to light and heat the sky city from below. These were the very energies that we once distributed in harmony over the surface. Smaller beings could prepare our food and clean our living spaces. The smallest could learn to crawl throughout our structures and provide repair services and ensure our controls over the resources and interstellar entryways were intact. It seemed so reasonable and righteous."

"Righteous? So you felt you had the right?"

"Of course. We were the Children of the Founders. We had every right. Who but we who had kept life evolving for so many hundreds of millions of years? We were recognized as the *Great Guardians* by all the alien species we dealt with—and those who didn't respect us..."

"Don't tell me, you loved them into submission."

"No." Lili yanked his consciousness to an area near the polar ice. A black, cracking rip appeared in the skies over the ice. A fleet of black and silver ships roared through the rift, filling the skies with an ominous hum as they spun over the ice and began to carve it into pieces. A mother ship was nosing through the dimensional passage when the black, crackling iris around it slammed like a mousetrap. The front end of the ship and its inhabitants were swallowed up in a huge explosion of red and blue flames. The other nearby ships tumbled and disintegrated in the shock wave. The doorway was simply gone as the ice rose up to swallow and crush the remains of the fleet and any of its survivors that fell to the surface.

"That was horrible," Richard complained as he could see the bipeds from the craft being devoured by the elemental forms of water within the ice flows.

"Yes, but necessary. We believed that as we commanded the elements that there was no weapon or power that could stand long against us."

"So how does this bring us to our time in the present?"

"Impatience is one of the characteristics that led to our second fall from grace. You could learn from that."

Sinclair could feel a pressure around him from Lili's energy. It was not pleasant. "I regret my poor manners. Proceed as you like." He stilled his thoughts and listened.

They moved away from the ice caps far into space above the Earth in a long, rolling curve. A bright snap of light occurred over the scene. For a second, Richard could see thousands and thousands of Earths, all spinning in their own orbits in separate solar systems, in separate time frames. It was exhilarating but confusing. Each planet was the Earth but a little different in the shape of the land and seas, the color of the sky and the number of moons. Some had none. Some had three or four.

"It's spectacular. What is it?"

"This is the *corridor*. Those who travel the dimensional trails can pick not only where, but what, and when. It is the multiverse. Few have seen this. The Lilith's guard this vision and knowledge. It allowed us to control who traveled through our space. Certain places in the universe are just created to become the elevators to the cosmos. Earth is one of them."

"This is . . . well, beyond belief."

"Perhaps this voyage will open your eyes. Let us go back to our Earth and the time before we forgot the way. That can happen when one becomes impatient."

They pulsed in spurts back through a tunnel of multi-colored hues spinning around them in an illuminated tube. They entered and settled on a forested zone near the delta of a great river.

"You just passed through what your sciences refer to as a worm hole."

"Amazing. We can do all of this and I am solid . . . but you are, well, outside of Lili's body. You aren't physical, are you?"

"No. You have not seen our true form. We have moved out of the physical world but evolved into a dark form that is not like our forbearers' silken existence. We are now subject to anger, violence, and even pettiness. That is how the Templars became involved."

"I cannot imagine how."

"Watch as the story unfolds," she commanded.

Richard watched the light-skinned Liliths herding mammalian workers in vast quarries. The giants struggled with the tonnage of raw rock. Occasionally there would be a series of smaller beings, little hairy men, coming up from holes in the ground with piles of ore they had harvested in the mines. A two-hundred-foot-long spacecraft landed near the site. It was sparkling, smooth silver with an ornate cladding atop the craft in the form of a cornucopia of wild beasts, giant snakes, and violent screaming faces of an alien race. The craft's surface was festooned with illuminated symbols that were unintelligible to Richard. A large entry ramp opened from the bottom of the ship from which a wondrous entourage emerged.

The occupants mesmerized Sinclair; they were living duplicates of the drawing on the Sumerian clay tablets and Babylonian friezes he'd looked at in the British Museum while he was training in London. All that was known for sure was that in ancient times these entities were known as the Annunaki, but their origins could not be defined by current archaeologists.

Richard focused on the bearded aliens wearing ornate head pieces with tubes and lines running into their necks and sides. Their procession was accompanied by the loud sounds of music from warbling horns. All the workers in the area lay prostrate, including the giants and the Liliths.

"I don't get it. Your people are acting like slaves."

He watched as the Annunaki of Sumerian mythology descended to inspect their offerings. The male leader held a metal rod forward over the cargo. Blue laser light passed from the tool over the tons of ore and raw stone, which then disappeared without a trace. The lead alien then spun around quickly, pointing the rod at the nearest giant humanoid. The Annunaki vaporized the dumbfounded giant as though it were nothing of importance. The Lilith rose and protested. This led to a general display of arms by the invaders. In a few seconds there was no life left in the mine quarry except the group of Annunaki. All other living things were vaporized. The marauders walked slowly back aboard, trumpets blazing. The doors closed and the ship hovered over the remaining trove of raw materials. A light penetrated from the bottom of the ship and the wealth disappeared. The vessel flew off into a black, willowy rift in the sky.

"So they killed your people?"

"For tens of thousands of years we became subservient to a race that was simply more technologically evolved, and who were absolutely ruthless in their resolve. They knew how the *corridor* worked. We had manipulated the entryways. They had mastered them. They also did not fear our control of the elements. This was child's play to them. Once again we had lost our sense of humility and our advantage.

"As we declined in numbers and powers the planet became more and more hostile. There were horrific wars between the new sky gods and other alien races that had lived here at peace with us. Our genetics experiments were out of our control as the visitors . . . and that is all we ever call them . . . advanced our efforts with the lesser life forms to do even more skilled work for them. These intergalactic pirates were desperate to obtain gold and uranium. They bred the various hominids like ants. Millions and millions died every year from terrible toils put upon them. They made these imprisoned workers, whether great in stature or small, build giant palaces of worship to the masters of the skies. But to them . . . to these monsters . . . none of this mattered next to their greed for ore and more ore. Worst of all was their gluttony for fresh water. Before they finally departed they had stolen almost twenty percent of the Earth's fresh water for their own needs.

"We did not know why they left. Eventually it may have had something to do with the increasing solar flares. In just a few days they completely abandoned all the outposts and monuments they'd built. We acted swiftly to gather up their technology with the resources we had left, burying any remnants of their existence deep in the Earth where these contraptions could never be discovered.

"We also pulled back to our last bastion to preserve our race: the original location of our first colony . . . the one you saw at the beginning. Now we were hidden beneath hills heavy with cedar trees above rolling valleys. We thought it would be safe forever. However, with time, as we became less of this world, the original pure vibrations of that holy spot drew the attention of genetics experiments the Annunaki had left to die. The manipulations of the visitors helped the mammals gain consciousness and they began to advance faster than was the natural order of things. They battled each other for space and food. They ate each other. They gave themselves privilege over others they could manipulate or destroy. The very worst characteristics of their founders became their primary way of life. Brutality was their only code of existence."

"As a hominid I find this all rather intimidating and difficult. It doesn't agree with any of my research or my beliefs, for that matter," Richard said, his sense of outrage clear in his tone.

"Richard, we cannot manipulate these records. You know that. We understand your discomfort. We tried to prepare you for your travels to places and times outside of your racial memory or your written histories. Few souls dare to come this far back. So let us move to the time that will answer more of your questions."

The scene turned to absolute blackness. There was nothing but the heavy scent of dry, stale air. There were no sounds. There was no sense of time or space. A light began to flicker in the distance. It bobbed and weaved about and became clearer and larger. It was a flame from a torch followed by other torches behind it. Richard could see the outlines of the small group of men bearing the lights. Their hair and beards were long and disheveled. He could smell their sodden clothing now and the sordid body odors accumulated through the struggle of months of digging. There was both urgency and fear in their faces as they crept forward through the darkness. The cavern they had located was huge and led off in many directions. The scoria was carved out not by water but by some other force that had designed the passages in patterns of interlocking spokes. This labyrinth style had a single purpose: access for the designer, and entrapment of fools who might break in. The design had failed against human cunning and commitment.

The band of men finally stopped at the bottom, at the hub of the tunnels. Each step forward was marked in intervals with chalk on the walls. Eventually they stood before a cache of objects the likes of which Richard was totally unfamiliar. There were long, shining shafts that continued to glow once the torch lights struck them. There were additional piles of the short rods the Visitors had used in their battles with the Liliths. Short, opalescent blocks were stacked in lines. Beneath the blocks were globes of liquid metal floating without visible support, holding up the blocks. A humming rose in the cavern as the men approached the globes. There was an increasing radiance of blue light that expanded to eventually light up much of the cavern. Richard could hear them cry out in shock as the light exposed a mountain of purified gold ore. Hundreds of tons were piled to the ceiling. In addition, the men looked over golden tablets with ancient writing, lighted chambers with seats that activated vistas of great histories of this world and others, and powerful communications tools that allowed visual and oral contact with distant civilizations. A green, rotating face of an Annunaki was projected as a holograph from one of the communications beacons. It spoke unintelligible commands. The men kneeled in reverence, but when nothing changed and the same noises continued, they grew braver and rose to walk through the holograph. Its magic was powerless to prevent their plunder.

The leader of the party picked up one of the foot-long rods. It immediately shed the same blue laser light Richard had seen earlier. The explorers knelt again as if in the presence of God.

A high-pitched shrieking echoed through the chambers. A host of Liliths, black and vicious in their gaseous form, rushed forward from every direction. Richard could hear the men yell out. He understood their ancient French dialects decrying demons.

"Now, Richard, you will see what caused this awful battle between us."

As the Liliths rushed to attack the interlopers, the French leader raised his rod out of some odd instinct of self-defense. In a blink the first three attacking Liliths were destroyed in mid-flight. The assault broke off immediately. The cries of the lost Lilith souls rose up around the knights who were now too frightened to run. Several of them took heart and gathered up other rods as their leader had done. There was a burst of blue light from the four newly activated tools. The light exposed some of the Liliths that had not retreated. The men held their new weapons forward and again dissolved the defenseless spirits.

For a while there was silence.

CURSE OF THE 8ᵀᴴ BUDDHA

Richard watched as a giant centipede quietly crawled down the walls behind the men and rushed forward into the smallest of the Frenchmen.

"My God!" Richard cried out. "Is that what got inside me? Is that what you did to me?"

"Quiet, Richard." Lili stroked his forehead until her anesthetic touch calmed him. "We kept those creatures captive from the earliest time on Earth. They are our contact to our ancient past. You might call them our familiars that allow us to go within your human form."

The knights pulled back away from their comrade as he rolled and struggled with his possession, his face was an array of strained expressions. Spittle flew from his mouth and his eyes rolled back, white and threatening. He then began to speak to the other men in their own tongue. Richard listened as the Lilith made a pact with these graverobbers through the body of their captive. If the knights agreed to not attack the Liliths, then there would be a peace.

The men agreed conditionally, full of their newfound power. In return, they demanded that the ancients explain everything in the cavern, and explain what the Liliths were, why they were there, and how this place came to be. The intruders were searching for the Holy Grail and the Arc of the Covenant.

The Liliths refused to provide explanations for all of the alien technology simply because they had no idea what these articles were or why they were important to these crass little monkey people. In negotiations, the Lilith demanded the life of one of the knights every fifty years or they would fight the humans until both sides were decimated. The Lilith would choose the knight of the purest heart to be their vessel and to serve their ranks as a consort, so the Lilith line could continue to reproduce. This seemed to the Templars like a small price to pay for so much wealth and power, so the agreement was struck.

"That fellow first possessed by our pet became the exchange to start the process. He was the father of my line of the Liliths."

The scene passed. Richard found himself moving quickly again, back toward his body and into his shell on the bed in his condo.

"So," Lili said, still stroking his forehead, "after several months of teaching and sharing, the men brought down their comrades-in-arms to move the great treasure out of Jerusalem to Rome, where it would remain hidden. Of course most of the gold did not go to Rome. The Templars formed a secret bond to withhold the truth of the enormity of what they had found. They would not expose the pact made with the Liliths. Instead, the Templars became the protectors of the fortune of gold, silver, gems, and ancient technology.

"Meanwhile, the Roman Catholic Church went about changing the entire history of our race, rewriting the ancient texts, and spewing hate and filth about us. We became the scourge of the night, the devourers of men and children in their sleep. The Lilith became the lowest form of life. Our real crime was falling into the darkness instead of rising upward. Now we had given greater powers to inferior creatures.

"The Templars cursed us for the price they had to pay. Eventually they declared they would not pay us or they would destroy us. What they forgot was that we agreed not to battle with them, but we did not say we would not influence others. It was easy to manipulate the mind of a petty French king and the corrupt Pope to strike against the Templar cabal. Our vengeance was nearly complete, except for those who were clever enough to escape with their lives and their treasures.

"So, they have hated us to this day and cursed us as they now must give up their own and their best as a sacrifice. They know we still influence others to hunt them. There is no forgiveness between us. There cannot be. No one will give quarter."

Richard rolled his head back and forth, loosening up his stiff neck. He had a throbbing headache, which was a typical after-effect from visits into the forbidden Akashic records. Such travels bore a severe trial on the body. He sat up, through Lili's grasp, and rushed into the bathroom to vomit. His solar plexus was particularly sensitive to the returning spirit held to the body by the sliver cord of his body's ethereal center. Lili did not interrupt but remained as a watchful guardian outside the room that now held her treasure.

Chapter 13

She helped him crawl back onto the bed. Only one woman had shared that space since the epidemic, but Mary Beth was just a brief fling. And here was Lili, the poster child for attraction-compulsion. Richard was too weak to put up much of a fuss. So much information was rolling through him. At least he no longer held the internal pains from Marie Halleran's forced abortion. He didn't even have strong residues from the *Pelican* and its rotting bilges. The mystical time voyage had cleared his new memories. *Perhaps,* he thought, *the monster left me at last when it saw its own heritage.*

"I must go now, Richard. It is not right for me to be here alone with you, although you are just the sweetest little 'ol thing." Lili's voice was smoother and softer than earlier, with that twang of Georgia. The overtones of gravel had dissipated. The Lilith was gone.

"Don't you ever get pissed, I mean, really? They use you like a frickin' hand puppet. I never know when you're going to pop in like a bad dream. Obviously they can move you through walls and through great distances at a whim. Why don't you fight this?"

"It is out of my hands, really. Being chosen does not mean you have choices. It means you have duties. You are in the same boat. You just don't know it yet."

"Well, if you say so." He shook his head, took a deep breath and then settled his gaze on her again. Richard reached out to her and pulled her closer. There was a slight resistance at first but it faded quickly. "Don't go. I won't harm you. Please."

"You know I can't. My role—"

"Is to make my life a living hell, yes, I got that picture already."

She turned away, letting her long wall of black hair hide her expression. "Richard, you cannot think that way about me after what you have seen. Please tell me you don't think I am like those who flow through me."

He let his grip loose and fell back on the pillows, exhausted and dehydrated. "You're right. I'm an adult and I need to start acting like one. But I'm also damn lonely right now. I don't think I have a friend left. The State is ready to fire me. The Master wants my balls on a rack. Alex treats me like his pet poodle . . . oh, yeah, he doesn't have a dog. I probably don't sound very polite."

"Not very." She kept her back turned to him as she let her legs hang off the edge of the bed. Her silk dress was a splash of cherry blossoms and tree branches over a cream colored background. He reached out and rubbed his hand over her spine, forgetting about the ring.

"I would like you to stay. Just to hold me and keep me warm. For all you've put me through, just a little spooning won't hurt. I promise, no funny stuff. No intimacy other than two people traveling through the night wrapped around each other for comfort and some dignity, in a time of trouble."

She slid around quickly, almost mechanically and faced him, holding his tired face in her hands. "I love you, Richard Sinclair. I will do anything you wish of me." With that she slithered out of her dress. Sinclair was speechless. He pulled the sheets away from his side and covered her.

"Do I not please you?"

"Jesus. This is too much. Oh, crap, the ring. I wasn't thinking." He tried unsuccessfully once again to remove it. She moved forward, throwing off the sheets and then prostrating her lithe form atop his chest and legs. He touched the back of her neck with the ring.

"I can please you any way you would like."

"Lili, listen carefully. It would please me very much if you would put your dress back on, call a cab, and then go home. Could you do that to make me very happy?"

"Yes, Richard. I will do whatever you want, my dearest honey bear."

He studied her in amazement as she moved her sleek, golden frame off of him and off the bed. She dressed quickly, directly in front of him as if he were not in the room. He was bewitched by her supple arms and legs spinning around as she wriggled swiftly back into her clothing. He wondered if he were being a little foolish. Her breasts were small and firm, pushing high into the air like orchids seeking jungle rain. With flawlessly shaved legs, and little pubic hair, she appeared glossy and disquietingly young. Richard had not been with a woman like her before. She was exotic and entrancing, but his stomach and head told him this was not the time. Besides, misusing this new power from the ring, or wherever it was coming from, bordered on the Black Arts—something he had sworn never to perform.

His commands were carried out in robotic simplicity. Phone call. Walk to door. No goodbye. No smile. No glance backward. All Richard knew for sure was that the front door made a hard click as she pulled the knob. He shook his head again as he lifted up the double-wrapped viper ring on his finger for a closer look. It was somehow reminiscent of some new experience. *The ship*, he remembered. *It's like the snake designs on the ship of the Visitors—the Annunaki.*

"Huh," he said, admiring it with the realization it might never come off. "Perhaps the Master would get his head on straight if he had to kiss my ring." He chuckled and rolled over into the mess of linens as he prayed for a long stretch of unconsciousness.

Thunderclaps rolled through the condo. Richard thought they were parts of a dream as he rolled over. His legs were still not responding from his slumber. He forced one eye open as his head squeezed out of the pillows. He listened again. Nothing. Then the thunder roared again, but not from the sky.

The voice of the god of storms followed closely. "Sinclair, open the door! Open the door, Sinclair! I know you're in there."

"Why didn't he just call or use the damn doorbell?" Sinclair complained to the empty room. He pulled the pillows over his head again after letting loose some muffled expletives.

The thunder continued. "I swear, you open this door or I'll kick this bastard in!"

Richard knew Bisol could do it. "Okay. I'm coming, goddamn it." As he crossed the room he realized how light it was. He took a quick peek at the stove's digital clock. It was two o'clock. He'd slept through almost a half day. It certainly was Alex on the other side of the door. Richard could smell the acrid cigarette stench rolling off his teacher's clothing and under the door jamb. It was not the best fragrance to encounter on rising.

"Christ, Alex, don't you ever fuckin' sleep?"

Richard turned his back after opening the door, a definite mistake. Alex stepped in quickly and wrenched Sinclair's shoulder as he swung him around to face him. Bisol's face was flushed with excitement and rage. "Listen, asshole, I've tried calling you for two days. Don't you ever answer your calls? Didn't it wake you up?"

"Hey," Sinclair snapped back, whipping Alex's hand off him as if Bisol were a child. "What are you talking about? What's today?"

"Friday the sixteenth, you idiot. You didn't feel the quake two days ago?"

"Shit, I've been out for over two days? I can't believe it. No, what quake? God, I've gotta take a leak." Bisol followed him to the outside of the door to the bathroom.

"It's the only news in the country. The south end of the Calaveras Fault let loose Wednesday morning about ten-thirty. An eight-point-three and damned shallow. Three of the big bridges are down in the Bay. Fires everywhere. Berkeley's a mess. Oakland's a hell hole. Thousands dead and wounded. It's a total cluster fuck. The Governor's down there now. Where the hell have you been?"

"Alex, honest, I've been right here. Passed out. I told you I was sick. God, the area must be a mess. They were just starting recovery from the Daly City quake. It's got to be hell down there."

"Forget all that. Don't worry. You don't work for the State anymore. They aren't looking for you now. I need you to help me . . ." Alex sounded terrified.

"Pull yourself together, Alex. I'm sure everything that can be done is being done, and there isn't much we can do from here." Richard washed his hands. He exited to face a pale Alex Bisol.

"You don't understand. It's Marie. She was at the clinic late last night and she got caught in some falling debris. Mother of God, she's gonna die and she never forgave me. I never told her, never really told her how much I was really sorry. You can help me. I won't ever ask anything again. You can touch her and get in there before she's gone, even in a comma. I've seen what you can do. I know you can do this. Please."

In the last two months of hardship and training he had never seen Bisol show a shed of weakness. He simply didn't buckle or give quarter. He didn't ask for boons. Alex kicked ass and didn't wait for formalities. Of course, what Alex was asking was impossible. Richard was still mentally and spiritually fried after the adventures with the Liliths and the unexpected rebuke from Eli. There was nothing he could do for anyone until he recuperated. Alex was looking for miracles. Richard had none, but he also had great respect and a deep caring for Marie, after holding her memories so near.

"Sure," he said, pulling Alex's clutches off his right arm. "I'll go, but I'm doing this for her, not you. This might not even work, but I feel I owe her a chance to connect one last time. Let me get dressed and we'll go. How are we going to get into the Bay with that many bridges down, and with the area secured for entry and exit for air support?"

"You let me worry about that," Alex replied as he began looking for an ashtray.

Richard was trapped again in the Buick smoke chamber as they rushed down Interstate Five and then across Fruitridge Boulevard to the Sacramento Executive Airport. Richard was unfamiliar with the Templar flight capabilities. Everything he'd traveled on in the past had been commercial out of Sacramento. Alex drove with reckless abandon as they rolled into the driveways between the hangars. He headed the car straight toward a line of parked private planes including one Lear Jet. To the side was a small helicopter waiting for them with its blades already in full rotation.

They ducked down as they ran to the cockpit. The pilot was missing. Alex directed Richard to get in the passenger side as he pulled himself up into the pilot's seat.

"Can you fly this?" Richard was surprised again at Alex's secret skills.

"Look, it's a 206B3 Jet Ranger III. It practically flies itself. Hell, I could fly this in my sleep. Let's get going."

They both buckled in. After donning their head sets and sunglasses, Alex pointed to the map in the front pocket. It was tucking in tight with a vial of Dramamine and a fresh bottle of water. Richard noticed the vial was already half empty.

"Better charge up, kid. I know you don't like heights but there's just no other way. Don't piss me off and puke all over my baby."

Unlike the Buick, the chopper was immaculate. Not even a speck of dust on the dials or windshield. This was another side of Alex that he'd missed.

Alex chattered with ground control as he lifted off. Richard was not accustomed to the constant vibration running up through his butt, or the noise level. It was not as quiet as he'd thought it should be on a chopper. His conversation with Alex would have been tough without the head phones. He kept adjusting them as the head piece squeezed his temples, pounding from his voyage through time. The activities were a bit distracting but would never have been enough to keep the terror of flight like this from tearing Richard's guts out. This time there was no concern. It was almost enjoyable.

Alex, however, was sweating profusely and seemed a bit shaky. He kept sipping from his water bottle.

They drifted featherlike over the interstate highways heading toward San Francisco. The effects of the earthquake waves were visible everywhere across the land. Cars and big rigs were tossed around the ditches and off the bridges. The beginning of the damage to homes was evident as they flew over Vacaville. There were trees and power poles down everywhere. Richard could see the flames and smoke rising from the refineries in Martinez as they passed over Vallejo. He feared the worst. He directed Alex to go up and avoid the plumes drifting toward their craft. As they went farther south they could see the destruction at the Carquinez Straits Bridge. The middle section was torn away. A dozen ships had torn loose from the mothball fleet anchored nearby. The steel flotsam had played havoc with the bridge supports as the aging victory ships were tossed freely in the current.

"Must have been a seiche," Sinclair said to Alex as he maneuvered around the dense black smoke.

"What's that?"

"It's when you trap the energy of the quake in water trapped in a Bay or Lake. It rocks back and forth in the closed space, like rocking a full bathtub. We do planning for this called slosh modeling. See those hillsides below with nothing on them? That used to be expensive real estate in Benicia. Some of the most expensive. The seiche waves stripped them clean. Oh geez, look over there."

They could see a huge oil tanker pushed into a small town's streets. Everything was covered in six-foot-deep crude as the hull spewed its contents over the land.

"My God! My family and I lived there in Crockett. It was such a cute little town back in the 'eighties. Our salad days while I was finishing up at Berkeley. All of our artsy-fartsy friends and their little galleries and boutiques. It's all just swept away. Ruined."

They flew farther south over San Pablo Bay. Hundreds of roofs of homes floated in the mixed debris. Dozens of small boats and some Coast Guard rescue craft wended through the tangled remains on search-and-rescue missions. Richard had little hope in his heart for anyone thrown into those Bay waters.

Sinclair did a quick analysis of what he'd seen. This was more than the Calaveras Fault could create. Someone was not telling the full story. The Hayward Fault must have gone off again.

Alex followed Interstate Eighty over Hercules and almost to Richmond. Everything below them was devastated, with endless puffs of smoke and towers of rising flame. It was a battlefield. The natural gas pipeline along the interstate was burning in several places without any firefighting attention. Even flying at several hundred feet above the ground they could still make out the shapes of the bodies in and around the menagerie of car crashes and burning wreckage.

A plinking sound struck behind them. Alex turned an immediate sharp right to dive the copter hard toward the ground. Sinclair felt his stomach coming up to his throat as he cried out.

"That was a close one. I should have expected it." Alex's voice was trembling but still direct. He was clearly agitated. "Oh, yeah. Gunfire. You never forget that sound after combat. I heard that the area anywhere near Oakland was a real shooting gallery all night. We're cutting across the Bay now."

They climbed and headed straight west. The helicopter traffic over San Francisco looked like a swarm of bees coming into and out of beekeeper's smoke. Above the main traffic were swarms of mosquitoes: the blood-thirsty news helicopters getting the best shots for national and international coverage. The seiche damage was striking along the piers. The waves had cut a furrow deep into the Financial District. The Transamerica Building had significant damage but was still standing. A giant U.S. flag cascaded from one of the upper floors stripped of windows.

Some other landmarks hadn't done as well. Coit Tower was down. Trolley cars were askew on many hillsides. To the south they could see major damage to the Richmond-San Rafael Bridge. Several sections were simply missing. The water below them in the San Francisco Bay was filled with boats and ships. Many were capsized and on fire. Many smaller craft were still attempting rescues. The Bay Bridge seemed amazingly unscathed, though some of the side rails were missing.

As they rushed toward San Quentin, before veering south to the hospital, it was obvious that the worst shockwave had hit the south end of the Golden Gate. The bridge's support cables were strewn out like errant hair in a sea breeze. A southern support column, damaged years before by a barge strike, had collapsed onto the tidal flats, not far from where Richard had first battled the Lilith at Crissy Field.

His heart pounded hard; tears came easy. It was clear this wasn't from an 8.3. *Many* faults must have slipped— something the Governor had sworn could never happen after the Daly City Shaker.

A bump, another bump, and the helicopter was solid and steady on the top of Mercy Center Hospital. Alex went through an abbreviated shut down. He pulled at Richard's shirt, holding him from trying to exit until the rotors slowed. Eventually, he popped open the canopy to indicate it was now clear to exit. From their rooftop perspective they could look across and evaluate all the damage and turmoil below. The Marina had sunk into a pit of rubble. Much of it was under the Bay waters that had rushed in. The remaining visible debris was on fire. Thousands of sirens and car alarms filled the steel canyons. The drifting smoke and cacophony made the scene a Bruegel's nightmarish impression of hell.

After a quick entrance through the roof door, they found a working service elevator and headed to the fourth floor. A sharp jolt rocked the elevator. It stopped abruptly. The lights went off. Emergency lights flickered on.

"Aftershock."

"No shit, Sherlock."

Then it was still. The elevator regained power and ran directly to the first floor where it then locked open, no longer responsive to button-pushing passengers. They exited quickly only to find the stairwells packed with fleeing visitors, some medical staff, and even a few terror-filled patients. It was awkward and difficult forging a path upward through the morass of screaming evacuees who had returned to the building for treatment after the major shock two days before.

Alex made his move at the fourth-floor exit doors. He had to punch an orderly to make a path through the doorway and onto the stairs. This didn't seem to be a problem for Bisol. He had but one goal and that was all that mattered. Sinclair followed him: a fullback behind his lineman blocker. In a few minutes they were finally at Marie's room, but exhausted from the struggle.

"How is she?" Alex asked, rushing to her bedside.

Richard was surprised to see Edmund Turner sitting at Marie's side. His head was heavily bandaged and his left arm was in a brown-and-white sling. Turner's clothes were not just rumpled and ragged, his shirt and pants were splattered with bloodstains. His glasses were taped in the middle to hold them together. The left lens was cracked and splintered.

"Alex. Richard. How did you—?"

"Never mind that," Alex interrupted, sitting on the other side of the bed while he looked over the monitors. The respirator pumps forced air in and out of Marie's lungs through the ventilator tube stuffed through her mouth.

"Did she revive at all? Say anything?" Bisol practically begged for a positive sign of any kind.

Sinclair could see the disfiguration on the left side of Marie's face. The head wound was covered, but blood was seeping slowly through the bandages. There was no sign of her left arm, just an empty sleeve covering a wad of gauze and wraps near the end of her shoulder.

"Holy shit, this is really bad, Alex, I had no idea. Marie was a good person. She didn't deserve this."

"What do you mean, was?" Alex cried out. "You ass! You blithering ass." He shook Richard hard.

"Alex he was only trying to support you," Turner said, wiping the new tears from his eyes with his free hand. He stood away from the bedside and moved to support Sinclair by the shoulders.

"She was fond of you, too, in her way. You would have liked her if you had gotten to know her better. Of course, part of you knows her better than any of us. Thank you for coming. It was a brave thing to do."

"Richard, get over here, now." Alex was in desperation mode. "I want you to hold her hand and mine. You can hook us together."

"I don't think it works like that, Alex." Richard did not move forward. This request was just too strange. There was no way to be sure that any of the powers still remained after the last contact with the Liliths. Maybe the energy would backfire and harm Marie. It just wasn't worth the risk.

"I ask by the Blood of the Lamb." Alex lowered his head and kneeled before Marie. Richard sighed deeply as he was now compelled to perform any act a Templar member requested when the blood of Jesus was invoked. Those words could only be asked once between two brothers of the Order. It was usually in the act of saving a life.

Alex stuck his right hand forward. Richard did not grasp it. Instead, he walked past Alex and put his hands around Marie's face and held her gently, just as Lili had held his face so gingerly two days past. Richard touched his forehead to Marie's and whispered the new blessing, "Walk Thee in Perfected Light."

Alex stood, upset, reaching for Sinclair's shoulder. He was instantly thrown by an unseen force against the green tiles of the room's wall. The power of the Annunaki was raging through Richard's body. The energy roared through every cell in his body.

Again and again Richard repeated the mantra of the blessing. His face paled and sweat ran down his neck. His breathing expanded and contracted with the pace of the ventilator. After a minute of this he pulled his head and hands away. He reached over Marie's mouth and deftly removed the corrugated hose that had traversed into her face and down into her lungs. She no longer required the assistance. Her color returned. The depression on the left side of her face expanded outward.

"Richard, what are you doing?" Turner was pushed backed away from his niece's bedside as a blue light began

CURSE OF THE 8TH BUDDHA

to emanate from within her skin. At that moment Sinclair put his left hand and then his right hand directly over her sternum. He felt the warmth and tenderness of her breasts as they heaved with the new strength entering her body.

"I pray for all that was, and all that is, to be balanced and whole as it will be, so help me God!" Richard screamed the prayer at the top of his voice. A wind began to spin from the center of the room. It created a tornado of papers ripped from the diagnosis clipboard at the foot of the bed. Dixie cups flew into the maelstrom from the unused feeding table.

Marie gave out a groan, followed by several high-pitched cries of agony. Neither Turner nor Bisol could get through the blue force field that surrounded Marie and Richard on the hospital bed.

"I don't believe it." Turner pointed at Marie's arm. The bandages fell away revealing a bloody, torn stump. In seconds it twisted and turned in a rose-gold whirlpool of light. Tissue and bone emerged in a twirling mass out away from her body as the blue glow filled in an invisible mold that once held the shape of her arm. Soon there was an elbow, then forearm, and then a perfect, delicate left hand to match her right. A pulsing orange globe remained on the end of her new fingers as the recreated limb returned to a normal color and began to move under Marie's direction.

Her eyes were now open. They projected blue flares of light shooting upward like Roman candles.

Sinclair slipped down the bed toward her abdomen. His hands moved swiftly from her chest to just above her uterus. Marie buckled and appeared ready to levitate. This time a forest green canopy of radiance formed within the blue bubble. It pulsed separately and produced a low hum. Sinclair was also making some kind of noise or musical tone to harmonize with the light. Marie lay still again as he pulled back his hands and crossed them over his chest in the Egyptian Pharaoh's crook and flail position. He muttered a few undecipherable words. Then there was absolute silence and no wind, no humming, and no blue field. The room was a sacrosanct fortress of peace and healing. No voice could be raised. No emotion stirred. It was an empty beach after a storm. Richard sank to the floor on his knees, bent forward and spent.

"Alex," Marie spoke, finally, breaking the stillness. "I forgive you for everything. I am here again. I'm alive. And Richard, you dear friend, look what you've done. All things are possible again. He is the *Lantern* to lead the way." She reached out for Alex. He rushed to her, sobbing into her chest and shaking like a leaf. She pulled his head up and stared deep into his eyes, allowing his tears to fall on her face. "There's a surprise. God's grace is on us both." She pulled his left hand down to her abdomen. Alex leaped backward, away from the twisted sheets and through the hospital drapes.

"Impossible! Impossible!" Alex shook so violently he wet himself.

"Richard, come with me. They need to work through this. Let's step outside." Turner pushed at Sinclair's arm. There was no resistance. Sinclair was as dumbfounded as everyone else in the room. They were quickly outside the room and the librarian closed the door.

"Was she . . .? Did I . . .?"

"Well, it wasn't Santa Clause. I don't know what you've become, but I thank you from the bottom of my heart. I mean, if there is anything, ever—"

"I couldn't have. She was dying. I just—that's not possible. It wasn't me."

CURSE OF THE 8ᵀᴴ BUDDHA 211

"I don't care if it was Winnie the Pooh. Whatever you did in there has not been done since Jesus walked the Earth. No Master of the Order has ever achieved such greatness. Oh, we talk about those Masters that have ascended in a flash of light, but those are probably just stories to keep the new members in line. You, Richard, are the real thing: A real saint with godly powers of healing, like none other in the Templar society. You are the Lantern we have waited for these past seven hundred years."

"The Lantern," Richard sneered, looking away. "I've heard that from Eli. I didn't find it comforting. I don't know what happened in there, but I accept it. Marie and Alex will have to deal with the consequences. It's beyond me. I just want to get out of here. I need to just get away for a while."

"You've picked a bad time for that. The city's a mess. I don't know how you two got here, but don't expect to make it back tonight. It's a nightmare no matter where you go on the streets. The dog packs are out now, too, and they've attacked a lot of people. Should have expected it."

"How far are we from the Command Center? Do you know where it's set up? I suspect the original is down in rubble. I might be able to make that."

"There's not a lot working in Frisco right now. The Main Library is being used for the Emergency Operations Center until they can recover the Moscone Center."

"That's a pretty long walk from here. I'll have to take care with all that rubble. It wouldn't hurt to have a police escort. We almost got shot out of the sky near Richmond."

"Oh, Alex flew you. Well, I'm not surprised," Turner led Richard to the stairwell. There was still a great deal of commotion as the upper floors continued the evacuation. "We'll get Marie out of here soon. We may be able to go up and fly her over to Daly City. That's still got a hospital up and running. It didn't get hit nearly as hard. Isn't that weird? They took the hit last time. San Francisco ate this one."

"I've still got my State Emergency Service Worker ID. I can probably pull up a cop somewhere on the street to get me over to Main. I'll bet they've got every beat cop and his brother out for this, just like the Daly City quake last year."

"More than that. They've called up off-duty, recent retirees, and hell, they've pulled them out of nursing homes. Anyone ever sworn is out there trying to keep order. I kept up through the radio reports. It's pretty grim. You won't find much law and order at street level."

"You and Alex watch your ass. Don't let anything happen to Marie and the baby. I still just can't believe it." Sinclair paused as he waited for a space in the herd that would allow him to open the stairway entry door.

"Wait. Before you go, I've got to tell you about some of the other stuff you asked for, about that Mint bullion."

"I think it can wait, Turner. Really. It can't be that important in the middle of all this."

"Now listen," Turner said in a controlled whisper as he pull Sinclair back to a corner. "There was a lot more to this than I thought. After the Treasury boys got done with me I thought the probes would be over. Hardly. I had some really tough guys from the Chinatown gangs catch up with me in the library basement. It wasn't pleasant. Of course I dummied up and saved my ass. But that got me really going. So I did some really serious digging in places even the rats don't enter. You gotta be careful, Sinclair. There is a secret society out there we have never penetrated called the Green and Red Dragon's Breath. Most just call them The Breath. It's an unusual collaboration of the Yakuza and the Tong. There is a war going on here that is ancient. It is way over and beyond the

CURSE OF THE 8TH BUDDHA 213

influences of the Order. I believe that if they could have proved I was a Templar they would have killed me, right there in the Greek classics section. Just horrible! Just think, blood all over those one-of-a-kind collections.

"Anyway, this secret society was the one responsible for overthrowing the last emperor of China and putting Sun Yat Sen in place. They hate the communists. They need more funds to support their ends and overthrow the PRC leadership. They have absolutely no fear and are totally focused on this task of freeing the Chinese mainland from both communist and Western cultural influence. They really moved up their game after the Olympics ended. I swear, Richard, if you know anything about them and this missing Mint treasure, you'd best leave it behind you. We need you now, alive. Now go."

Turner and Sinclair pushed the door open just in time to make a space in the downward flow of frightened bodies. Richard held tight to the wall. Once into the crowded lobby he navigated around fallen wheelchairs, broken glass, and an array of medical equipment left behind from the mad rush outside. He hesitated by the metal frame of the exit just long enough to get his bearings and to make sure nothing else was falling from the upper floors. He could see several victims on the front entry skewered into the concrete by large chunks of falling glass that had crashed onto and through them. As the lines progressed out it appeared clear so he covered his head and rushed into the melee.

He stayed in the center of the street whenever possible to avoid fallen glass, light poles, and power lines. The roads were not passable anymore as the cars and trucks were strewn about like dominoes. An ambulance was tipped over in some short shrubbery. He did a quick look in the back to make sure no one was trapped. It was an empty shambles. A broken gurney was lying off to one side.

Richard knew the advance life system rigs well from his emergency training. He pulled back some of the debris and sought out the Class II drug locker. It was still intact. He pulled out a tire jack from under the wheel cover to jimmy open the lock. He filled his pockets with the syringe packs and vials. These might be critical as the days rolled by without enough medical support. The Command Center might need them just to continue operations. Sinclair crawled out from the back of the ambulance but was impeded by the pressure of something metal at the back of his head.

"Don't move, motherfucker, or I'll blow your goddamn brains all over the place!" Richard froze and instinctively fell to his knees and crossed his hands behind the back of his head.

"Officer, I am an emergency responder. I'm headed to the Emergency Operations Center at the Main Library. My wallet is in my back right pants pocket. In it is my State Emergency ID. This is my job. I've just pulled out the controlled meds from this ambulance before someone on the street gets them. There's no one to call on in the hospital. They're all over the place running down the street."

"You move an inch and I'll splatter you." The deep, booming voice loomed over him. Sinclair could feel a huge hand reach in his pants and rip his wallet out. It was deathly still, even in the hysteria around them. He wondered why the energy wasn't protecting him now.

"I'll be go to hell. Get up and turn around, you sorry sack of shit."

Richard complied as the pistol barrel was withdrawn from his skull. He turned, looking up into a dark, menacing face. The officer was covered with dust and sweat. His outfit didn't fit that well, and the shirt tails were pulled out, but the name plate was still visible over his pocket. It read, simply, "Johnson."

"As God is my witness, you've got a lot of explaining to do. I'll get your sorry ass down there because they want you hung by your nuts from what I hear. The Governor really wants a piece of you, big time. And I'll be glad to let him have it. But before the State gets you, you're going to tell me I'm not crazy and I mean *right now*." He pulled Sinclair upright and pulled him by the collar, close to his face.

"C'mon. Let's hear it. I'll stay here all night even if I need to protect your dumb white shit until I can get you to clear me. You ruined my whole goddamned life."

Sinclair wasn't sure if he really wanted to reach the Command Center now. Unfortunately the ring had worked. He had his police escort.

Chapter 14

"So, let's get down to it. You're all over me and I don't even know you? I mean, what's with all that?"

"More than that, buddy. I'd like to piss on you and whoever protects your white ass."

"Ooh, a little personal there, don't you think? You don't know jack shit about me. And really, I could care less. It's too bad you got caught up in the crap down in that hole, but Johnson, whatever you saw after that, and how it affected you—well, that's none of my goddamn business."

"You believe in God? I mean, do you know what Jesus taught us about forgiveness and turning our cheek to our enemies?"

"Look, I'm not your enemy, but I don't have time for this. I've got to get to the Command Center now, bow my head, and kiss some serious ass to get my stupid, meaningless little job back. What do you expect me to do for you? I can't do a damn thing to fix your problems. I can't even fix my own."

"I'm a deacon," Johnson continued, looking down at his feet while he pushed little piles of rubble about. "That means I have responsibilities. I was a great father and damn near retired. What came out of that ground and into you wasn't right. Maybe a demon, I don't know. I have to tell the truth. I had to say what I saw and what I did. Do you understand that? That's called testifying for the Lord. You didn't come back to clean up your mess, whatever you got into down there. That night beat the hell out of my career. You have any idea what happens to a short-timer on the force once they put a psych evaluation in his record? Hell, I could hear them whispering 'fifty-one-fifty' behind my back at the station."

"Huh? You *are* old school. Nobody uses the fifty-one-fifty code for psych cases anymore. Shit, I'm really sorry. I had no idea, but I've been going through a whole life of bullshit the last month. Hell, even the Guv wants to gut me."

"Know that feeling."

"Look, what you saw was real. You did the right thing. What could I do, anyway, to change any of what happened? Nobody would believe either one of us."

Johnson leaned back hard against the ambulance and stretched his head farther back as he took a deep breath before he let it out in one deep puff. "My wife kicked me out. My kids won't talk to me. Even the congregation closed the doors because I had been touched by the devil. But I have to be honest to my God. Do you understand that? Jesus never lied to the Pharisees. He didn't deny his truth to the Romans. How can I lie about what I saw and what I know? No, I needed someone else by my side who could witness to my truth. I had to stand alone like this. I just can't anymore."

Sinclair bit at his lip, thinking about all the innocents who'd been wounded on this trail of Drake's treasure hunt. It wasn't his doing but they were on the same roadway, just innocent pedestrians left after a hit-and-run.

"All of this reminds me of what the good Dr. King once said. 'I believe that unarmed truth and unconditional love will have the final word in reality. That is why right, temporarily defeated, is stronger than evil triumphant.'" Johnson clasped his knees and leaned forward.

Sinclair could see tears rolling down his cheeks. "There might be another way, if you're willing. I don't have any credibility with any authorities right now. And as far as someone standing in my corner, well, I've got zilch in that score right now. You up for another answer?"

Johnson didn't say anything at first. As Sinclair waited they both jumped a bit as a large piece of plate glass fell to the ground from an office building just a block away. The echo of the shards bouncing on abandoned rooftops of cars and trucks, and then the pavement, was a wild translation of a wind chime, yet edgy and profound.

"Guess that's an omen. Seven years of bad luck for that building. Doesn't mean I have to eat it forever."

"No, and you can still be true to yourself and your God."

"How's that?"

"I'll tell you once we get to the Command Center. It's getting dark. We can finish this inside once we arrive where it's safe and protected." Sinclair used his right hand to point the way north to the Library.

It wasn't easy for Sinclair to hike up and down the hills of San Francisco, especially while inhaling the heavy, billowing smoke filled with choking dust. His knees were once again wracked with shooting pains. The clanking of the vials in Sinclair's pockets was in syncopation with the percussion section from Johnson's pistol clicking against the metal on the Motorola radio attached to his belt.

"Give it a rest, buddy." Johnson motioned for Richard to take a seat on the hood of an abandoned Prius. He checked it first for glass and other debris. The break was welcome.

CURSE OF THE 8ᵀᴴ BUDDHA

They'd traveled without a word between them all the way to edge of the Mission District.

"Need to find some water soon. Maybe get into one of these corner stores if some Pakistani rag head doesn't shoot me first." Johnson rubbed the globs of sweat rolling across his forehead. Fine, white airborne dust and ash muddied his face. He was taking on the appearance of a jungle fighter.

"I don't think they'd shoot a cop. Not even in this city."

"Yeah, well, I've seen 'em shoot a kid for stealing a pack of gum. Don't ever let down your guard in a convenience store." They caught their breath while listening to the continued din of emergency vehicles, alarms, and now the cries of dogs, the wild ones and runaways already forming new hunting packs to find prey. Some wild, feline screams identified a cat becoming pack food.

"In an hour or two I'll be shooting muffy out here. Even the Pekinese are vicious after they've missed a few days of chow. C'mon, let's saddle up."

"Wished I'd brought my Go Kit. Could have really used it."

"What the hell is that?"

"That fits," Sinclair said with heavy disappointment. "Years of trying to get the public to prepare a quick pack of critical food, water, flashlights—you know, the good stuff—and even the cops don't know about it. You're supposed to have one at home or in your car, and another one at the office. Maybe one in a hundred even have one. Not one of the better projects I worked on."

"Should have called it 'I done left the fucker' kit. Yeah, that would have got the attention of the press."

Sinclair laughed for the first time in days. He needed the release. He and Johnson pilfered a few bottles of water from an abandoned market and then continued north.

After they reached Larkin Street, within site of the Library's elevated columns, Sinclair turned and pointed for Johnson to take a break this time. A nearby bus line bench was empty. There was no one waiting. It was a perfect place for a miracle in the middle of the metropolitan chaos.

They checked the bench for debris.

"You learned from the last quake, huh?" Sinclair finally sat against the hard, cold steel. The green plastic sealant was worn in the center from the bottoms of the poor urban dwellers forced to use mass transit as their only way home.

"More than that," Johnson said, wiping the seat with his handkerchief. "You have to check anything you sit on in this part of town for needles and condoms. This City has really turned into a shit pile."

"Let me pose a way out of this mess you're in, since we're on a little break. If you had absolutely no memory of the event or of anything that happened that night, then you wouldn't be able to worry about telling your truth. In fact, if you had a completely different memory of that night then you could tell your new truth and you wouldn't be lying."

"I don't think that would be possible, unless you plan to rip my brain out and put in a mindless piece of meat in there, like my ex-partner Pfeister. That dog shit left me hanging like yesterday's laundry. I'd like to pole-axe that boy."

"Give me a little trust here. It's not good for a deacon to go around with that kind of hate. You've got some good works to do. Let me clear the path for you. What d'ya say?"

"Deal." Arnie stuck out his huge hands and shook Richard's. Richard didn't overreact but hoped for a transfiguring experience for Johnson, even though he risked having one of Johnson's nightmares for a lifetime. Nothing happened. There was no exchange. He had none of Johnson's memories from that night. Johnson did not react, either. There had been no exchange.

"Okay," Johnson said, breathing in again and letting his shoulders relax. "So how can we get this done? You got a shrink in mind?"

Actually, Sinclair had nothing in mind. At the moment he was fairly convinced he had just walked into a quicksand trap of his own making. The transfer powers of the centipede within were his ticket to free Johnson. Of course, he might have left something just as volatile behind, but at least Johnson's centipede memory would vaporize. Now he had no solution.

"Can you trust me for just a minute? Before we think about some of the more complex solutions, I want to just bring down your anxiety a bit. You're pretty tuckered out, even sitting here. I'm thinking you weren't expecting to be in the middle of this calamity."

"Hell, no," Johnson shot back, turning to look at Sinclair directly. "I was on damn medical leave, looking at losing my retirement pension. This hits and the Mayor's calling up the blind, crippled, and crazy to come out and help. I'm too old and tired for this. I had to arrest a looter last night and the kid almost took me. If you've got a valium, I'll take it."

"No drugs right now. Just sit still for a second. Let me use some pressure points on your brow to release some of the tension." Sinclair reached over to Johnson's dust-encrusted forehead without hesitation. "Walk thee in perfected light."

At first there was no reaction as Sinclair started the blessing, but by the last word Johnson's eyes were rolling back in his head, revealing nothing but the whites. Sinclair was frozen, unable to decide what to do next. His concern was he had put the officer in shock or maybe a seizure. Johnson's huge frame trembled as his lips opened and rivulets of spittle ran from the sides. Sinclair could feel the heat growing from the snake ring. A high-pitched whine rose from nowhere as a micro-flash of blue, neon light enveloped them both.

"What have I done?" Sinclair stood and looked down at the man as if viewing his murder victim. Johnson was still, his eyes and mouth closed, with no apparent breathing. Then a smile formed on the officer's face as his eyes fluttered and his shoulders rolled forward. He stretched his arms upward and pulled his legs up as if starting the day out from his bed at home, arching like a cat.

"Officer Johnson?"

"Yeah," he replied, smacking his lips and clearing his palette.

"I think there's some commotion down the street. A big piece of glass fell. Could you check it out?"

"Okay. I just thought I'd take a rest here for a second. It's been hell these last couple of days, huh? You with the City?"

"No, State. I was just coming out of the EOC for some air. Saw you over here and thought I'd let you know what I heard."

"Good enough. You better get back in. Those damn dogs are a real menace after dark. I wonder why Pfeister isn't down here. He's got younger legs. Oh, man, why don't they tell you when you're a kid how getting old sucks?"

"I'm with you." Sinclair raised his pants leg and revealed the surgical scars on his knees. Johnson reciprocated, showing his scars from parachute jumps for the Army. They laughed and parted ways. Richard sighed

CURSE OF THE 8TH BUDDHA   223

with relief and looked down at the ring again, wondering what surprises it still had for him.

The tightness in his chest still moved a bit, letting him know he wasn't totally alone. The curse remained.

Sinclair ran in short bursts up the stairs towards the EOC. He felt the hammer in his stomach as the acid rose up to his mouth. It was going to be a mess when he showed his face. The State representatives from the Governor's Office would be there, worn out, whipped and frustrated. The challenges in the Bay Area would be overwhelming. He'd be like gasoline thrown on the fire already burning their feet. The way things were headed, he might even be arrested by the Highway Patrol or the city cops. It didn't matter. It was his duty. That was what he was trained to do in disasters, no matter the personal cost. He pushed at the revolving doors at the entryway into the great city library. Its stacks of wondrous knowledge were strewn about the floors.

Richard was about to enter the auditorium when he felt several men's strong hands grab him from behind. A rag was spread over his mouth and he fell back into their control.

"Can you hear me now, Richard?" The gravelly voice greeted him as he was able to open just his right eye. His head felt heavy and thick as though a pillow was stuffed between his ears. There was a dreadfully bitter taste in his mouth from the asphixiant his kidnappers had used to subdue him. It was cloying and metallic. He could make out Lili's form in front of him. Her face bore a sardonic grin.

"Don't you ever give up? I thought we were done with all this. I have nothing left for you. You know what happened. The Templars are no longer after your treasure. Why torture Lili like this? She is so—"

"Sweet? Tender? Desirable?"

Richard thought the Lilith's speech particularly offensive coming out of another innocent forced to suffer through this menagerie of conceit. "You may have been great once, whatever you call yourselves now, but you have degraded into a lowly form of consciousness. No evolved being would do the things you purport to be justified. You disgust me." He stopped in the middle of his diatribe after receiving a hard blow to his right jaw by an unseen assailant behind him.

"Stop." she commanded.

He could hear a number of people moving behind him. A door closed, leaving him alone with the brutal Lilith. It was the first time he'd truly appreciated the ring that was tight to his finger. He might suffer, but she wouldn't dare kill him.

"Oh, don't think for a moment we didn't consider hacking off that digit—and maybe more. But without knowing what repercussions that remnant might bestow on us, well, it wasn't worth the risk. We saw what happened on the bench with that black person. You'll have to tell me more about that experience."

"Go fuck yourself." He pulled at his bonds but they were both secure and painful to test.

"I think you may change your mind, or would you like to see your Pygmalion with her skin sliced off down to the bone?" The Lilith guided Lili's hands to a knife on a table. Richard could see the blade flash under the subdued lighting of the dim confinement. The blade came up, pointing at Lili's neckline. The Lilith guided it slowly. It began to cut as it meandered toward her left breast. A river

CURSE OF THE 8TH BUDDHA

of fresh blood spurted from what was still a shallow fissure.

"For God's sake!"

"God's sake? How perfectly pedestrian of you. Now, we can start to share some information or this little scratch will become a river. I feel none of it. This is just a vessel for my communication to you, a lesser. My sisters made an unfortunate pact with this maniacal little society of power-hungry Asian men long ago, otherwise I would certainly have disposed of them. They are so tiring and just as shallow and useless at times as your own Templar trash. Unfortunately, the ultimate goals of the Red and Green Dragons meet our needs. For now we tolerate their childish passions and intrigues."

"So what do you want from me now?" Sinclair sat upright, clearing his head from the potion's control. He was astonished to see the wound on Lili's chest disappear and heal shut without a trace.

"Before we digress to that night in our hiding place, it is time you knew that you have already been given up by your dear Order. Oh, yes," she stressed, noting the shock on Sinclair's face, "your master Eli has given you up to us as our tribute. He only seemed concerned for your well being as long as the Templars were not tampered with and you were the key to finding their silly gold. Now they'll give you to use with ease. Amazing how a good housecleaning changed their opinion so many centuries ago in France. No matter what they say of fearlessness in the face of death, the reality is that many of their leaders fear their own mortality more than anything else. Regardless, you come to us a bit damaged but truly the most promising offering since our agreement. You are now so deeply changed by our dear pet, and that horrid little ring you wear, that your value is far greater than any price we might have demanded. So, dear Richard, you were given away. Surely they told you this was coming."

"Not really. But I also have no reason to trust you."

"Did the old buzzard ever mention to you that you might be the *Lantern*?"

"And if he did?" Sinclair tried to conceal his terror at the knowledge the Liliths had of Templar secret business.

"No doubt he did. I can see it in your eyes and feel it in your pulse. The Lantern is nothing more than an old medieval term for a victim burned at the stake to free them of evil and to release those present from the Dark Lord's influence. You shall be the Templar's karmic debt repaid: A final vengeance for that ancient travesty against us."

"Gee, I just can't tell you how special you make me feel. You've got me connected to aliens with this ring. You've got me living the life of some Taoist saint's hubby and now I'm a team-trade late in the season. Who writes your stuff, the Marx Brothers?"

Lili shuddered and then fainted to the floor. The black cloud lifted out of her and rushed to Richard, the struggling captive. The ancient creature's screams rolled through the room, pulling sound tiles off the low ceiling. A pounding continued from the closed doors behind them, giving some indication that the Chinese captors could not enter the killing field. The Lilith would not allow the undisciplined and un-evolved to see her pure form, especially as it fed on the blood of this fool who dared heresy against the Lilith.

His bonds vaporized and his ring hand jerked up without his control. Just as the spiny, violent cloud reached his face an orange and red fire flitted through the air from his ring finger. The effects were like a laser concert he'd seen at the coliseum in Oakland. The Lilith was perforated with hundreds of laser-filled voids in seconds. Her screams were unbearable, tearing at his eardrums. He feared he might be deaf and dead as the battle continued. She backed into a dark corner and made another charge for Richard as he stood up.

This time the ring slammed his right and left hand together, palms locked, with arms straight out. His arms formed a lance in front of him. A spinning circle of blackness rushed from his hands, even more terrifying than the Lilith's wraith form. The Lilith could not resist the magnetic compulsion of the void. The scream rose to a fever pitch but disappeared just as her vaporous mass was sucked to pieces into the spiraling trap. The sound of a vacuum seal followed as the cosmic doorway compressed to nothingness. The room was left still and abandoned of the foreign force. Only Richard and Lili remained to face the marauders behind the door.

He rushed to her and held her in his arms. There was no breathing. She was unresponsive to his revival efforts. Richard wept openly, completely, letting this and the loss of his wife and daughter come out of him. The loss of his job, his Templar devotion, and his trust of everyone around him wrenched out of his psyche. Lili rested calmly in his arms as he cradled her to his chest and rocked back and forth in the room, sobbing to whatever gods might be left to listen to his prayers. There was no concern in his world for the wood splinters flying from the door as desperate men forced an entry into his prison.

A new quiet rose around him and his newly beloved. A pathway of lights stretched out and pulled both of them through the walls, out of their prison, and far beyond. The oppressive stale gloom sped away as a white, milky light swirled around them. He could feel the intense pain from his cuts and bruises dissipating. A joy rushed up through his skin, bones, and through his mind. The dense fog swept into his nostrils and through every pore of his skin. His tears dried as he felt a relief from all the wounds he had ever experienced mentally, spiritually, and physically. A foreign sense of ecstasy overcame him. Time stopped its passage around them. Lili rolled back and forth in a stream of the life force and then slipped out of his arms. She was now standing above him—floating. Her eyes opened and met his in perfect concordance and oneness. There were no words. No outbursts of emotions. They were simply souls bound in silent harmony, pulled swiftly into a tunnel of light.

A casual observer just entering the Chinatown prison chamber would have noted a brief flash. There were ropes and duct tape on the floor and on the single chair. The swinging fluorescent fixture twisted back and forth on dusty brass chains covered with webs. The solid-core oak door shattered and then burst into the vacancy. The explosion was followed by a tide of angry, armed pugilists desperate to defend their powerful leader. But there were no captives and no goddess to guide them.

Richard shuddered, opened his eyes, and found himself in Lili Zhang's gentle embrace. The stench of the fires and choking smoke forced him back into the physical world that was still very populated by mankind. He pulled back from her warmth to investigate their new surroundings. It was only vaguely familiar at first until he turned around. The crane was lying collapsed on its side like a brontosaurus fallen into a tar pit. Dark fluids were still running out of the bottom of the main control room and around the generator. Below him were the remains of the excavation site. There were only six feet of dig wall still uncovered. The rest of the pit was filled with a thick muck of drainage water topped with rotting timbers, construction debris, and garbage that had floated out of the containers the quake swept into the hole.

"What happened?" He twisted to right himself and the help Lili up.

"Even as an acolyte of the Tao I have no understanding to answer those questions. How we were brought here and why are mysteries to me. I do know I have loved you forever. Does anything else matter? You brought me back to life. We have blended our energies into something even the Temple masters cannot conceive. Does it matter *where* we are, really, since we just are?"

He leaned to kiss her lightly and then deeply without any hesitation for the first time. They both shuddered as their energies readjusted to physicality. It was a heady voyage of pure longing and fulfillment. Then they pulled away. They stood confused next to the starting point of Sinclair's dreadful adventure into the land of the Liliths.

"I can feel it pulling at me, Lili. You can't imagine. The thing in me is compelling me to go into the water. This is madness."

"I don't know what to do." She pulled back from him in terror. She could not hold him as he began to twist and transmogrify. A long, rolling beard sprouted from his chin and cheeks. His eyes doubled in size, with nothing but coal dust filling them. Richard's brow widened and gills opened on both sides of his neck. His hands grew extra fingers and his legs pushed out, leaving him slightly bent.

Richard, or whatever he had become, stepped over the edge of the chasm. As his webbed feet touched the mire, a powerful crackling sound ripped across the filth. The depths of slime and debris were frozen in seconds into a skating rink. The icy walkway held him up as he moved to the center over the original collapse location. His right hand rose out from his body as a purple beam shot from the palm of his hand, from the ring, down and into the brown iceberg.

"Lili, step back and turn away." The voice warned her, but it was not Richard. Some other entity commanded with a power beyond the mere forces of men and Liliths. She obeyed.

Ice shredded and screeched as it split apart. Richard could sense something rising up to his feet. There was resistance from whatever was emerging, but it could not resist the powerful being above. The top layers of frozen fudge exploded up and the small golden statue, no longer than Richard's forearm, flew up to face of the alien intruder that commanded its presence.

The malevolent ornament gnashed its metallic teeth while powerful shafts of laser-red fire flashed from its emerald eyes over the ice and the construction site. Whatever it struck burned or evaporated, except Richard. The violent bursts bounced away from him and were neutralized into harmless glittering refractions. The golden statuette attacked again and again with no effect.

The figurine attempted to escape. A beam of purple flashed from Richard's ring and held the attacker suspended in mid-air. This restriction brought even more screams and cries out of the relic's metal belly. Richard's hand reached toward it. The struggling effigy twisted, squirmed, and splattered green, glowing sputum in resistance. It was fruitless. Finally, Sinclair's hand, with all seven fingers, wrapped around the demonic figurine and closed hard. The denizen's metallic face froze. The fury subsided. Then, without any fanfare or flash, the guardian figurine disappeared in a blink.

Richard backed away from the spot, leaving a huge void remaining below in the frozen mass. With each step back toward the edge, part of the "Visitor" drifted away from

Richard's body, until at last he crawled over the berm at the edge and rolled, fully himself, under the gaze of the Taoist priestess.

"Well, I think it's safe to look now." He laughed and reached up for her hand. She supported him upward with surprising strength. She was not quite the helpless waif he had imagined.

"What was that all about?" She inspected his neck for any remaining gills.

"I haven't got a clue. I do remember it all, but as an external viewer. Probably like you and the Lilith. I was there but not as the participant. It felt like there were two of me, but the other one just pushed me into the corner to wait until they were done playing."

"It is disturbing, isn't it? Like I told you, Richard, there is nothing I could do to resist the Lilith, either. Do you know exactly what that thing was that came out of the water? I saw it for a second before I turned away. I might have an idea."

"All I can tell you is that I've seen that object before. It was a vicious curio made of silverfish-green metal. A real nasty bit of work. It bit me here on the wrist when I was deep underground." Richard pulled his sleeve back to reveal his wrist and found that there was no bite mark remaining. No scar. He curled his brow and then jumped up and down, followed by a succession of deep knee bends.

"What are you doing?" Lili stood back and evaluated the middle-aged leprechaun before her, doing his dips and jigs to a non-existent fiddler.

"Well, I'll be damned. Unbelievable. It's wonderful, Lili, just wonderful." He was like a child again. He grabbed her hands to join him is a quick spin, just barely keeping them from the precipice. They now looked over a deep crevasse empty of water, of pilings, and of all evidence that anything but dirt had ever existed in that space. The pit was simply an excavation site, and nothing more.

"Wheee!" He lifted her off the ground and into his arms unafraid of his knees or back failing him. Everything was clearer. His vision was perfect. His lungs were full and open. There was blood flowing everywhere, and he felt that as well.

"Please, Richard, put me down. Are you going crazy?"

"No, not mad. I've just gone happy . . . happy here in the middle of the fires of hell. What a macabre turn of events. Pinch me, would you?"

"I'll do no such thing." She put her hands to her hips after he set her safely back on the soil. "So you really have no idea what that object was that attacked you?"

"Not a clue."

"Well, I have never seen one, but it matches the stories I've heard. It is said to be a curse for life to encounter the golden *ganyan*. The Liliths were probably bound by it to protect the treasure. Only the Red and Green Dragon Society know how to use the *ganyan*. If you removed it, or destroyed it, then the bond of duty is over. This will be very bad for us, Richard. The Liliths will be free, but the Society will hunt us like rabbits, whether or not they ever get their treasure back. We have interrupted hundreds of years of planning."

"Well, so will the Order. I guess we get a two-for-one on this journey. Ha, I laugh at them both. As long as I have this—" He stretched out his right hand to show the ring to Lili, but there was no ring. There was no sign a ring had ever graced his hands.

"They took it. That Annunaki bastard took it back!"

"Who?"

"The Visitors. The Annunaki. I have no mystical powers left. God, I even had to have you lift me up. We're really screwed."

"We should leave this place now. There is nothing left here for either of us. If those warriors from the Society find us we will die very badly."

"And today is not a good day to die, my dear Lili, I assure you of that. Let's go."

"I agree."

"I think running, carefully, would be good. Where the heck can we go? Everything's torn up. There's not going to be a lot of safe places for us."

"There is one safe place I know that was unharmed in the shaking. There are many reasons to go there now."

"Okay, where to?"

"North. I'll lead. We'll be safe at the Taoist Temple on Broadway. There are people waiting there who can help us and give guidance. I want you to meet them and someone else staying there."

"So who else do we need to pull into this soap opera, and excuse me for being dramatic, but this is just all a bit too much, don't you think?" They started to move quickly through the rubble and north to central China Town.

"My mother and father. . . they are there. I think it is time."

Richard hesitated, wondering how much more stress he could take in one week, or one lifetime. The distant baying of dogs interrupted his concerns about Lili's family gathering.

"If you know a short cut that would be good. If that's a pack of wild dogs we're in real trouble, and I mean right now."

"Yes, there is a way, if it is still clear. It made it through the last quake and the one in nineteen o'six. I hope you aren't claustrophobic."

"Oh, please don't tell me we have to go underground. I get so tired of this."

"Don't worry, I'll show you the way. Just hold my hand. As long as we support each other we'll be safe for lifetimes to come."

He looked behind and saw the last glints of light reflected from pairs of bouncing red eyes, as a dog pack to the south rushed toward them through the scattered cars and trucks. He prayed they could outrun the predators. Richard and Lili linked hands as they raced up Montgomery to Columbus Avenue. The night was closing in around them in the unlit steel canyons of a devastated San Francisco.

Chapter 15

Richard let out a yelp as he helped Lili pull some fallen ceramic overhangs away from the front door of an abandoned realtor's office. The searing pain from the fresh cut on his right hand distracted him from the approaching dog packs.

"Damn, I should have brought that Go Kit. At least I'd have some gloves and first-aid supplies." As he rubbed the fresh blood from his wound on his shirt he jumped back. A fresh piece of overhang fell across the street. Scattered piles of red brick were splayed on the cracked streets; their sources were the tipped-over two and three-story commercial buildings on Montgomery Street. There were scatterings of broken supports and shingles from beige apartment buildings that cascaded to ground level. Some of the apartment remains were still on fire. No traffic, including fire engines, had been able to negotiate a pathway through the tangled menagerie. Lili and Sinclair were alone except for the predators on their trail; blazing eyes were again popping up like fireflies in the dimming shadows around the scattered vehicles just a block behind.

"How bad is that cut?" Lili stopped for a second and pulled his right hand up. The incision ran across his palm and oozed heavily. She tore a strip from her dress and wrapped it around and over his hand, making a quick bandage. "Now put some pressure on that so it doesn't get worse. We're going to be a long way from medical help for a while." She pressed a point hard on his elbow, then one on his wrist. The bleeding slowed immediately.

He resisted as she pulled him into the wrecked realtor's building through its damaged interior. "No time for this. The dogs smell the blood. We'd better move faster or we're going to need a lot more bandages." He could hear the growling moving toward them. "Are you sure this is the only way in? We're somewhat off track by my reckoning."

"This is the best way. Trust me." She yanked him through a tight passage around tossed desks, file cabinets, and ergonomic office chairs. The once tranquil office was now the leftover scene from a Western bar fight. "The steam tunnels are right below. We are trained where to hide in case there is a riot against our people."

"Are you kidding me? Man, this is a tight fit." He had trouble getting through some of the wreckage she slid past with ease. His height and slight pudginess wasn't helping. "Guess I have to get back in the gym." His balance was off a bit as well since he couldn't grasp anything with his right hand while maneuvering through demolished interior. Glass from the storefront windows and framed art work was scattered throughout, as were sharp spikes of metal from various pieces of overhead supports and torn piping.

"We have learned for centuries that the white overlords in America fear us and hate us. It wasn't that long ago in your history that my people were lynched not far from here for drunken fun. We have made it our responsibility to ensure safe havens." There was a strong bitterness in her words.

They reached a stairwell. Richard was quick to pull the door shut behind them with the hopes it would hold off the pack if it entered the buildings. He was surprised the entrance to the downstairs was made of steel, not wood. There was a small mesh-reinforced security window that let them peer back out into the work floor. He jumped forward as a set of angry jaws filled the window behind him. Claws scratched and beat against the metal.

"Christ that was close! I didn't think they were anywhere that near."

"Come. We can't think about that now. I know where the flashlights are—here."

Lili pointed a beam down the stairwell so they could see the floor below them. She then pointed to a spare light fastened to the wall so Sinclair would have a light of his own.

"Can you hold that with your right? You should hold onto the rail with your left. Some of these stairs were twisted in the quake."

"Yeah, I'm fine." Sinclair proceeded slowly, still protecting his new knees even though he was fairly sure they were permanently healed. Any travel down stairs had been his painful curse, but now he moved down with shocking ease.

"We tend to be a bit shorter, so watch your head." Her warning was timely as they moved past another doorway and into the steam system beneath the city. Some of the lines had main feeder trunks dipping down to his forehead level. Fine threads of old asbestos linings hung like cotton string drifting over his hairline.

"If you only knew how much I hate going underground. Almost as bad as heights—well, how I used to feel about heights."

"It's probably from another lifetime. Maybe you died in a fall?"

"I don't really care that much about what happened back then, I'm just trying to cover my ass now. Say, how far have we got to go to reach the Temple using this route?"

"Maybe another half hour if the passage through the Old City is intact. Why do you ask? There are no dogs behind us now."

"I don't mean to be indelicate, I mean, really I don't know that much about the *you* here and now. But hey, I really have to go like a race horse. That last run and then the stairs. Any ideas? Maybe I could just stay behind a couple of minutes and then catch up?"

"Please. I don't want you embarrassing yourself in front of my parents." She giggled. Considering where they were, and the recent events, her comments were charming but somehow inappropriate. He watched as her flashlight flitted about and then disappeared as she turned a corner. In a few minutes he caught up with her as she waited outside a rusted iron plate that was slightly extended from the tunnel wall.

"I'll need your help pulling this open."

"Lili, I don't think dynamite would get that open. You must think I'm superman."

"No, we have a Chinese lock on this. We have protected parts of old Chinatown for over a hundred years. Even the Mayor's Office doesn't know about these old passages. We have people, like those in real estate office, who watch over these sites."

"Any nasty, fat, redheaded guys?"

"I don't understand."

"Never mind. So what do we do?"

"It takes two people to open the latch. There are a few still left from the last century still installed in the tunnels. We replace them with something more modern when we need to, but as long as they are still working we leave the old double dragons in place. Now, let me tell you the order and I'll press the latch here under this pipe."

They worked in concert and the rusting plate snapped open just an inch or two. They pulled back the outer casing. This movement released a hidden lever, followed by some muffled clicking as a passageway door slid open. As they entered Lili took a match from a case mounted on the inner wall of the adjoining entrance. She lit a single gas lamp which started a slow, jumpy chain reaction of ignitions down a series of century-old gas lamps along the walls.

"Is this old system safe, especially after the quake? That's natural gas."

"Not a problem. We use small, metal containers for only a block at a time. If there is any break it automatically seals off the fractured lines from the bottle that fed it."

"Never heard of that before. Really smart."

"We don't plan like typical Americans. We look at the long road."

"The Tao, right."

"No, not the Tao. Just the path. They're different. Let's get to the Temple. We can talk philosophy later. I don't like spending that much time in here, especially after a quake. We'll have to watch carefully for damage and water."

The walls narrowed and then opened to a familiar site. The rotting smells of decay were identical to those underneath Old Sacramento. The beam work and layout of the hidden streets were identical, dating from the same period of the Gold Rush. Some of the buildings still had glass window fronts and signs for their wares, including a dentist, a barbershop and what appeared to be parts of an old bordello.

"There's something I didn't expect—a whorehouse in Chinatown."

"What did you think men would do when they couldn't bring their wives here? Could you go for decades without sex?"

Richard winced at the remark and was glad the semi-darkness hid his blushing.

"This used to be the end of Sullivan's Alley. Since most Chinese men were restricted by Congress from bringing their wives, they ended up here, often extinguishing their desires between the legs of Chinese girls who had been stolen as slaves for prostitution by your trade vessels."

"Could we change the subject or something? Maybe discuss the Liliths and what they have in mind? I really don't want to get into all this social awareness stuff right now. We've got to have a plan to get the hell out of this city."

"Here we are, trapped in an ancient battle. Who knows how old it is? The Templars are really just children in the middle of this. You were used just like I was—as a vessel for their evil. But we are together now, at last. This is our time—time for humanity to take back our rights. It's our world now, not theirs. We'll have our day, again, just as the Native Americans will have theirs."

"Who knows how long all of this has been going on? After that journey back in time the things we do now seem insignificant. Look, I'm really just a simple guy caught up in something way over my frickin' head. I'm really not that excited about getting into a three-way conflict where we're the little guys. Those don't turn out so well for the little guys. By the way, I think you can leave the Indians out of this. At least they aren't involved in this mess."

"Oh, but they are."

"Do I dare ask? Oh, go ahead. If we have to talk about something down in this mausoleum I might as well hear it all. Is this weirdness ever going to end?"

They continued down the streets, following a pathway lighted by gas lights strung on a series of tall, round wooden posts that smelled of creosote.

"It is no mystery, really. In fact, the Templars caused a lot of this mess, thanks to Marco Polo, their emissary."

"Yeah, we covered that ground before. So he blew the lid off your discovery of the New World. That's long past. We need to move ahead."

"Ho, easy for you to dismiss. Those men kidnapped you—you do remember them as real, don't you?"

"Very."

"The Red and Green Dragon's Breath will hunt us until they fulfill their mission. They have a commitment by blood and honor. The Emperor's envoys made treaties with the native people here sometime in the twelve-hundreds, hundreds of years before that silly Italian erupted on San Salvador like a wet boil. The Emperor had planned to start new trade and colonies. The idea then was for a golden era to begin. The Chinese people did not treat the natives as your explorers did later. We were partners. Our treaty is still our bond, no matter how the communists now lord over Beijing. The Breath are here to retrieve that treasure so that the Chinese homeland can rise up to new freedoms. It will also be used to help return the land here in America back to the rightful owners."

"You must be delusional. You can't possibly hope to get all the lands back to the Indians. Even if you could get some back, well, you've seen how they fight with each other over stuff as mundane as casino rights. You really think the Governor is going to stand by and let you carve up his state?"

"He won't have much choice if a three-million-man army comes marching down the coastline from Canada."

"I don't think we live in the same world. That's just not likely no matter how you draw up the scenarios. It's pure fantasy. You might as well ask to see the Wizard."

"Perhaps you need to see reality and your environment through new eyes. Surely someone whose culture believes their messiah can bring the dead back to life is not one to wag a finger at the unlikely."

"Well, like the Wicked Witch of the West said, 'What a world, what a world.'"

"Yes, this last two months has been like Oz to me, long before you entered the picture, my white wizard."

"I'm afraid that without my ring that my days of wizardry are over. We've got to find a way out of Frisco and fast are on our own. I'm sure those thugs won't give up on finding us that easy. It won't matter what I say about the treasure and the fact that it's gone now, for good. They won't believe what we saw and neither will the Templars. We're really SOL, unless you plan to swim over to Oakland."

"We need to find a way over to the piers once we get to the Temple."

"I don't think that's such a great idea. That's too close to the Bay. I saw a lot of that torn to pieces from the slosh from the quake when I flew over today. What's so important over there?"

"We were ready for this event. I know where we have a boat nearby in a safe area. It's above all that threat area just off Calhoun Terrace."

"Please tell me it's not a row boat. I couldn't row with this hand."

"Hardly. We can get into the pier and launch from there. I've got the pass code to the launch site."

"There's likely to be a real mess when we get close to the piers. I'm not sure an outboard prop will survive in that water. If you had seen what I did you'd know."

"We expected that. The craft has been converted to a jet-ski drive as part of an inboard motor. There's titanium plating on the hull as well."

"I'm impressed. Who did all this planning?"

"My father. He was an engineer before he got involved in the State Department. Many of our people were saved these last two days because of his efforts."

The lights of the flickering gas lamps did not illuminate far back into the side streets and alleys, so they stayed to the center of the once well-traveled thoroughfare draped in the gas lights. Still, it was so dim that the posts' flickering could only be seen for two blocks ahead or behind.

Lili stopped walking and lurched to her left. "Do you hear that? Richard!" she screamed. She dropped the flashlight and rushed to his side. His light revealed dozens of rats moving quickly in their direction from a side street.

"I'm terrified of them. That's why I hate coming down here. I just hate them. Hold me up while they run past."

"No, Lili, we need to run, and I mean faster than we did up top. I learned one thing in search and rescue—when the rats are leaving you better be ahead of them. Now move." He could feel a cold air moving ahead of the rats, which meant one thing: underground flooding.

He picked up her flashlight and they ran parallel with the poles between them. None of the overhead beams had fallen on the gas lines or lights so there was little to hamper their dash.

After flying four blocks, Richard broke the silence while still in stride. "How much farther? I can hear things collapsing behind us. We've got to get out of here. I can't keep this pace up much longer."

"Just ahead. See where the lights turn right?"

They followed the turn and came to a winding metal staircase. Richard shook it with his right hand to ensure it was still secure after the quake. He surveyed it with the flashlight as far as his beam would allow. It would be a climb.

"You go first."

"I know the way at the top. It takes about five minutes to get up there."

"Go. We don't have five."

The two pounded up the iron cage. Their hands pulled desperately at the railing to pull them up even faster. Cold air rushed upward when they were only halfway to the landing. Richard's wounded hand ached and the bandage tore open in his scramble.

"Faster, Lili." He was already thinking about how long he might last under water, and if the gas lines might not hold, adding poisonous gas to their breathing space at the top of the escape route.

Rats fought for a foothold from the turbulence below them. Some rodents fell screaming off the staircase as the dark water swept over them, carrying them far away into the preserved streets that were now collapsing.

They were both just on the landing, on a three-foot precipice, as the stairwell began to rock and pull out of the corroded iron connections below them.

Lili pushed hard on three pressure releases of another iron plate. "Richard, pull the lever over there. The dragon statue on the wall."

He slammed the orange, crusted lever back. It covered his bleeding palm in rust and mold. A cover plate moved forward just enough for a handhold. They peeled the cover back as adrenaline pounded at their brains.

"Can we close it off once we get in?"

"Yes, but quickly."

It was pitch-black inside the space beyond the cover. They dropped the flashlight to the floor as they struggled furiously to close the doorway behind them. It finally engaged the inner pins and sealed inward with a whooshing sound. Some water was already coming over the lip as the corridor plate closed. The cover snapped and popped as it held the water back as the current pounded on their escape hatch.

"Any idea where we are?"

"I haven't been in this part of the tunnels. Steam corridors are common throughout the City. There are concrete walkways for maintenance crews to work on all the piping, electrical and plumbing hidden underground. We should be close to the Temple entrance."

She inspected some of the numbers on the piping above them. Here the tunnel ceiling was higher. There were Chinese characters on some of the pipes that led to the floor before disappearing.

"We're in luck. This is under the bank. We're just two streets over."

They reached a split in the tunnels. Lili directed Richard to the right. After forty feet they stopped.

"This is it."

"Lili, there's no entrance."

"Not like the others. Here, hold the light on this wall." Richard laughed as she pushed against a set of pipes.

"Going through solid walls, are we?" He quit laughing as the entire wall moved back ever so slightly on a set of bearings, like the wall at Lake Tahoe. The entire surface was a clever trompe L' oeil.

"You could help me, you know."

He put both lights behind him under his belt. They began pushing inward. A bright light broke through as access opened for a well-lit conference area. They stepped in and pushed the facade of a six-foot, golden yin-yang circle back in place to seal off their entry.

"Oh, that was very nice." He had trouble speaking; he was spent from the near escape and the final exertion of reconstituting the steam tunnel wall.

"Keeps out the rats. I'm just so glad we made it out of there in one piece."

"I know, the rats."

"Oh, maybe some other things much worse than rats. Not to worry." She smiled and snapped her head back to push her long back hair behind her face, revealing her flashing green eyes.

"Oh, now you tell me." He stared at her again, now in bright light, as they rested with their backs against the yin-yang. "I think I could get used to loving you. You are really amazing."

"I only hope my father feels the same about you, Round-eyes."

"Oh great. That'll just end a perfect day. Maybe I better go back and face the dogs."

Lili led him through the wide expanse of the workout area and several internal gardens with sand meditation zones filled with gigantic, black volcanic rocks. The white and black walls were a stylized contrast to the cedar and walnut walkways and room dividers with their silk-screen sliding doors.

As they entered a corridor Lili turned and put her hand flat against Sinclair's chest.

"Listen carefully. My father is old school. He won't tolerate any nonsense, so please be on your best behavior.

This is where my family has always agreed to meet during a major crisis in San Francisco. I'm sure they are still here. They don't know anything about you yet so please give me a little time to prepare them. Sit here and I'll call you when I think the time is right."

He sat on a low meditation bench as Lili continued on to an open doorway in a long hallway. At first it appeared there was a bright-red splash of formal Chinese calligraphy on the panel at the entry, but it was in an odd location.

Richard was thinking about what he would say to his new in-laws. Lili's scream cut through the silence. He tore through the hallways. Sinclair stood over Lili, stunned, as she cradled her mother's blood-soaked and mutilated body in her arms. He could see the attached office where an elderly man was spread out on a desktop, still piled on dark pools that were running off the side. His right hand had been cut off and thrown to the floor. His ears and nose had also been sliced away. There were no eyes left to stare into space.

Richard pulled Lili up and away. She struggled and fought back with her arms striking at him. "It's your fault! You and those damned Templars! You did this. You! You! You!"

He didn't fight her but allowed her blows to continue against him until she could strike no more. She collapsed into him, weeping and sobbing out of control. He let her go on as long as he dared, just holding her as she emptied her rage. He slowly descended to the floor with her, rocking her against his body. They sat huddled for a time in the field of carnage.

"Lili, listen. We've got to go. I am so sorry. So sorry. But those bastards who did this will be back. They haven't been gone long. They expected us to be here. Someone told them. We've got to get out of Frisco right away. There's nothing more we can do here. C'mon, Lili."

She crawled back to touch her mother's head one more time, running her hand through the gray hair.

"Lili, please," he begged. He watched her pull a little hair out and roll it tight into her palm. "We'll come back for them. I promise."

"I promise, too," she said, rising up and putting her hands out in a blessing. "They are gone. There will be justice someday for this—someday. My parents are here, in us, and in all things. We are not separate. The river always flows, always flows."

She did not look back again as Richard lifted her to her feet. They moved to the front of the building and finally to the front doors. The entrance was no more than twisted steel and aluminum frames lined with shards of glass poking out from their edges.

"Does your flashlight still work? We had them on a long time in the tunnel. God only knows how old the batteries are."

"Yes, I've got plenty of light left, but won't that draw the dogs?"

"I'd rather take that risk. There's too much damage out here; it'll be too easy to get ourselves cut up or fall. It's a lot worse than on the streets we came from. There was more fill used here to build on. Look at that building across the street." He turned the light across the street level, revealing a series of cars crushed under fallen brick. A set of lion-dog statutes lay motionless on their sides by broken glass and rubble from a neighboring grocery store that was completely flattened. The canine effigies' ivory-white paint made them ghostly twins piled in the earthquake ruins. They were the only dogs visible for the moment.

"We'd better move. It's to our advantage to move the boat in the dark. There will be others trying to get out of this mess and they'd kill to find an escape route."

"This isn't going to be easy but I'm not afraid when we're together. Yes, Richard, with you by my side. I also know now that my parents are looking over us." She reached her left hand up and shined the beam on her palm. "Here, will you put this in your pocket for me?" She put her mother's hair in his hand. He nodded and secured the remembrance.

They ventured into the destruction with their meager lights against the threats of the fallen city.

Richard had no sense of direction in the quagmire left in the area torn apart by the waves that had rolled back and forth in the Bay as part of the seiche. Blocks of buildings were stripped to the foundation. Oddities remained: a lone tree near a missing park bench, a mailbox beside the roof of a house from a distant residential area, and thousands of books piled in a soggy mess as they plugged the storm drains along the remains of the sidewalks.

"I hope you have a recent tetanus shot. This is a mess in here. We could be stepping on almost anything."

"We'll have to take the risk. There's little time with the Breath chasing us. They know of some of the preparations as well. The boat might already be gone."

"Where are we headed, anyway? Most of the street signs are gone. By the time we get to the Bay there won't be any landmarks to help navigate."

"See if you can find Broadway."

"Well, there's an omen of good luck, look straight up." She looked up at the sign illuminated by his flashlight.

"Now we just need to move east to Davis and we'll be close. I have no idea what these side streets are with all this damage. It's like a jigsaw puzzle."

They continued through the wreckage. Lili gasped and held her hand over her mouth. Sinclair turned his light to find her staring into a yellow cab filled with crowded passengers torn in various pieces; part of their torsos were sticking through the remains of the front windshield.

"That may not be the last we see down here. There's a big expanse opening up just ahead. We may be close to the piers."

In a few minutes they were standing on an open roadway littered with vehicles, lumber, boats, and floating garbage the seiche had torn away from Sausalito.

"This is probably the Embarcadero. That looks like the Pier Nine building, at least the remains."

"And the torn away walkway for Pier Seven, directly ahead. I just pray it didn't collapse on the exit grate below."

"What are you talking about? That's just a fishing pier. There's nothing under it."

"Let's turn back to Davis. Look for a two-story concrete building with thin windows. It looks like an old church, but square."

They moved back through the piles of flotsam thrown up along the exit to the next street behind them. Lily moved north, adroitly, through the debris field.

"Here. This is it. Amazing. So little damage."

Sinclair looked at the side door. It was ripped open off the top hinges. He and Lili were able to pull it back and enter the site.

"God it smells like hell in here!"

"The toilets in this building tie directly to the Bay. I'm sure the surge pushed everything right back in. I agree.

Very bad." She covered her nose with her arm. There was little benefit.

"What next? I don't see this getting us anywhere but stunk up and infected if we get cut."

"See that stairwell over there? Yes, that one. If we can get through and down below we may be out of here."

Richard slipped a bit on the slimy floors as they fumbled forward for a safe path to the entry. There was an absolute darkness around the opening. A warm, salty breeze rose up and pushed at them when they entered.

"That's good. We still have access to the Bay or we wouldn't have that sea smell."

"I'm game. Let's keep going."

They worked down the slippery stairs while sliding their hands over the rounded walls fresh with Bay bottom clays and silt pushed up during the invading waves. Their lights played across two quays at the bottom that stretched out from a partially blocked and tattered steel grating. Lili's flashlight revealed a corrugated door to the side of one of the wharf abutments.

"At least it isn't destroyed like the others. All of our other boats are gone. Probably sucked out with the first wave's return. Let's see if we can get that door open."

"But the gate goes down into the water. The mechanisms are likely broken."

"No, it's designed that way. The boat is inside, if someone hasn't already made off with it."

The lines of the corrugated steel were buckled and penetrated at several of the folds. One pleat in the metal was skewered with a half-inch-thick spike of rebar.

"If that went through to any hull on the other side it isn't floating anymore."

"Just pull it up. The chain and pulleys are still here to open the door when power is out."

Sinclair wrestled the iron rod back and forth until it gave way, pulling out of the gate. He barely missed tumbling into the water below. He could hear the chains moving to the side as Lili worked the chain gang. He joined her. The door groaned and shook as the chains continued to fling over the pulleys, clattering and banging on the wall of the hidden dock. After twenty minutes the steel covering was up about five feet over the water line.

"That's enough," Lili said, turning the light onto the new opening.

"See anything?" Richard rested from the effort, waiting to see if they were truly stranded in a septic tank.

"The moorings still look solid. She's there. Have a look."

Sinclair peeked back into the locker to find a coal-black speed boat without a single piece of chrome or reflective surface.

"Is that a Cigarette?"

"Oh, you know a little about boats? Yes, a thirty-six foot Racing Gladiator. It's got beautiful twin inboards with seven-hundred-fifty horses of water-pony power."

"Yikes, I thought you were a TAO priestess, not an announcer for ESPN."

"Yes, I'm a priestess of my temple, but I'm not an idiot. Let's see if she's still running or if she's taken on water."

A thin walkway inside the storage cove allowed them access alongside. Lili went below and began a brief inspection.

"Untie the lines, if you know how."

"Yeah, well, I'm old, but I'm not *stupid*." Richard worked at the ropes along the seawall but couldn't quite master them in the dark. He soon felt another set of hands over his.

"Don't know what a double bowline is, do you?" She made a quick move with her hands and snapped the line open, tossing it to the boat.

"Okay, can we just go?"

Lili laughed lightly as she turned from him, gently tugging him into the canopy. Richard knew nothing of boating. When he rented the small craft in Catalina he knew just enough to get him out to the channel current with the hope he'd be pulled out to sea. He'd never tied as much as a half hitch his entire life.

"Is this normal to have the wheel on the right side? We're not in England." He shuddered as the engines roared to life, thundering under his seat. Lili turned on the search beams on the front and the entire quay lit up.

"It was just fine in Hong Kong."

"So this isn't from the U.S.?"

"No, it's a gift to my father from a cousin in the business." Lili engaged the throttle, slowing, moving the silhouette craft into the main entrance.

"I never heard anyone refer to the State Department as a business."

"No, no. The old family business: smuggling."

"You're not for real, are you? Really? Priestess, boating aficionado and a smuggler? Hard to fathom all that."

"Better get used to it. We have a long life ahead of us. You didn't think I was just some simple little flower of the Orient, did you? If so, you have a big surprise coming. Southern Belle and South China—that's pure fire. The Lilith's just made me look like a Barbie."

"Well, Miss Fireball, how do we get out of here? I may not be a merchant mariner, but I know that hull won't last in this crap left over from the tide. We'd be lucky to get a hundred yards, not to mention the garbage getting pulled up into the engines."

"My father took care of all of that. Hull looks like fiberglass but it's lighter and stronger—a special alloy of aluminum and titanium developed in Lawrence Livermore Labs. She could cut through diamonds at 100 knots. The intakes for the engine have a special breathable high-pump filter. That was a little invention from my uncle."

"Let's hope we don't need it. I'm not sure about that exit. When we came in it looked pretty rough."

Lili turned the spotter beam on the helm towards the outer wall. The exit was a turmoil of twisted metal and pylons contorted into an impassable barrier.

"She won't cut through that."

Another blinding, blue halogen light pierced through the other side of the maze. A voice yelled something unintelligible through a bull horn. Lili yelled back and immediately reversed the boat's thrust.

"What's up? Who was that?"

"Uncle Harry. He knew I'd come here with my family. He's been waiting."

"I don't think there's much he can do. Hey, this thing is backing up. I didn't think a boat could—"

"There you go, thinking again. Okay, we're back in. Do exactly as I do. Cover your ears with your hands and open your mouth, and then close your eyes. Then curl down in a ball. Now!"

Lili took the position and Richard followed just in time for the explosion. The pressure rushed the air out of Richard's chest. A flash sent light through his closed lids. Even with his ears covered there was a low hum and ringing when he pulled his hands away. The biting after burn of cordite sizzled in his eyes and throat.

"What the hell was that?"

"I'd guess C-4. Uncle is very good at that."

"Speak up. I couldn't hear all that."

She pointed her light on her face and motioned in sign language for him to buckle up into his seat. She turned the spotter back on and eased the Cigarette out into the fresh fragments from the explosion.

A man's deep voice cried out again from the other side of the new, wide passage. Lili answered and moved forward, following the guiding blue beam from under Pier Seven.

A scraping sound screeched along the hull on Richard's side of the boat. He pulled away, even in his straps, toward Lili.

"Don't let that little contact worry you. You better get ready for worse."

Lili's left hand pulled back the dual throttles on the panel between them as she monitored the rows of gauges along the fine inlaid wood instrument panel. The narrow prow pointed to a parallel path with her uncle's lights as both boats rumbled like suppressed Indy cars under the pylons of the long fishing pier. Their paths veered sharply left, to the north. Sinclair looked behind to see that the tongue of Pier Seven's walkway was folded and descended precipitously into the crowded waters. The brief glaze of light from the two boats revealed little of the cause, but the results were evident. He thought about the souls that might have been out there for a quiet day of fishing when the quake tore apart their footing, and then the wave followed to swallow them alive.

They headed to open water moments later, their lights off. Conflagrations still gutted the structures along Yerba Buena Island and ahead of that Treasure Island.

"Those poor bastards never had a chance. I can't imagine many survived."

"We've haven't heard from any of our friends on Treasure. The news reports were frightening."

Lili turned on the spotter beam to identify some of the materials blocking the path ahead as they motored away from the shadows of the silent Bay Bridge behind them.

"Shit!" Richard turned his head away. Hundreds of bodies banged against the hull. The two boats split them apart like a fresh fish die-off along a beach. Full rotting had been delayed in the water, but there was enough to wrench Sinclair's stomach. His last meal covered the control panel on his side of the console.

"Richard, get a grip." The resolve in Lili's voice settled the troubled Templar. He settled into a dulled daze, trying to look way from the carnage. Lili shut down the lights after a warning beam passed over them from her uncle. They were soon out in the main channel of the Bay.

The vista from open waters revealed the fires along the Oakland shore. Every hillside had a flare. Some rose and fell. A few moved along a line—a sign of an uncontrolled brush and possible forest fire. Smoke drifted from a few of the larger blazes, concealing smaller pinpoints level with the water; likely bonfires for survivors along the shoreline using the plentiful driftwood.

"Where are we headed?" Sinclair yelled. "I can't read that compass."

"It's not a compass. You might call it a fish finder."

"Your family uses this for fishing, too?"

"No, it was for detecting mines."

"Great. Just what we need."

"Hang on! Uncle Harry's in a bit of a rush."

Sinclair reeled back against the hard seat. The head rest was too low to support his neck. He wiggled down in the seat belt, against the acceleration, so the next jolt didn't decapitate him. The thunder of the engines shook him. His teeth knocked together. He clenched his jaws.

A huge shadow was gaining on his side of the boat. In a moment it covered the few lights remaining from Frisco. It was big. It was too big.

"What the hell are you doing?" he cried out over the din of the engines.

"We've got to get past some of the Coast Guard patrolling the Bay right now. We're about to become the remora to a very big shark."

The Cigarettes aligned along the starboard side of the huge emergency supply ship as it cut a huge wake. Uncle Harry and Lili road the wake like surfers. Up and down; rise and slam—but they made their way quickly and discreetly until they were close and parallel to the Berkeley shoreline. The tiny shadows then veered hard right and sped pell-mell to shore without regard to the treacherous objects floating on the path.

"I can see the outline of the hills. I know where this is. There's nothing out here."

"Oh, are you so sure?" Lili pulled the throttles back. The boat rumbled low and heavy. Richard could smell the oil and tar and other solvents in the water. The risks were high for a fire when the refinery products were mixed with the Bay water.

"Christ, that's Seawall Drive, or what's left of it. I don't even see the outline of the labs. That's University Avenue, I think. But there's nothing over here, except..."

"A big hole in the ground?"

"Well, yes. The quarry. There're a lot of folks in Berkeley who don't even realize there's an open pit right on their front door. But it's not open anymore, as far as I know."

"That would be wrong. We owned the pit. It was a perfect place to build underground facilities, right off the water. We're coming along the little spit. That's Interstate Eighty, directly to our right. If they knew what to look for and when, they could look right down our throats. The best place to hide something is right in front of people. Don't you agree?"

"Yeah, I've heard that somewhere recently. I just want to get off the water. I don't feel well. I've seen plenty already. Can we just get ashore?"

"Look to your left."

Richard watched the two boats approach a derelict ship's frame wedged against the spit. The hull moved aside and opened up a waterway directly into the spit wall, directly on the other side of the deep quarry. They motored slowly within the pirates' den as the camouflaged wreckage closed behind them.

Chapter 16

Richard and his new love arrived back in relative safety to a condo still littered with Richard's scattered dirty clothes. There was no time to tidy the place for Lili. *She's probably seen worse here*, he mused.

"I couldn't say a lot when your uncle's thugs were driving us back here, but I've got to question riding alongside a ship like that so the radar wouldn't catch us. How could you trust being in that wake, in the dark?"

"My uncle was the best pirate in Oakland for many years. And you should be very polite and thankful his guards risked bringing us back here through all of that turmoil in the Bay area."

"Lili, in all the time I spent in the Bay Area, I still can't recall anything about Chinese pirates—or any pirates."

"I said he was the best. Now, don't you think you should rest?" Richard flopped down on the couch. He adjusted the pillow under his head and pulled a nearby blue thermal blanket over him.

"Well, I suppose. I'm buzzed up and exhausted at the same time. I don't care what you say; I don't think he liked me. If I hadn't given him those drugs from the ambulance for his wounded men . . . well, I might be hanging in one of his underground meat lockers."

"You're still overreacting. He's grumpy about strangers coming near his private dock without first being introduced somewhere else first."

"You realize how close his knife came? God, Lili, you were almost a widow before you were a wife."

"Is that a proposal?" She smiled as she rubbed his forehead.

"I'll let you know. Maybe not, if your uncle's opinion continues to be that hostile. He wouldn't even shake hands. Imagine if I'd tried to hug him."

"I don't think you'd want to imagine that, my love. That would be thoughtless."

"Thoughtless? Keeping me on that boat for an extra half hour, throwing up over the side, while you two talked. That wasn't thoughtless?"

"He just had to be careful. Telling him about his sister and my father was not easy for either of us."

"I understand. I wasn't thinking. Bad call."

"Richard, if he didn't like us he wouldn't have given us his truck and an escort through Oakland."

"You mean thugs."

"Now who is being harsh?"

"Well, that big guy's tattoos weigh more than I do."

"Sounds like a little size envy to me."

"Hey, this is getting personal. You win, just wake me by seven. I'm going to call in to the Sacramento headquarters and see if they'll let me come in to help with the disaster response. At least that's something I'm good at."

"If you must. Don't you think a little rest is the first order? I mean, you are an older man." Sinclair could hear the same drifting giggle that had unarmed him during their first encounters.

"I need some more Dramamine. Can you help close the shades? I'll never get on another boat as long as I live.

Never." The calm of his own condo was salve for his tortured soul and body.

"You are such a baby, Richard. C'mon, rest here on your couch. I'll take care of everything. I think you need a mother more than a lover."

"I don't remember reaching the lover part yet. Are you sure that Lilith isn't still in you?"

"I'll never tell." She closed the drapes as far as she could reach and then walked to the bathroom. There was an irritating crescendo down the hallway of cabinet drawers opening and closing, along with bottles and cans being moved about the shelves.

"They're not in there. Please, look in my jacket pocket hanging on the back of the bathroom door."

"Got it."

"Don't shout. I can hear perfectly well now. Uh, bring the aspirin, too. That explosion was a real ass kicker."

"Okay," she whispered before she tiptoed back over the creaky flooring.

"Even the damn floor is against me."

"Here, take these. I got some nice cool water from the tap."

"I hate tap water. Who knows if they're trying to poison us or something, between the chlorine and the fluorine and the lead?"

"You'll live. Now take these and swallow. Just be happy I didn't pick any of the pills up off the floor, where you seem to be keeping a collection."

Richard lifted halfway up just long enough to swallow the pills and the drink. He made a growling gopher face, exposing his teeth as he puckered his mouth.

"Maybe you were once Lucrezia Borgia, too."

"Just lay back there and rest a bit. I'll take the bed for a while after I meditate."

"Meditate? After everything you've been through?"

"My parents and I were very close. My loss is mine to bear, but as a priestess I have a larger picture of reality. My loss is real, but my understanding is a bulwark against sentimentality. In the Tao we cannot be destroyed, but only change form. I cannot be separated or lost from those I love. We are ever one, like you and I."

"You're amazing. When I lost my. . . look, if you need me to just be close, let me know. Oh . . ." He reached inside his pockets and removed the hair from Lili's mother. "Maybe this isn't the right time, but I want to make sure you have this. We're still in danger. I don't think there would ever be a good time. I'm so sorry about your folks. I mean it. If you want me close let me know."

"I will. I think we'll be safe for a while now. Although I do have this nagging sense something else is wrong. Perhaps it is my parents trying to warn me."

"Yeah, I felt the same sense of doom since we left the harbor. I've never had these kinds of abilities before all of this. It's probably just leftover from all the horrors we've gone through. It's all just a bit much. But now I'm just desperate to get some sleep. If you get up first would you wake me about seven?"

"Okay, seven it is. I'll leave you to. . ." She was interrupted by the phone ringing. The ring tone was set at maximum. It sounded like a claxon on a destroyer going to battle stations. "How horrid! Did you set it that way?"

"Just an oversight. It was an old set I hooked up after the last one that got fried. You should know; the damn Liliths melted it."

She picked up the receiver and greeted the caller. "Yes, he's here. May I ask . . . all right, I won't." Lili brought the phone over to Richard who was now sitting upright

CURSE OF THE 8ᵀᴴ BUDDHA

against the arm of the couch. "It's some woman. She sounds, well, a little giddy."

Richard curled his brows in a frown and took the cordless. "Sinclair. Who's this?"

"Meeeee!" The long, childish burst of energy was not typical of anyone he knew. "And your little buddy Eddy. He's a real blast. Why didn't you tell me you had such smart friends?" She tee-heed a few times.

"Eddy? I don't know an Eddy. I don't know who you are but . . . Oh, God, it's you, Mary Beth. Where in the hell are you? Are you drunk?" He could hear the phone moving around on the other end and voices warbling in the poor connection. "Look, I can't hear you all that well. It's probably the phone system after the quake. If you call back—"

"Ho, good buddy. I got it covered. Quite a little fireball, this little archeologist. Sorry to surprise you like this. We couldn't find you anywhere after they evacuated the hospital. That's how I met her. Weird how we got together and we both knew you. The State sent her over to look at the hospital foundation since she used to be a structural engineer at one time. Imagine that, and what a structure."

"Edmund? Edmund, are you drunk, too? This has got to be a nightmare." He thought about the two of them, drunk, rolling on the floor, wrapped around each other. The Dramamine was overtaken by his new nausea.

There was a low knock at the door, but Sinclair's attention was elsewhere, as he stared the other way outside the apartment window. "Lili, could you get that and just send them away? It's probably the neighbor wondering why she can't find her cat. Cats tend to hide out after quakes." He turned his back away from Lili and began interrogating the librarian in hushed tones.

"Turner, are you insane? You don't ever call here unless you were requested to find something. And you're with Mary Beth? Are you nuts? You could expose use all."

"Oh, I fully expect to expose some of us, as soon as I can find a hotel room."

"*Please*," Sinclair responded with disgust. "You're crazy. How could you both go out and get tossed like that? Who's watching Marie, for God's sake?"

"I suspect she's watching herself—and the baby. A real beaut. That's what we're celebrating. I caught that bastard Bisol when he was trying to suffocate Marie. Didn't know I had the fight in me. Really laid him out with a bed pan. Works just like in the movies. It was great. And then ten minutes later and poof, there's a healthy baby boy. What a miracle—a twenty-minute gestation."

"He's a hero, and he really knows a lot about horsies!" Mary Beth was screaming wildly in the receiver over Turner's shoulder.

"Whoa, Poncho. You want to step back a few there? Alex tried to kill Marie? He tried to kill her—a Templar superior?"

"Damn right. He's a wanted man by us and the police. The cops are looking all over for him. I don't know how he escaped later or got out of here without that helicopter. I just needed to warn you. No telling where that asshole might show up. Want to know about the baby, buddy? Hey, it's got your eyes. Just kiddin'. Richard? Hey, Richard, you still there?"

Richard was there but frozen in place as the Luger pistol's barrel tapped against the center of his forehead. Sinclair recognized it from the collection his mentor had once pulled from a suitcase in the back of the Buick. Bisol was proud to note that his prized Nazi weapon was his favorite for close-up wet work.

"That's a good boy. Just put it down, nice and slow. And keep your damn hands to yourself. I won't shoot you first. It would be my pleasure to slam that slope over there into hell, though, before I spread your brains all over this shit hole you call home."

The wounds on Bisol's right crown and cheek were swollen and still bleeding through the rough bandages stuck to his face.

"Alex. What the hell?"

"Oh, you haven't seen hell yet, my friend. If I didn't have my orders I'd carve both of you little hamsters up. Did you really think you were going to get away with the treasure, all by yourself? You know what happens to traitors to the Order."

"He's no traitor. You are wrong!" Lili shouted back as she stood back against the curtains.

"And you, rice nigger, you open that bitch mouth of yours again and I'll cut it wide open just like your old lady's! You gooks really stick together. They wouldn't say a goddamn thing. But you, Sinclair, you were so predictable. I figured you'd come back here, just like a trained rat."

Richard rose up, enraged, realizing who butchered Lili's parents. Alex pushed back hard against Sinclair's head, hard enough to bruise him.

"Last chance, champ. You even fart sideways and I'll just do you right here. Maybe you'd like to watch while I rip up your little coolie whore?"

"I swear, Bisol, this will be the end for you. You've raised your hand against two of the Order. I heard all about Marie. There won't be a hole deep enough."

"I know a lot about holes, partner, and so do you. Seems we're going to go back to one for a little reunion. It might not be quite the family gathering you planned on, you and your new friend. Now get up and get your stuff on. We've got a long ride up the hill. If Eli didn't want both of you alive I could have had some real R&R tonight. Taking out an entire Chink family, hey, that would have made up for Turner and his blond bitch of a niece getting the best of me. I'll take care of his ass later, and hers."

"Who gave us up? Eli? The cops?"

"Guess it won't hurt to tell you. You're just tomorrow's leftovers anyway. I cut a deal with those Red and Green idiots. Those Chink bastards knew exactly where you and this piece of garbage were heading. I had some trouble beating you there. Those old folks held me up longer than I figured. I thought maybe they were covering for your escape."

Lili quickly rushed to attack Bisol. As her hand reached his face he side-kicked her back across the room against the couch. She lay still, moaning.

"I need you both or she'd be out the goddamn window. Yeah, the Breath want her real bad. See, that's why I'm working both sides of the bench. They're both basically stupid, but one of them was bound to find the treasure sooner or later. When they did I'd just take it and head for places even they don't know about. Oh, but then you had to get in the middle of my perfect plan and fuck it up. Damn, I hate college boys like you." Bisol kicked Sinclair hard across the ribs.

The room was spinning and narrowing in Richard's field of vision. Breathing was difficult as tightness in his chest joined the pain rolling through his ribs. Whatever dizziness remained was pushed aside by his bound rage. Only the single, narrow pistol barrel kept him from going for his captor's throat.

Richard complied with Bisol's orders, dressed, and led the way to the door. Bisol yanked Lili up from the floor.

He held her tight to him with the gun pressed against her back as they exited the disheveled condo and headed for Alex's Buick. They were soon driving up Highway 50 on the same dreaded route Sinclair had come to hate. This time, however, Richard was driving with Lili and Richard behind him in the back seat. Sinclair stared ahead in silence as his guardian watched, his gun to Lili's head as he chain-smoked.

"You know, she's not that bad for a rice ball. Really. You could have done worse."

"Why don't you just shut up, Alex?"

"Just keep driving, smart boy. I never trusted you Commie sympathizers from Berkeley."

"So this is how it is? The Brotherhood doesn't mean a damn thing to you? It's all about just whatever Alex wants?"

"That's right, wise guy. I do what I'm told and I go up the chain until I get the pot of gold. I'd of had that pile stuck in the shoals, too, if it wasn't so well guarded. You were just a temporary assignment anyway until it was time to pay the price. Do you get it now, smart guy? You're the payoff for the contract with the Liliths." Bisol's announcement pulled Sinclair's throat tight, his breathing was labored. The road narrowed as he concentrated his rage and terror.

"That makes the Templars pretty stupid. Why send me all over the world? Why the months of training and the readiness? That's a real waste."

"That's part of the deal. The Liliths didn't want an idiot; they wanted a real prize. Your bloodline is what cast you in the role. They knew for a decade that you were the one. The Masters just waited for the right time."

"Like I had no choice? It was just ordained?"

"We didn't ask you. You were told. The Order demands; it doesn't beg."

"You'll regret this some day. You all will."

"I've heard that a few times from a long line of young pups just like you. Some made it. Some didn't. I could care less."

"And Marie? That was all just an act you put on?"

"I wanted to see if she actually had any memories that would be a problem for me after I skipped out. She wouldn't hold a vendetta for me for something she couldn't remember. Man, did you fall like a rock for that performance. Almost had her down, too. Didn't expect that paper-weight uncle would have the cajones to pull one behind my back."

"You are a pig."

"Can it, pal. We're only about twenty minutes out now. If we weren't pressed for time I'd stop for some pie. Might as well do the next best thing. Let's see what we've got here."

Bisol stuck the barrel hard against Lili's right ear as his hands began to fondle her breasts. She cried out.

"You asshole! I'll kill you!" The car swerved.

"No heroics. Keep your eyes ahead and forget the funny stuff. Remember, you don't have any seatbelts on. None of us do. You want to commit suicide, go ahead. Or, you can just grit your teeth and suck it up. I'm just exploring over here a little. Let's see what this cunt has for tits."

Richard squeezed his hands hard on the steering wheel; his knuckles went white. He had to endure the cries and protests from Lili while driving the hard curves near the summit.

"Not even a decent handful. Shit. You wasted your time on this. Might as well be a fuckin' pedophile. Now Marie, even when she was just a kid, there was some real buds.

She was fresh, too. Let's see if this little kimono's been picked yet."

Bisol struggled with his weakened captive as they wrestled across the torn leather back seat. He finally ripped the left side of her dress up and pushed his hand into her crotch. Lili turned, eyes on fire, spitting in his face and biting his hand. He struck her a violent blow across the temple. She fell silent against the back door window, bleeding from her head wound.

"Lili!" But before he could reach for her he felt the pistol against his head.

"Now it would be a stretch for me to evade the cops and Eli, but if you tempt me, I may have to. You do one more stupid thing, like she did, and here's how it's gonna go: I stop this car and stretch her out on the hood. After I'm done no man will ever want to touch that spiny little squint-eye again. You got it?"

"Okay," Richard sobbed. He could see her in the rearview mirror. Blood rolled down her face in several rivulets until it dripped over the front of her torn dress.

"Never mind the blood. It'll stop pretty soon, especially at this altitude. You'll be carrying her down into the Castle, anyway. I'm not going to touch her anymore. Lost my taste for sushi for now. She bites like a fuckin' bulldog." He looked down as the blood from his own arm oozed from the fresh row of teeth marks. "Just keep driving up the west side of the Lake."

"We're not going to the Lodge?"

"No, were going directly to Fannette Island through Vikingsholm on the land side of Emerald Bay, right through the damn front doors. No sneaking around the back this time. The Governor shut all the State parks down and put the Park Rangers on earthquake response. Vikingsholm will be empty. I'll tell you where to turn.

Take Highway Eighty Nine north along the lake when we get to the cut-off to go Eighty-Eight to Nevada. And don't screw around and do anything weird to grab attention at the three-way light. I can always change my mind about your little China doll."

"Do geese see god?" Sinclair said aloud now, praying for some divine guidance to save them.

"What a pussy. You and your goddamned geese. Well, I think I know two geese who are going to see God soon enough." He laughed deep, loud, and demonically as he lit up another cigarette.

Chapter 17

"Pull in over there." Bisol pointed the pistol at Sinclair as he shook Lili. "Hey, wake up."

Lili groaned lightly and turned her head just a bit.

"Let her alone! I'll take care of her."

"Sure, buddy. You go ahead and do the heavy lifting."

Richard carried her semi-conscious body through the parking lot. They proceeded slowly down the steep driveway to the Vikingsholm Mansion. Even in the growing darkness the building was impressive with its tall, deep-set granite windows. A massive cone of dark shingles capped the tops, like a miniature castle.

"We won't have to worry about this." Bisol tore the "Closed for the Season" sign off the front door casing. He had a key that opened the massive oak door. He was quick to turn on the interior lights as they passed into the foyer, with Richard still in front, carrying Lili.

"How far are we going?"

"Not that far. The old lady put in a nice little elevator, if you know how to find it." The interior of Vikingsholm was an interwoven design mixture of a Scandinavian lodge and a Victorian manor. The features were made from the finest and rarest woods, from the expensive mahogany paneling to the inlaid cedar floors. They finally stood in the main entertainment room looking over Lake Tahoe. The trio rested between a walnut grand piano and an Italian writing desk carved with its recessed scrolls around the sides and base. Below the corbelled ceiling, highlighted even in the dimmed table lamps, was a sculpture of two giant snakes, the smaller atop the larger. What was odd was that they both had two heads. Richard thought of the ring immediately and wondered if the Templars knew about the Annunaki.

"You can set her over there." Bisol pointed at a mauve-colored, overstuffed settee curved into the wall behind the writing desk. "You go over to the fireplace and when I tell you, pull back on the carving of the Green Man, you know, the one that looks like a guy covered in leaves and ivy. That old codger over there. Just reach behind it when I tell you."

"Why use the Green Man for the secret doorway?"

"Wouldn't know. Don't care. I just know the trick. Now get ready."

Bisol moved to the piano and lifted the keyboard cover hard, letting it slam against the rest. He struck a C note, then F sharp, and then played the E minor chord. Richard could feel a low rumbling under his feet. There was a dull click behind the carved face above the fireplace mantel. He pulled forward on the marble carving when Bisol pointed at him. A dull sound of sliding chains and rolling bearings vibrated the wall under his hand. The entire fireplace moved forward some three feet into the room, knocking over one of the matching Edwardian chairs. Sinclair jumped back, avoiding the chair's fall.

"Oh yeah, forgot to tell you about that. Too bad it didn't take a toe off. I'd love to see you hobble with your bad knees and a bum foot. I figured carrying the bitch this far would have damn near crippled you. Acting the tough guy, huh?"

"So now what?"

"Carry her behind the case. It'll be tight, but you can do it. I've carried bodies in there before."

Richard had some difficulty squeezing Lili through the space without hitting her head. She was groggy but coming around. He did a quick check of her eyes when he took her from the couch. They confirmed his fears of a concussion.

"Just make a little room. We'll all have a nice, slow ride down." Alex pushed his victims deeper into the small alcove. There was a recessed fluorescent panel above them providing soft lighting for the controls on the inside, behind the back of the fireplace. Bisol pressed a blue and then a red button protruding from a small brass plate cover. The wall pulled back in to them, compressing them into the elevator. A short jolt was followed by the sense of movement downward with a slight rocking motion accompanying the descent.

"You mean for months we had to row out to Fannette Island, claw over those steep rocks and trees in the dark, while there was an elevator going to the same cave?"

"Well, we couldn't just walk through the damn place full of state park ranger pukes. There was this little cutie stationed there, though, for a while, had hair like Niagara Falls . . . given half the chance . . ."

"Is there anything human left in you, really?"

"You know your problem, Sinclair? You think the good guys win. Maybe that's why you thought you could get away with the treasure. Did you think you could do something good in the world? What a child you are. Disgusting. It's my gold, not yours."

Richard felt the elevator slow and then stop with a light thud. The wall pulled back and revealed the familiar carved walls from past visits underneath the lake.

"I told you already; Drake's treasure was never here. Besides, the Templars stole it from the Jews. And you know what? The Jews stole it from all the warring tribes and nations they slew—and on and on. That's all this has ever been about: who can kill more effectively to get that little pile of shiny metal."

"Great, gritty stuff, Sinclair. I'll use that in my autobiography when I write about this adventure. Of course, I'll leave you and this Oriental trash out of it."

Lili turned in Richard's arm, awakening slightly, but aware enough to spit on Bisol.

He coiled back, ready to hit her again but held back. "No, that would just make me too happy. Eli said keep both of you awake. I guess I can wait until he's done with you, Sinclair. Then maybe I'll get a shot at taking care of Mary friggin' Poppins here."

Richard cradled her over his shoulder, feeling her shudder in pain and disgrace.

They entered the main meeting area. Eli was joined with two other Templars Richard did not know.

"Alex, you've done well. At last, Richard, you'll fulfill your destiny along with that useless detritus in your arms. After tonight, we'll know exactly where the treasure is and you'll be returning what you've taken. We saw what you did to the treasure site. We don't know how you did it, or why, but be assured we were not amused."

"I couldn't give a shit what you think. You're nothing but a snake. I hope you and your asshole Templar brothers rot in hell. There isn't a hair of wisdom or worthiness in any of you."

Bisol struck Richard across the shoulder. Richard fell to his knees. Lily rolled forward and onto her back. She was still bleeding from the head wound. She stared silently at the cavern ceiling. Her shallow breathing indicated the brink of shock.

"Enough!" Eli commanded. He and the other two Templars stepped down from the raised stairs of the platform below his throne. They stopped finally to tower over their prisoners. The long, black Templar cloaks indicated positions of authority in the Order, as did their golden wristbands, beards, and scarlet red tattoos across the top of their right hands. They were the three Grand Masters in a rare gathering.

"You're the other Masters," Sinclair said, looking up at their wizened faces.

"Yes, Richard, and now it is time for you to leave our Order. Alex, wait outside and make sure nothing comes through that door."

"Yes, Master." He holstered his pistol quickly and walked briskly to the doorway. Richard could hear the bars clang against the rock on the other side as Alex sealed them in.

"Now my brothers, let us call on our most hated partners and seal our pact."

The Grand Masters raised their right arms, combining hands in a triangle over the heads of Richard and Lili.

"*Yamanash ach tanu. Aband ebufore!*" Eli commanded three times. The trio then repeated the phrasing over and over in deep, trembling harmony. A wind rose through the room with a screaming sound carried in its passing. Richard remembered it from Crissy Park by the Golden Gate Bridge. The remains of the Lilith clan had arrived.

"Lili. Lili. Wake up."

"Good, Richard. Good. She needs to be awakened. They need to speak through her to finish the transfer of property."

Richard reached to her and pulled her across the smooth, white floor. He raised her to a sitting position. She flickered her eyelids, barely able to move. "My love."

"How touching," Eli interjected. "Now my brothers, we stand on his right while she is the vessel on the left. The Liliths will take what they want. We will also get what we need as they know how to force the location of our treasure from this reluctant jackass." The tall, cadaverous figures strode to Richard's side. They intoned the ancient ritual mantra again. Richard recognized it as the Aramaic he had heard in Malta. Templars had discovered the true pronunciations of that powerful and terrible language. They reserved it for their most secret rituals.

Liliths filled the ceiling and alcoves with their tarry ethers. The feathery rhizomes of their essences crawled over the floor and impregnated the air until their tributaries of filth narrowed to a fine point above Lili's arms. A tornado of pitch formed above her. Her left arm rose, without her volition, to meet the turbid convolution of darkness. At the same moment the interwoven hands of the Masters grasped Richard's right shoulder.

He surprised them by reaching up himself and squeezing their thin wrists hard together.

Lili also surprised her invaders by winding her right arm around Richard's left leg, holding tight.

"Hold on, Lili. Let them in. Now!"

The Templars struggled like trapped beasts in a leg iron. They could not strike him as their feet and hands froze in place. A blue light surrounded both Sinclair and Lili as he bound the Masters in his grip. The black umbilical on Lili's arm turned and writhed madly as the Liliths tried to extricate themselves. Flashes of lightning and rolling thunder filled the space along with the cursing from the Masters.

Richard looked up, stretching his and the Masters' arms to their maximum. He took a deep breath and screamed out with his all, "Walk thee in perfected light!"

Everything stopped. The flow of time suspended. Everything in the cavern went motionless, yet Richard could travel about the room with his mind, rotating his perception to inspect every aspect of the scene. Yellow light poured from Lili's mouth and eyes. There was nothing visible from her head but the illumination. Lighting bolts stopped halfway out of the turbulence formed by the Liliths. He could see that the Liliths were just three entities, equaling the force of the Templar Masters.

He called to Lili in his mind—*Hold on!*

An explosion of matter swirled in a blast of speed. The room melted in concentric blurs. Black Lilith clouds rolled up through Lili and into Richard. The Masters' bodies and robes shriveled into ribbons of latex and black silk. The snake-like remains of the Templars sucked into Richard's fingertips and into his torso. All the perpetrators were now within him, caged and raging for escape. He drew another deep breath and pulled the light from Lili's face into his heart.

"I forgive you. I forgive you all." Richard's words completely silenced those within.

A cascade of spinning lights roared like cannonades out of Richard's torso. The hostage couple disintegrated in a flash. Nothing remained. Then the cavern shrank to a single point of nothingness—not just a hole, but absolute nothingness. In the nothingness a pressure built until the nothingness erupted in one tone, in one light, in one cacophonous reentry.

Richard and Lili stood, whole and conscious, before a twelve-foot-tall Annunaki warrior covered in scale armor over his blue flesh. He had only pools of midnight for eyes. The hollows of the wide, full face projected an opalescent glow that filled the cavern. The giant's banded arms and shoulder-length hair matched the Sumerian tablet drawings, but the rest of his form was grotesquely disproportionate to human life. Lili and Sinclair faced the titan now standing beside the cavern throne.

"You have by honor broken the ancient wheel sown so long ago. I am whole again, only through the act of forgiveness by two innocents. Now I can return and leave you to your race—a race we tampered with but did not create. I call forth the Lilith scimitar."

There were no words spoken. The pronouncement was solely within their heads, in telepathic clarity. As the behemoth recalled its tools of power, Richard fell to the floor in agony, writhing and twisting while holding his chest. A clicking and snapping followed as amorphous plasmas drifted up from his solar plexus to form a giant yellow centipede. It emerged through his clothing, stretching out across the pale stone. In moments the full length of the beast was revealed as it hardened its plates and reared back with menace toward the terrified couple.

"Lili, help me!"

She rushed to his side.

"I don't know what to do."

The centipede was fully turned now, ready to strike at the pair. The Annunaki raised its left arm and made a decisive motion with a closed hand. The centipede immediately jerked backward. An invisible rope yanked its head to the wrist of its new master. The beast rolled up

CURSE OF THE 8TH BUDDHA

into a yellow ball as flashes of electricity rolled across its plates. With another snap of its arm the alien tossed the golden ball to the wall where it burst apart, falling as a massive pile of yellow dust. The glittering mass was hundreds of times the size and volume of the vanquished monster. The Annunaki stepped down slowly from the high point of the cave and reached over to the top of cowering couple's heads. The scaly hands rested gently on each of them.

"You are now responsible for these ancient powers on your world. I will leave you with this burden. You did not abuse them in the past. You have proven your worth."

Richard sat upright as the giant hand pulled away from his skull. He looked down to see that he and Lili had matching double-snake rings, she on her left middle finger, and he on his right. He was now dressed in a black robe of pure silk with a silver lining on the collar and cuffs.

"I don't understand." Lili had tears in her eyes. She was clothed in a brilliant white gown of pure silk with gold epaulets and a golden trim on the hem.

"You are both pure of heart. Now you bear the gifts misused by your predecessors. The resources we brought from this planet lie behind you. Come, I will show you."

They walked slowly to the mountain of glowing gold.

The Annunaki giant pulled Richard's right hand out and over some of the fine powder. The pile transformed into hundreds of gleaming blocks in lines of perfectly stacked columns.

"You can use your love," the giant continued, "to remove the hate that has filled this material. You can be the rulers of mankind if you so wish."

"For me," Richard replied, quietly, "I would rather rule over just Richard Sinclair. That is the true mastery. That won't take your gold."

"And that, dear Lili, pure of soul, is why we picked you both, and why you picked him. Your tests were beyond the means of most beings to survive. You are the ones who were strong. You have inherited." The word 'inherited' echoed and ricocheted about the cavern as the huge form of the ancient being became opaque. The alien image drifted away into a dimension invisible to the newly anointed.

Silence came again as only two souls remained. He held her tight to him this time. "I vow I won't ever let you go again in this life or any other." A surge came from their embrace, giving a new glint to the treasure of treasures beside them.

He pulled back, fully healed and reenergized through her essence. "There is work to be done. We have to remember our duty first, always."

"Always," she replied, softly.

"But we are one again, as it should have always been."

"Always. But what's to be done with all this?" she asked, pointing at the gold.

"We'll find those answers as we walk the world together. Right now we need to escape back to the surface and leave this place for a time."

"You seem worried. Nothing can harm us, Richard."

"The Visitor never said that. We aren't immortal in these bodies, or protected." With that he pinched her arm.

"Oh, that was awful! How could you?"

"Just a reminder to keep our balance. We are as fragile as the rain. Our rings give us an edge, and our love gives us strength, but we are still only human."

"That's enough for now."

"And now, we must show our grace and strength as we leave here. Will you trust me to deal with Alex as we open that door? I have a responsibility from the oaths I swore as part of the Templars. Whether their leaders were corrupt or not, I gave my word of honor."

"I don't know if I can be that magnanimous."

"Then let your love for me be your shield. Let what he is drift away from you. Please."

"This once. I mourn my parents deeply, but I will let your justice rule this time."

Richard led the way to the chamber exit. He pounded hard on the wood beams. The bolts pulled back to reveal a shocked guard.

"You . . . you aren't dead." Bisol pulled his firearm.

"It's too late for that, Alex. The Masters have ascended."

"Oh, horseshit! That's an old wife's tale for young recruits. No Master ever did that. How'd you get this far? No matter. You're both dead." He raised the pistol at Lili.

"But first," Richard interrupted, raising his right hand toward Bisol's pistol, "do geese see God?"

"To hell with you!" Bisol squeezed the trigger but there was no report. The bolt didn't move. He pulled back the weapon to check for a jammed bullet.

"Alex, I do think geese can see God. I think that might help your perspective."

Bisol's eyes sank back in his head as the pistol dropped. He could no longer hold the weapon as his hands shrank into the arms of his jacket. His pants collapsed under him. Bisol's neck extended and twisted like a cobra as his skin bubbled and popped. Feathers rushed out of his muscles and through his skin, but he could not scream as there was no human mouth left to shape his fright. In moments the once violent mercenary was simply no more than a small, fat Chinese goose. The long, slender white neck bobbed back and forth as the tiny black head, with its secondary hard black crown, opened to release a series of plaintiff honks and hisses. Richard gathered the protesting fowl up inside Alex's empty leather jacket so only its head poked out from his control. He and Lili made their way back to the elevator entry.

"Will these controls work the other way?"

"I don't know, Lili, but we don't want to go out the other way. It's too rugged and we don't have a boat."

"If we leave, are we ever coming back to this inheritance?"

"I don't think that will be our biggest challenge. There will be time. Press both buttons and let's go. We've got unfinished business to deal with. First we'll need to get back to Frisco, with your Uncle's help, to honor your mom and dad. But right now, we need to get out of here in one piece."

Lili reached out but the elevator energized before she could reach the brass plate. The ring on her finger felt warm as it hummed. "The ring did that. I didn't. I guess we'll learn more about these rings as we go."

"I suspect. I wasn't sure about the goose thing, either. I just knew that somehow I could do it."

Once outside Vikingsholm, Richard escorted Lili to the east of the grounds so they could look out on the ruins atop Fannette Island. They walked to the end of boat ramp facing the western rock walls of the island as Lake Tahoe's waters lapped gently below them.

"What do you have in mind for your Templar? I'd like to just stomp him to pieces."

"Oh, I think Alex should do just fine up here, with a little adjustment." Richard pulled the goose out of the jacket and moved his hands over its wings. He ripped the right wing off in one hard tug. The goose honked and hissed fiercely, rolling its neck around in agony.

"Why do that?"

CURSE OF THE 8TH BUDDHA

"Because," he said, tossing the stunted bird with superhuman strength toward the ruins. "He raised his arm against a Templar. There was a price to pay for that. Now he won't be swimming back. He doesn't have the lung capacity. He won't be flying, either. I can never punish him enough for what he has done to so many others, including your family. However, I am required by my oath to take the appropriate action against him. In that, I have been true to my word."

"Hardly enough of a punishment for all he's done."

"Well, that would be true if it weren't for that fellow." Richard pointed to a splotch of black moving among the rocks below the Tea Garden walls. They watched as the goose struggled to barely reach the safety of Fannette Island's shoreline. The goose dropped from exhaustion after Richard's toss and its short, desperate swim. "Do you suppose bears like smoked meat?"

"My, that is rather awful. Perhaps he would have been better off if I had punished him."

"Perhaps, but like Alex told me, only the tough survive. Maybe he'll improve his character. He once said it was an honor to face one's fears. Enjoy your honor, Alex."

They turned and strolled back to the car, ignoring the violent bird cries behind them.

Lili rested on the open car door for a second, tilting her head in thought.

"What's up?" he asked.

"I'm thinking you should not use that goose adage again. Maybe it's too dangerous."

"Okay. I'll do that as soon as I get a new car and take this old Buick to a recycling center. Ah, in fact, I have just the saying: another palindrome from my teacher on Malta."

"Dare I ask?"

"Madam, in Eden I'm Adam."
"That, my dear Adam, will do very well."
"Well, my dear Eve, it's a start."

The Author

Rick Tobin is a professional emergency manager, author, radio personality, and owner of High Hope Publishing. Rick lived in the San Francisco Bay Area and near Lake Tahoe for three decades. He currently resides with his family near San Antonio, Texas and far from the influence of the California Templars and the Annunaki.

Made in the USA